THE FOURTH Galaxy READER

By H. L. Gold

THE FOURTH

Edited by H. L. Gold

Galaxy READER

Doubleday & Company, Inc., Garden City, New York 1959

Copyright, 1956, by Galaxy Publishing Corp.: NAME YOUR SYMPTOM, Jim Harmon, and HORRER HOWCE, Margaret St. Clair, reprinted by courtesy of the authors. MAN OF DISTINCTION, Michael Shaara, reprinted by courtesy of Harry Altshuler and the author.

Copyright, 1957, Galaxy Publishing Corp.: I AM A NUCLEUS, Stephen Barr, and THE BOMB IN THE BATHTUB, Thomas N. Scortia, reprinted by courtesy of the authors. YOU WERE RIGHT, JOE, J. T. McIntosh, reprinted by courtesy of Willis Kingsley Wing and the author. WHAT'S HE DOING IN THERE?, Fritz Leiber, reprinted by courtesy of Harry Altshuler and the author.

Copyright, 1958, by Galaxy Publishing Corp.: THE HATED, Paul Flehr; KILL ME WITH KINDNESS, Richard Wilson; THE GENTLEST UNPEOPLE, Frederik Pohl, and MAN IN A QUANDARY, L. J. Stecher, Jr., reprinted by courtesy of the authors. THE MINIMUM MAN, Robert Sheckley; THE GUN WITHOUT A BANG, Finn O'Donnevan, and BLANK FORM, Arthur Sellings, reprinted by courtesy of Harry Altshuler and the authors. OR ALL THE SEAS WITH OYSTERS, Avram Davidson, reprinted by courtesy of John Schaffner and the author.

To Joan and Van
with love and gratitude

CONTENTS

In this corner

Just recently the wife of a U.S. diplomat called, said her husband was to meet with an Iron Curtain official known to have a fondness for "space" fiction, and what could I suggest as a politic gift of books?

Politic!

Political is the word.

Like all overlords before them, the Communist chiefs consider everything to be political; the differences between democracy and autocracy are immense, but this is the biggest, the multi-trap-doored labyrinthine arena in which democracy continually finds itself emerging unaware, to be thwacked humiliatingly before the laughing world—simply for want of knowing that everything *is* political, or can be made so if that's how one operates, and that this is how autocracy *does* operate because it must.

Brink of war and Olympic games, steel-production figures and Nobel prizewinners, U.N. debates and ballet for export, alphabet-bomb bans and world fairs, Arab nationalism and music contests . . .

And, of course, science fiction. Why not? It falls into the *everything* classification.

Not long ago, newspapers picked up a Moscow story in which Russian writers of science fiction were ordered, as the headlines something less than accurately stated, to "Think, Damn You!" (We in American science fiction would say *extrapolate*, which is the process of taking a known fact or theory of today and carrying it just as far as imaginative logic can take it, only we don't have to curse or command our writers into doing so.) When Russian politniks make a political statement on something, how else should we regard that something but as political, even if it's something as seemingly unlikely as science fiction?

This is no call to Washington to mobilize science fiction into diplomatic and military legions. We need them not. But let's be a bit smart about this literary force we so casually own, which so unthinkably outclasses the antagonists in the arenas they invariably choose, and in which we go on being surprised to discover ourselves, a force that exists right now, with no subsidies for research and development being required, no aid programs for allies to import it at our expense. . . .

Most U.S. science-fiction magazines have foreign editions in one or another country—and *Galaxy* has editions all over the British Empire, France (which includes Belgium and Switzerland), Italy, Germany, Sweden, Finland, with more being negotiated—items of democracy, far superior by the Russians' own yelped admission, imported by other nations at not a penny's cost to government or, for a glad change, taxpayer, and at every level, of course, as private as enterprise possibly can be.

And there's the accounting for the superiority of American science fiction. When a dictatorship settles on a crash priority, it can get an awesome lot of things done, but thinking isn't one of them, and science fiction—good science fiction, not filmonsters and cinemarmageddons—is the product of thinking. Lone thinking that is done by individual writers at individual typewriters, for science fiction produced in any collective fashion, whether by a bureau of literature or a board of directors, collapses into a puddle of effects, Technicalorific in Hollywood, black-and-white politicalumnies in Kremlinland.

Prove that latter charge? As easily done as said. *Galaxy* was approached by the Soviet Embassy for an exchange of Russian and American science fiction—story for story, even-stephen, no money to change hands. We naturally said we would be glad to take a look, and on came the flaccid flood, and here is how the swap would have worked out:

Their timid venturings to the edge of space, for our bold explorations of planets in this solar system and elsewhere, commutings between the galaxies and even other universes—which, regard you well, are actual mathematical concepts that have been created out of necessity to account for observable and duplicable phenomena.

Their forcibly constrained Utopian views of Communistic society a few years into the future, for our bravura forays into social setups of every conceivable kind for more millenia and light-years than mankind has recorded hours of history and sea-leagues and land-miles of voyaging.

Their tinkerings with the sciences of today, and only today, with a worried eye toward coming Lysenko-like dogmas, for our daring construction of disciplines as much beyond today's as space-ship construction is from the building of rafts, and many that are no more than guesswork hazards that may prove true—*may*, mind, not *will*, a word that belongs in science fiction only until the end of any given story, for the next, or one soon after, is sure to contradict it as thoroughly as the author is capable of, as, to be sure, he should, else what is science fiction for, if not to come up with every imaginable answer?

Their . . .

Well, the one attractive piece of Russian science fiction did not come from the Embassy. It came from an American translator who happened on it back at the end of World War II, when it went on sale briefly—very briefly. A competent novel by a competent craftsman, its scientific premise was acceptable enough, though nothing to create an uproar past the Jules Verne era: a tunnel through the earth, large enough to accommodate considerable passenger and freight traffic at railroad speed, which is faster but costlier than shipping, slower and less pleasant and convenient than jet flight. The scientific premise, however, was much more credible than the political one: the U.S.A. and U.S.S.R. built the earth tunnel as a joint project!

Only two conjectures seem less likely: that the author escaped exile or execution; that the book would now be allowed Iron Curtain publication.

On the other hand, there would be just one reprisal if it were brought out here: who'd buy anything so pathetically outdated?

You probably would like to know if the Russians still wanted American science fiction. Well, yes. If they didn't have to pay for it. And if they could make certain changes.

They can't make those changes. But if there are enough U.S. diplomats bringing enough "politic" gifts of American "space" fiction to enough Red officials with a taste for it, they could have the entire edition of this volume of freely enterprising stories without its costing them a cent.

Not a bad idea, is it?

H. L. GOLD

THE FOURTH Galaxy READER

I AM A NUCLEUS

×∞∞∞∞∞∞∞ by Stephen Barr ×∞∞∞∞∞∞∞

WHEN I GOT HOME FROM THE OFFICE, I WAS NOT SO
much tired as beaten down, but the effect is similar. I let myself
into the apartment, which had an absentee-wife look, and took a
cold shower. The present downtown temperature, according to
the radio, was eighty-seven degrees, but according to my Greenwich Village thermometer, it was ninety-six. I got dressed and
went into the living room, and wished ardently that my wife
Molly were here to tell me why the whole place looked so woe-
begone.

What do they do, I asked myself, that I have left undone? I've
vacuumed the carpet, I've dusted and I've straightened the cush-
ions . . . Ah! The ash trays. I emptied them, washed them and
put them back, but still the place looked wife-deserted.

It had been a bad day; I had forgotten to wind the alarm clock,
so I'd had to hurry to make a story conference at one of the TV
studios I write for. I didn't notice the impending rainstorm and
had no umbrella when I reached the sidewalk, to find myself con-
fronted with an almost tropical downpour. I would have turned

back, but a taxi came up and a woman got out, so I dashed through the rain and got in.

"Madison and Fifty-fourth," I said.

"Right," said the driver, and I heard the starter grind, and then go on grinding. After some futile efforts, he turned to me. "Sorry, Mac. You'll have to find another cab. Good hunting."

If possible, it was raining still harder. I opened my newspaper over my hat and ran for the subway: three blocks. Whizzing traffic held me up at each crossing and I was soaked when I reached the platform, just in time to miss the local. After an abnormal delay, I got one which exactly missed the express at Fourteenth Street. The same thing happened at both ends of the crosstown shuttle, but I found the rain had stopped when I got out at Fifty-first and Lexington.

As I walked across to Madison Avenue, I passed a big excavation where they were getting ready to put up a new office building. There was the usual crowd of buffs watching the digging machines and, in particular, a man with a pneumatic drill who was breaking up some hard-packed clay. While I looked, a big lump of it fell away, and for an instant I was able to see something that looked like a chunk of dirty glass, the size of an old-fashioned hatbox. It glittered brilliantly in the sunlight, and then his chattering drill hit it.

There was a faint bang and the thing disintegrated. It knocked him on his back, but he got right up and I realized he was not hurt. At the moment of the explosion—if so feeble a thing can be called one—I felt something sting my face and, on touching it, found blood on my hand. I mopped at it with my handkerchief but, though slight, the bleeding would not stop, so I went into a drugstore and bought some pink adhesive, which I put on the tiny cut. When I got to the studio, I found that I had missed the story conference.

During the day, by actual count, I heard the phrase "I'm just spitballing" eight times, and another Madison Avenue favorite,

"The whole ball of wax," twelve times. However, my story had been accepted without change because nobody had noticed my absence from the conference room. There you have what is known as the Advertising World, the Advertising game or the advertising racket, depending upon which rung of the ladder you have achieved.

The subway gave a repeat performance going home, and as I got to the apartment house we live in, the cop on the afternoon beat was standing there talking to the doorman.

He said, "Hello, Mr. Graham. I guess you must have just have missed it at your office building." I looked blank and he explained, "We just heard it a little while ago: all six elevators in your building jammed at the same time. Sounds crazy. I guess you just missed it."

Anything can happen in advertising, I thought. "That's right, Danny, I just missed it," I said, and went on in.

Psychiatry tells us that some people are accident-prone; I, on the other hand, seemed recently to be coincidence-prone, fluke-happy, and except for the alarm clock, I'd had no control over what had been going on.

I went into our little kitchen to make a drink and reread the directions Molly had left, telling me how to get along by myself until she got back from her mother's in Oyster Bay, a matter of ten days. How to make coffee, how to open a can, whom to call if I took sick and such. My wife used to be a trained nurse and she is quite convinced that I cannot take a breath without her. She is right, but not for the reasons she supposes.

I opened the refrigerator to get some ice and saw another notice: "When you take out the Milk or Butter, Put it Right Back. And Close the Door too."

Intimidated, I took my drink into the living room and sat down in front of the typewriter. As I stared at the novel that was to liberate me from Madison Avenue, I noticed a mistake and picked up a pencil. When I put it down, it rolled off the desk, and with my eyes on the manuscript, I groped under the chair for it. Then I looked down. The pencil was standing on its end.

There, I thought to myself, is that one chance in a million we hear about, and picked up the pencil. I turned back to my novel and drank some of the highball in hopes of inspiration and sur- cease from the muggy heat, but nothing came. I went back and read the whole chapter to try to get a forward momentum, but came to a dead stop at the last sentence.

Damn the heat, damn the pencil, damn Madison Avenue and advertising. My drink was gone and I went back to the kitchen and read Molly's notes again to see if they would be like a letter from her. I noticed one that I had missed, pinned to the door of the dumbwaiter: "Garbage picked up at 6:30 A.M. so the idea is to Put it Here the Night Before, I love you." What can you do when the girl loves you?

I made another drink and went and stared out of the living- room window at the roof opposite. The sun was out again and a man with a stick was exercising his flock of pigeons. They wheeled in a circle, hoping to be allowed to perch, but were not allowed to.

Pigeons fly as a rule in formation and turn simultaneously, so that their wings all catch the sunlight at the same time. I was thinking about this decorative fact when I saw that as they were making a turn, they seemed to bunch up together. By some curious chance, they all wanted the same place in the sky to turn in, and several collided and fell.

The man was as surprised as I and went to one of the dazed birds and picked it up. He stood there shaking his head from side to side, stroking its feathers.

My speculations about this peculiar aerial traffic accident were interrupted by loud voices in the hallway. Since our building is usually very well behaved, I was astonished to hear what sounded like an incipient free-for-all, and among the angry voices I recog- nized that of my neighbor, Nat, a very quiet guy who works on a newspaper and has never, to my knowledge, given wild parties, particularly in the late afternoon.

"You can't say a thing like that to me!" I heard him shout. "I tell you I got that deck this afternoon and they weren't opened till we started to play!"

Several other loud voices started at the same time.

"Nobody gets five straight flushes in a row!"

"Yeah, and only when you were dealer!"

The tone of the argument was beginning to get ugly, and I opened the door to offer Nat help if he needed it. There were four men confronting him, evidently torn between the desire to make an angry exit and the impulse to stay and beat him up. His face was furiously red and he looked stunned.

"Here!" he said, holding out a deck of cards. "For Pete's sake, look at 'em yourselves if you think they're marked!"

The nearest man struck them up from his hand. "Okay, Houdini! So they're not marked! All I know is five straight . . ."

His voice trailed away. He and the others stared at the scattered cards on the floor. About half were face down, as might be expected, and the rest face up—all red.

Someone must have rung, because at that moment the elevator arrived and the four men, with half-frightened, incredulous looks, and in silence, got in and were taken down. My friend stood looking at the neatly arranged cards.

"Judas!" he said, and started to pick them up. "Will you look at that! My God, what a session . . ."

I helped him and said to come in for a drink and tell me all about it, but I had an idea what I would hear.

After a while he calmed down, but he still seemed dazed.

"Never seen anything to equal it," he said. "Wouldn't have believed it. Those guys *didn't* believe it. Every round normal, nothing unusual about the hands—three of a kind, a low straight, that sort of thing and one guy got queens over tens, until it gets to be *my* deal. Brother! Straight flush to the king—every time! And each time, somebody else has four aces . . ."

He started to sweat again, so I got up to fix him another drink. There was one quart of club soda left, but when I tried to open it the top broke and glass chips got into the bottle.

"I'll have to go down for more soda," I said.

"I'll come too. I need air."

At the delicatessen on the corner the man gave me three bottles in what must have been a wet bag, because as he handed them to me over the top of the cold-meat display, the bottom gave and they fell onto the tile floor. None of them broke, although the fall must have been from at least five feet. Nat was too wound up in his thoughts to notice and I was getting used to miracles. We left the proprietor with his mouth open and met Danny, the cop, looking in at the door, also with his mouth open.

On the sidewalk a man walking in front of Nat stooped suddenly to tie his shoe and Nat, to avoid bumping him, stepped off the curb and a taxi swerved to avoid Nat. The street was still wet and the taxi skidded, its rear end lightly flipping the front of one of those small foreign cars, which was going rather fast. It turned sideways and, without any side-slip, went right up the stoop of a brownstone opposite, coming to rest with its nose inside the front door, which a man opened at that moment.

The sight of this threw another driver into a skid, and when he and the taxi had stopped sliding around, they were face to face, arranged crosswise to the street. This gave them exactly no room to move either forward or backward, for the car had its back to a hydrant and the taxi to a lamp.

Although rather narrow, this is a two-way street, and in no time at all, traffic was stacked up from both directions as far as the avenues. Everyone was honking his horn.

Danny was furious—more so when he tried to put through a call to his station house from the box opposite.

It was out of order.

Upstairs the wind was blowing into the apartment and I closed the windows, mainly to shut out the tumult and the shouting. Nat had brightened up considerably.

"I'll stay for one more drink and then I'm due at the office," he said. "You know, I think this would make an item for the paper." He grinned and nodded toward the pandemonium.

When he was gone I noticed it was getting dark and turned on the desk lamp. Then I saw the curtains. They were all tied in knots, except one. That was tied in three knots.

All *right*, I told myself, it was the wind. But I felt the time had come for me to get expert advice, so I went to the phone to call McGill. McGill is an assistant professor of mathematics at a university uptown and lives near us. He is highly imaginative, but we believe he knows everything.

When I picked up the receiver, the line sounded dead and I thought, *more* trouble. Then I heard a man cough and I said hello. McGill's voice said, "Alec? You must have picked up the receiver just as we were connected. That's a damn funny coincidence."

"Not in the least," I said. "Come on over here. I've got something for you to work on."

"Well, as a matter of fact, I was calling up to ask you and Molly—"

"Molly's away for the week. Can you get over here quick? It's urgent."

"At once," he said, and hung up.

While I waited I thought I might try getting down a few paragraphs of my novel—perhaps something would come now. It did, but as I came to a point where I was about to put down the word "agurgling," I decided it was too reminiscent of Gilbert and Sullivan, and stopped at the letter "R." Then I saw that I had unaccountably hit all four keys one step to the side of the correct ones, and tore out the page, with my face red.

This was absolutely not my day.

"Well," McGill said, "nothing you've told me is impossible or supernatural. Just very, very improbable. In fact, the odds against that poker game alone would lead me to suspect Nat, well as I know him. It's all those other things . . ."

He got up and walked over to the window and looked at the hot twilight while I waited. Then he turned around; he had a look of concern.

"Alec, you're a reasonable guy, so I don't think you'll take offense at what I'm going to say. What you have told me is so impossibly unlikely, and the odds against it so astronomical, that I must take the view that you're either stringing me or you're subject to a delusion." I started to get up and expostulate, but he motioned me back. "I know, but don't you see that that is far more likely than . . ." He stopped and shook his head. Then he brightened. "I have an idea. Maybe we can have a demonstration."

He thought for a tense minute and snapped his fingers. "Have you any change on you?"

"Why, yes," I said. "Quite a bit." I reached into my pocket. There must have been nearly two dollars in silver and pennies. "Do you think they'll each have the same date, perhaps?"

"Did you accumulate all that change today?"

"No. During the week."

He shook his head. "In that case, no. Discounting the fact that you could have prearranged it, if my dim provisional theory is right, that would be *actually* impossible. It would involve time-reversal. I'll tell you about it later. No, just throw down the change. Let's see if they all come up heads."

I moved away from the carpet and tossed the handful of coins onto the floor. They clattered and bounced—and bounced together —and stacked themselves into a neat pile.

I looked at McGill. His eyes were narrowed. Without a word, he took a handful of coins from his own pocket and threw them.

These coins didn't stack. They just fell into an exactly straight line, the adjacent ones touching.

"Well," I said, "what more do you want?"

"Great Scott," he said, and sat down. "I suppose you know that
there are two great apparently opposite principles governing the
universe—random and design. The sands on the beach are an example of random distribution and life is an example of design.
The motions of the particles of a gas are what we call random, but
there are so many of them, we treat them statistically and derive
the Second Law of Thermodynamics—quite reliable. It isn't theo-
retically hard and fast; it's just a matter of extreme probability.
Now life, on the other hand, seems not to depend on probability
at all; actually, it goes against it. Or you might say it is certainly
not an accidental manifestation."

"Do you mean," I asked, in some confusion, "that some form
of life is controlling the coins and—the other things?"

He shook his head. "No. All I mean is that improbable things
usually have improbable explanations. When I see a natural law
being broken, I don't say to myself, 'Here's a miracle.' I revise my
version of the book of rules. Something—I don't know what—is
going on, and it seems to involve probability, and it seems to center
around you. Were you still in that building when the elevators
stuck? Or near it?"

"I guess I must have been. It happened just after I left."

"Hm. You're the center, all right. But why?"

"Center of what?" I asked. "I feel as though I were the center
of an electrical storm. Something has it in for me!"

McGill grinned. "Don't be superstitious. And especially don't
be anthropomorphic."

"Well, if it's the opposite of random, it's got to be a form of life."

"On what basis? All we know for certain is that random motions
are being rearranged. A crystal, for example, is not life, but it's a
non-random arrangement of particles . . . I wonder." He had a
faraway, frowning look.

I was beginning to feel hungry and the drinks had worn off.

"Let's go out and eat," I said. "There's not a damn thing in the
kitchen and I'm not allowed to cook. Only eggs and coffee."

We put on our hats and went down to the street. From either end we could hear wrecking trucks towing away the stalled cars. There were, by this time, a number of harassed cops directing the maneuver and we heard one of them say to Danny, "I don't know what the hell's going on around here. Every goddamn car's got something the matter with it. They can't none of them back out for one reason or another. Never seen anything like it."

Near us, two pedestrians were doing a curious little two-step as they tried to pass one another; as soon as one of them moved aside to let the other pass, the other would move to the same side. They both had embarrassed grins on their faces, but before long their grins were replaced by looks of suspicion and then determination. "All right, smart guy!" they shouted in unison, and barged ahead, only to collide. They backed off and threw simultaneous punches which met in mid-air. Then began one of the most re- markable bouts ever witnessed—a fight in which fist hit fist but never anything else, until both champions backed away unde- feated, muttering identical excuses and threats.

Danny appeared at that moment. His face was dripping.

"You all right, Mr. Graham?" he asked. "I don't know what's going on around here, but ever since I came on this afternoon, things are going crazy. Bartley!" he shouted—he could succeed as a hog caller. "Bring those dames over here!"

Three women in a confused wrangle, with their half-open um- brellas intertwined, were brought across the street, which meant climbing over fenders. Bartley, a fine young patrolman, seemed self-conscious; the ladies seemed not to be.

"All right, now, Mrs. MacPhilip!" one of them said. "Leave go of my umbrella and we'll say no more about it!"

"And so now it's Missus MacPhilip, is it?" said her adversary.

The third, a younger one with her back turned to us, her um- brella also caught in the tangle, pulled at it in a tentative way, at which the other two glared at her. She turned her head away and tried to let go, but the handle was caught in her glove. She looked up and I saw it was Molly. My nurse-wife.

"Oh, Alec!" she said, and managed to detach herself. "Are you all right?" Was *I* all right!

"Molly! What are you doing here?"

"I was so worried, and when I saw all this I didn't know what to think." She pointed to the stalled cars. "Are you really all right?"

"Of course I'm all right. But why . . . ?"

"The Oyster Bay operator said someone kept dialing and dialing Mother's number and there wasn't anyone on the line, so then she had it traced and it came from our phone here. I kept calling up, but I only got a busy signal. Oh, dear, are you *sure* you're all right?"

I put my arm around her and glanced at McGill. He had an inward look. Then I caught Danny's eye. It had a thoughtful, almost suspicious cast to it.

"Trouble does seem to follow you, Mr. Graham," was all he said.

When we got upstairs I turned to McGill. "Explain to Molly," I said. "And incidentally to me. I'm not properly briefed yet."

He did so, and when he got to the summing up I had the feeling she was a jump ahead of him.

"In other words, you think it's something organic?"

"Well," McGill said, "I'm trying to think of anything else it might be. I'm not doing so well," he confessed.

"But as far as I can see," Molly answered, "it's mere probability, and without any over-all pattern."

"Not quite. It has a center. Alec is the center."

Molly looked at me with a curious expression for a moment. "Do you *feel* all right, darling?" she asked me. I nodded brightly. "You'll think this silly of me," she went on to McGill, "but why isn't it something like an overactive poltergeist?"

"Pure concept," he said. "No genuine evidence."

"Magnetism?"

"Absolutely not. For one thing, most of the objects affected weren't magnetic—and don't forget magnetism is a force, not a form of energy, and a great deal of energy has been involved. I admit the energy has mainly been supplied by the things themselves, but in a magnetic field, all you'd get would be stored kinetic energy, such as when a piece of iron moves to a magnet or a line of force. Then it would just stay there, like a run-down clock weight. These things do a lot more than that—they go on moving."

"Why did you mention a crystal before? Why not a life form?"

"Only an analogy," said McGill. "A crystal resembles life in that it has a definite shape and exhibits growth, but that's all. I'll agree this—thing—has no discernible shape and motion *is* involved, but plants don't move and amoebas have no shape. Then a crystal feeds, but it does not convert what it feeds on; it merely rearranges it into a non-random pattern. In this case, it's rearranging random motions and it has a nucleus and it seems to be growing—at least in what you might call improbability."

Molly frowned. "Then what *is* it? What's it made of?"

"I should say it was made of the motions. There's a similar idea about the atom. Another thing that's like a crystal is that it appears to be forming around a nucleus not of its own material—the way a speck of sand thrown into a supersaturated solution becomes the nucleus of crystallization."

"Sounds like the pearl in an oyster," Molly said, and gave me an impertinent look.

"Why," I asked McGill, "did you say the coins couldn't have the same date? I mean apart from the off-chance I got them that way."

"Because I don't think this thing got going before today and everything that's happened can all be described as improbable motions here and now. The dates were already there, and to change them would require retroactive action, reversing time. That's out, in my book. That telephone now——"

The doorbell rang. We were not surprised to find it was the telephone repairman. He took the set apart and clucked like a hen.

"I guess you dropped it on the floor, mister," he said with strong disapproval.

"Certainly not," I said. "Is it broken?"

"Not exactly *broken*, but——" He shook his head and took it apart some more.

McGill went over and they discussed the problem in undertones. Finally the man left and Molly called her mother to reassure her. McGill tried to explain to me what had happened with the phone.

"You must have joggled something loose. And then you replaced the receiver in such a way that the contact wasn't quite open."

"But for Pete's sake, Molly says the calls were going on for a long time! I phoned you only a short time ago and it must have taken her nearly two hours to get here from Oyster Bay."

"Then you must have done it twice and the vibrations in the floor—something like that—just happened to cause the right induction impulses. Yes, I know how you feel," he said, seeing my expression. "It's beginning to bear down."

Molly was through telephoning and suggested going out for dinner. I was so pleased to see her that I'd forgotten all about being hungry.

"I'm in no mood to cook," she said. "Let's get away from all this."

McGill raised an eyebrow. "If all this, as you call it, will let us."

In the lobby we ran into Nat, looking smug in a journalistic way.

"I've been put on the story—who could be better?—I live here. So far, I don't quite get what's been happening. I've been talking to Danny, but he didn't say much. I got the feeling he thinks you're involved in some mystical, Hibernian way. Hello, McGill, what's with you?"

"He's got a theory," said Molly. "Come and eat with us and he'll tell you all about it."

Since we decided on an air-conditioned restaurant nearby on Sixth Avenue, we walked. The jam of cars didn't seem to be any

less than before and we saw Danny again. He was talking to a
police lieutenant, and when he caught sight of us he said something that made the lieutenant look at us with interest. Particularly
at me.

"If you want your umbrella, Mrs. Graham," Danny said, "it's at
the station house. What there's left of it, that is."

Molly thanked him and there was a short pause, during which
I felt the speculative regard of the lieutenant. I pulled out a packet
of cigarettes, which I had opened, as always, by tearing off the
top. I happened to have it upside down and all the cigarettes fell
out. Before I could move my foot to obliterate what they had
spelled out on the sidewalk, the two cops saw it. The lieutenant
gave me a hard look, but said nothing. I quickly kicked the in-
sulting cigarettes into the gutter.

When we got to the restaurant it was crowded but cool—although it didn't stay cool for long. We sat down at a side table
near the door and ordered Tom Collinses as we looked at the
menu. Sitting at the next table were a fat lady, wearing a very
long, brilliant green evening gown, and a dried-up sour-looking
man in a tux. When the waiter returned they pre-empted him
and began ordering dinner fussily: cold cuts for the man, and
vichyssoise, lobster salad and strawberry parfait for the fat lady.

I tasted my drink. It was most peculiar; salt seemed to have
been used instead of sugar. I mentioned this and my companions
tried theirs and made faces.

The waiter was concerned and apologetic, and took the drinks
back to the bar across the room. The bartender looked over at us
and tasted one of the drinks. Then he dumped them in his sink
with a puzzled expression and made a new batch. After shaking
this up, he set out a row of glasses, put ice in them and began
to pour.

That is to say he tilted the shaker over the first one, but nothing came out. He bumped it against the side of the bar and tried

again. Still nothing. Then he took off the top and pried into it with his pick, his face pink with exasperation.

I had the impression that the shaker had frozen solid. Well, ice *is* a crystal, I thought to myself.

The other bartender gave him a fresh shaker, but the same thing happened, and I saw no more because the customers sitting at the bar crowded around in front of him, offering advice. Our waiter came back, baffled, saying he'd have the drinks in a moment, and went to the kitchen. When he returned, he had Madame's vichyssoise and some rolls, which he put down, and then went to the bar, where the audience had grown larger.

Molly lit a cigarette and said, "I suppose this is all part of it, Alec. Incidentally, it seems to be getting warmer in here."

It was, and I had the feeling the place was quieter—a background noise had stopped. It dawned on me that I no longer heard the faint hum of the air conditioner over the door, and as I started to say so, I made a gesture toward it. My hand collided with Molly's when she tapped her cigarette over the ash tray, and the cigarette landed in the neighboring vichyssoise.

"Hey! What's the idea?" snarled the sour-looking man.

"I'm terribly sorry," I said. "It was an accident. I——"

"Throwing cigarettes at people!" the fat lady said.

"I really didn't mean to," I began again, getting up. There must have been a hole in the edge of their tablecloth which one of my cuff buttons caught in, because as I stepped out from between the closely set tables I pulled everything—tablecloth, silver, water glasses, ash trays and the vichyssoise-à-la-nicotine—onto the floor.

The fat lady surged from the banquette and slapped me meatily. The man licked his thumb and danced as boxers are popularly supposed to do. The owner of the place, a man with thick black eyebrows, hustled toward us with a determined manner. I tried to explain what had happened, but I was outshouted, and the owner frowned darkly.

One of the waiters came up to the owner and tapped him on the shoulder and started to tell him about the air conditioner, thus creating a momentary diversion, which did not, however, include the fat lady.

"He must be drunk!" she told her companion, who nodded contemptuously. A man carrying a stepladder came down the aisle from the back, his eye on the air conditioner, but not, it seemed, on the stepladder, which bumped the owner of the restaurant on the shoulder just as he was turning back to me.

It was not a hard bump, but it threw him off balance, so that he more or less embraced the waiter. Then he turned around and it was obvious he thought I had struck him. The room was now divided into two groups: ourselves and our audience, and those who were too far away or intent on other matters to have noticed the fracas, the chief of these being the man with the stepladder, who was paying undivided attention to the air conditioner. The owner was very angry with me.

"Mister, I think *you'd* better leave!" he said.

"He will not!" Molly said. "It was an accident, and *you*," she added to the fat lady who was about to interrupt, "keep quiet! We'll buy you some more soup!"

"Maybe it was an accident like you say," the owner declared, "but no one's going to push me when my back is turned! Out you go, mister! The drinks are on the house."

"We haven't had any drinks yet," I said. "There was salt in them."

"What d'you mean, salt? My bartenders——"

The air conditioner suddenly let out a loud whirring and I glanced up. The stepladder that the man was on began to slide open like an acrobatic dancer doing a split. I stepped past the angry restaurateur and put out my hand to stop it, but, as I did, the extension bar that was supposed to hold it together parted and it came down with a rush, knocking over several tables. The repairman pulled part of the works out with him as he fell, and the fan belt broke. The motor raced and black smoke poured out.

"What're you trying to *do!*" the owner yelled at me over the loud whine of the machinery. "God damn it, haven't you done *enough* already?"

I took two steps back, in dismay at what I was accused of, and stepped on the skirt of the fat lady's green evening gown. She in turn took two steps and was, as it were, laid bare.

The previous hubbub was as nothing to what now resulted and the smoke was becoming thicker. Then the door opened and, to my horror, Danny and his lieutenant came in, and I was the first thing their eyes fastened on.

Then the sprinkler system went on.

The cell was clean, although very hot, and I was not treated badly. There was, in fact, an air of superstitious respect, almost. A cop gave me some magazines and, against regulations, a late paper, but it was not late enough to carry the story of the restaurant mob scene. In it, however, was a garbled account of our traffic jam and a reference to the six elevators simultaneously and unaccountably stuck in the I.T.V. Building, but no connection was suggested.

My mind was in too much of an uproar to read, and I paced up and down. It seemed hours since McGill had called my lawyer Vinelli; some fantastic mishap must be holding him up, I thought. Then I happened to bump into the door of the cell and found the lock hadn't caught.

More of the same! But there didn't seem any point in trying to escape. Where would I go? Besides, I would have to leave through the desk room, where there would be at least the desk lieutenant and a sergeant on the phone. I began to wonder what effect it would have if I were to call out and tell them.

"Hey!" I shouted, but my voice was drowned out by a blast from the radio in the squad room. It died down immediately; someone must have hit a loud spot on the dial. I had an idea.

"Hey!" I shouted again, and again was drowned out. I opened the barred door and looked up and down the corridor. No one was in sight. Without making any unnecessary noise, but not stealthily, either, I walked as naturally as I could past the door to the squad room, where all heads were turned away, listening to the sensational pronouncements of Bill Bart, the radio gossip.

". . . and in your commentator's view, this man is dangerous! After attacking a woman and setting fire to a restaurant, he was arrested and is being held for investigation, but I predict that the double-domes and alleged scientists will come up with some more gobbledygook and we ordinary citizens will be left in the dark as to why or how Graham is causing all this trouble. So far, fortunately, no one has been seriously injured, but I predict . . ."

I left and went on down the corridor.

So Bill Bart was giving me a play! What kind of crazy guesswork was he foisting on his public, I wondered, and came to the desk room. I looked in at the door. On one side, a sergeant was talking to an elderly worried-looking couple and never turned his head. On the other, a gray-haired lieutenant sitting at the raised desk dropped his glasses as I came in. They fell on the floor and smashed.

"Mother of God!" he muttered, and gave me a cursory glance. "Good night, Doctor," he said. "Not that there's anything good about it." He was fumbling in the desk as I walked out of the door.

On the other side of the street, in the shadows, was a man who crossed over as I came down the steps. It was McGill.

"I had a hunch this might happen," he said, taking my arm. "The car's up ahead. Vinelli came here as quick as he could, but he slipped coming along the street and broke his ankle."

"Judas!" I said. "I *am* sorry! I feel responsible. Where are we going?"

He didn't answer me at first; he just kept hurrying me along. One of those New York siroccos was pretending to cool the city, and at the corner I saw his old coupé with the parking lights on.

A saloon next to us was closing up and a few late customers came out onto the sidewalk. One customer, on seeing me, stopped and turned to the others.

"That's the guy I was telling you about! That's Graham!"

I saw then that it was our telephone repairman from the afternoon. He looked reasonably sober, but his friends did not.

"Oh yeah?" one of these said, eying me belligerently. "I thought we just heard Bill Bart broadcast the cops had him."

"Right," said another of them. "He's escaped! I'll hold him and you go on in and phone 'em."

"Nah, the joint's closed. Police station's right around the corner. I'll go tell 'em. Hold onto him now!"

The repairman and three of his pals began to advance warily and the other one ran down Charles Street, but at that moment we heard excited yapping and a small dog chasing a cat came tearing up the street. The cat had a fish head in its mouth and, ignoring us, ran through the middle of the group, dropping the fish head. The dog followed almost instantly, only he ran between the repairman's legs, upsetting him. In falling, the repairman tripped his neighbor, who fell on him, and another one fell on top of them. The remaining one stepped on the fish head.

"Black cat!" he cried, as he joined the others on the sidewalk. "Crossed my path!"

We got into McGill's car and he pulled away fast. As I looked back, the four men were flailing around, but they saw the direction we took. I also thought I saw the street lamp behind us go out.

"That was a lucky break!" I said. "I mean the cat and dog."

"Don't give it a thought," McGill said, driving fast but carefully up Hudson Street. "You're being watched over and protected. We're going up to my office and have a conference and we're going to drive like hell. I have an idea this thing may not be able to do much more than hang onto you. Maybe we can even shake it."

"Hang onto me?"

"Yes, you're the nucleus."

We were at the top of the ramp to the West Side highway and he abruptly put on more speed: no traffic was in sight.

"But what is it?" I asked a little wildly. "How's it doing it? Why pick on me?"

"I don't know, but I'd say it picked you as the nucleus because you had just been the subject of various flukes—the taxi and subway and so on—so you represented a sample of what it's made of —flukes. I have a hunch you'll continue to be protected."

"Did you happen to catch Bill Bart's broadcast?"

"Yes, I did. On the car radio coming over. Not good. He said——"

In the rear-view mirror I saw a police car overhauling us. We were doing a good sixty-five. "Here come the cops," I interrupted, but before McGill could answer, there was a faint pop and the police car wobbled and slowed to a stop, and was quickly out of sight.

"Blowout," I said.

"See what I mean?" McGill answered, and turned on two wheels into the 125th-Street exit. Then he added, "Molly's waiting for us in my office."

I felt better.

We drove through some immortal gateway and McGill moderated his speed. He pulled up in front of a darkened building and we climbed the steps. It seemed cooler here and the wind was very strong. McGill tried the door, but it was locked. Then he felt in his pocket and swore.

"No key?" I asked.

He shook his head and then shook the door, and went through his pockets again. I reached forward and shook the door, too. The lock clicked and we went in. I made an apologetic gesture and McGill raised his eyebrows.

We climbed a flight of stairs, all dark except for a faint glow that came in from the campus lights, and then along an echoing hallway to an office in which were Molly and some unimportant items, among them a desk radio that she turned off as we came in.

She gave me her professional nurse's smile and I sat down next her. Molly's professional nurse's smile is not a phony "Everything's going to be all right," but a signal. It's supposed to mean "Never mind what these cretins are saying about you. You're okay."

I was a little puzzled that she showed no surprise to see me.

"Well," McGill said, "my hunch was right. He got out."

"So I see," said Molly, smiling at me proudly. "What happened? Knock over one of the jailers?"

I shook my head and told her, including the cat-and-dog episode and the police-car blowout.

"Don't forget the lock downstairs," McGill said, and when I told her that, too, he added, "You see, I think it's beginning to take sides. I think it's watching out for its nucleus. Alec ought to be rather lucky right now."

"Well, I don't feel it," I said. "I feel hemmed in."

Molly glanced at me anxiously and turned back to him. "What do we do now?"

"First, before any more funny stuff happens, I want to rig up a few tests and see what's with Alec, if anything. I'll even test for EMF, Molly, just for the sake of satisfying you."

"For what?" I asked.

"Electromagnetic force. Come and give me a hand, Molly. Alec, you stay put and relax. We'll call you when we get set. I only hope to God the cops and the newshawks don't tumble to where we are."

They left and I went to the window and looked out at the wind blowing papers and dust into miniature tornadoes in the dim light, and wondered whether it was going to storm. A few belated students on the way to their dormitories evidently were wondering the same thing, for they were all looking up at the sky. I went to the desk and turned the radio on, low.

". . . are doing all they can, which doesn't seem much," Bill Bart was saying breathlessly. "He was last seen speeding uptown on the West Side drive, but the cops lost him. The town is gripped in superstitious fear—it is now known that Graham was responsible for the elevators jamming in the I.T.V. Building this morning—but how did he do it? I ask you: how? And how has he turned off all the electric power in Greenwich Village? I contacted the power company for an explanation, but I was put off with the usual double talk. I say, and I repeat, *this man must be caught!* He is . . ."

I turned him off. So that was what the street light going off had meant.

In a little while Molly came back. "All right, duck, come and be measured. He's got galvanometers and electronic devices and stuff, and he'll be able to detect anything you're emanating down to a milli-micro-whisker."

I followed her into the lab where I was sat down, taped up and surrounded with gadgets. McGill tried various things and read various dials. There were buzzing sounds and little lights blinked on and off, but at the end he shook his head.

"Nothing," he announced. "You're married to a non-ferrous, non-conducting, non-emanating, non-magnetic writer, Molly."

"He is too!" she said. "He's as magnetic as the dickens."

"Possibly, but he isn't emanating anything. The damn thing apparently just likes him. As a nucleus, I mean."

"Is that bad?" Molly asked. "Could it be dangerous?"

"It's bad," I put in morosely.

"Also it could be good," McGill said, with a gleam of scientific enthusiasm. "Why, it wouldn't surprise me, Alec, if you could do anything you wanted to that involved chance."

I didn't like the guinea-pig's-eye view of him I got, and told him so. "Except for a couple of minor escapes, it's been highly inconvenient," I said. "I don't want to seem ungrateful, but I wish it would go and help somebody else."

"But, my God, man! Do you realize if you went to the track tomorrow, your horse probably couldn't lose?"

"I wouldn't get that far," I grumbled.

"And I bet if somebody threw a knife at you, it would miss!" McGill went on, ignoring me. "Here, I'd like to try an experiment . . ."

"Now, hold on!" I said.

"*McGill!* Are you *crazy?*" Molly cried, but he ignored her also and opened his desk drawer, from which he took a pair of dice.

"Roll me some sevens, Alec," he said, handing them to me.

"I thought we came here for a conference," I protested. "And I don't know whether you know about it, but there's been a Village-wide electric power failure and I'm being blamed, according to Bill Bart."

"Holy cow! When did you hear that?"

"On your radio just now. Furthermore, he says the whole town is gripped in 'superstitious terror.'"

"That could be true," McGill answered. "Most people haven't progressed beyond the Dark Ages. Look what happened with Orson Welles' broadcast about the Martians."

"Maybe we ought to leave town for a while," Molly said. "We could go to Oyster Bay or somewhere." Then she glanced up. "What's that noise?"

Outside, I now noticed, mingled with the soughing of the wind, a susurrus of many voices. We went to the lab windows. A crowd of two or three hundred people was standing in the campus, staring up at the sky over us.

"What are they looking at?" McGill asked. "No one can possibly know we're here."

I started to lean out of the window, twisting up my head to see what it could be.

"Don't do that, Alec! They'll see you!" McGill warned, and I pulled my head in.

"Can we get on the roof?" I asked, but Molly suddenly said,

"Look who's here." Three squad cars drove up and several police-men got out.

"Perhaps we ought to sort of very gently turn the lights off," I suggested.

Molly immediately snapped off the shaded bench lamp, which was all that was on in the lab. This left McGill's office light, and I started toward it.

"Hadn't we better run for it?" Molly said, but a loud banging on the front door downstairs answered her.

"I hope that damn lock doesn't give again!" McGill breathed.

"They'll break it down!" Molly gasped.

"Like hell. It's university property and they can't possibly have gotten a search warrant so quickly at this time of night."

From outside came a loud voice: "Alec Graham! Are you in there?"

"Don't answer," said McGill. "And keep away from the win-dows. I guess they saw the light in my office." He leaned out. "What do you want?" he shouted.

"This is the police. Open up!"

"I won't unless you have a warrant!"

There was no more shouting. They seemed to be parlaying among themselves, but the crowd had a menacing sound. A bril-liant light suddenly hit our windows, illuminating the lab ceiling —a police searchlight. I saw that Molly had disappeared and I assumed she had gone into McGill's office.

"These guys mean business," he said, "but what the hell brought them?"

"Something on the roof. That's what they're all looking at, so why don't we go up and see?"

"All right, but you'd better stay down here. There's no parapet and they'll see you."

He started for the door and I decided to follow—at least as far as the trap door, or whatever gave onto the roof—when Molly came in from the hall. She looked scared.

"My God! I climbed an iron ladder and took a look outside. There's a small cyclone over us—a ton of torn papers and dust and junk whirling around like a waterspout! They'd be able to see it for blocks!"

"Oh, great," McGill groaned. "Now it's playing tricks with the wind. That's how they spotted us."

"We've got to get out of here, McGill," said Molly.

"Maybe the best thing would be for me to give myself up to the cops," I said.

"I don't know whether they'd be able to get you through that mob," McGill replied. "Just listen to them. I only wish I could think of some way to satisfy the damn crystal or whatever it is. I have the feeling it wants something. It can't be merely fooling around for no reason. But there doesn't seem to be any motive beyond the fact that it's apparently on your side. How did it start? That's what I wish I knew."

He absently turned the bench lamp on again. I shrugged unhappily and scratched my cheek. In so doing, I pulled the piece of pink adhesive tape loose and it began to bleed again.

"Cut yourself shaving, darling?" Molly asked me.

"No," I said. "As a matter of fact, it was a kind of freak accident."

"Oh?" McGill lifted his head interestedly. "Anything involving you and a fluke I want to hear about. Tell Papa."

I did and McGill began to get his dedicated look. "You say this piece of glass just blew up? What did it look like? How big was it?"

"I only saw it for a second. It was dirty and I'd say about two feet across—more or less round and with flat places all over it."

McGill came toward me in a state of great excitement. "That piece that hit your cheek—did it merely nick you or is it embedded? If it *is* embedded . . ." He picked up a bottle of alcohol and a piece of cotton and took a lens out of a drawer. "Molly, there's a pair of tweezers in my desk. Will you fetch them?" He tilted the light up onto my face and dabbed the cut with the alcohol.

"Ouch!"

"Keep still. It'll sting a little. . . . Yes, I think I can see it." He took the tweezers from Molly, who had returned, and neatly removed something from the cut. He held it under the light and looked at it through the lens. Then he rinsed it under the water faucet, dried it on a piece of filter paper and looked at it again. "Well, it looks like glass. I don't know. Maybe it's the nucleus of the glass chunk and . . ." His voice trailed off and he frowned at nothing in particular, putting the fragment down on the filter paper.

I picked it up. It seemed like a bit of sand, only brighter.

McGill's concern over this new object of interest had been so intent that for a few minutes our attention was diverted, but now Molly began to pace up and down. There didn't seem to be anything for us to do, and, unlike most nurses, waiting makes her nervous. She was looking at the display of various chemicals and reagents on the shelves.

"What's that stuff?" she asked, pointing to a large jar of black powder labeled Deflocculated Graphite. "I bet those cops have gone for a search warrant."

"Finely divided carbon," McGill said. "Damn, I wish I could think of something! A chunk of glass . . . blowing up . . ."

"Graphite is carbon?" Molly said. "You don't think they'd actually *do* anything to Alec, do you?"

"It's another form of carbon. A diamond is still another: the rare crystalline form," he said. "I wouldn't put it past that mob to do anything."

"Oh yes. I remember that in chemistry," Molly said. "But the police wouldn't let them, McGill, would they?"

"I've got an idea——" I tried to break in.

"They might not be able to stop them," McGill replied.

"We've got to get *out* of here!" Molly said for the second time.

"If a diamond——" I began.

"With a helicopter, we might," McGill said. "Right now, we're surrounded."

"How about hiding Alec?" Molly asked. "You and I could act innocent."

"I don't *want* to be hidden," I objected. "My idea is——"

"Or better yet, we could act guilty. That would appeal to them, wouldn't it, McGill?"

"They'd tear the place apart if they got in," McGill said.

I took a surreptitious look out of the windows again. It seemed to hit me that our being surrounded was an exaggeration; most of the crowd was centered about the police car directly in front of the main door. They had an ugly look, and while I didn't like the idea of being alone, neither did I relish the thought of my presence possibly causing my wife and my best friend to be the victims of mob violence, for although the police might, in the absence of a warrant, refrain from breaking in, the mob might not. So I decided to leave, confident that some bizarre manifestation would lead them away from the lab, and that no matter where I went, I could hardly be worse off. To keep moving was my best bet.

Molly and McGill were still discussing the situation as I tiptoed into the hall. There surely would be a back door—probably in the basement—and I went down three flights to a cement-floored corridor. Then, with lighted matches, I found my way to a door at the back of the building, at the end. I opened it and peered out, to see a retaining wall and stone steps leading up to ground level. I eased out into the areaway and pulled the door shut, noticing that I still held the folded filter paper with the fragment in it. The lock clicked and I realized that my bridge was, as they say, burned behind me.

Two cops were talking together a little way to my right, but their backs were turned and they were looking up. I, too, looked and saw the whirlpool of debris, which was exactly as Molly had described and quite as attention-calling. Clutching the filter paper like a talisman, I climbed the steps and gumshoed away to the left, but as I got to the corner I met a group of young men, also looking up.

One of these was saying, "That's a lynch mob, if ever I saw one! I don't get it."

"Mob psychology, that's the answer," explained another.

My heart congealed, but they walked right by me. It suddenly occurred to me that any newspapers that had carried the story would scarcely have been able to dig up a photograph of me yet. All I had to do was to walk out of the campus, for who would recognize me? Where I would go then was something I could decide later.

So I started out with more assurance, but I took the precaution to act like an onlooker by glancing up over my shoulder now and then at the airborne maelstrom.

As I got to the other side of the open space I had another shock. A few yards ahead was another group of policemen, one of whom, I saw with dismay, was the lieutenant from Charles Street, and he was beginning to turn around. I barely had time to duck into a doorway to avoid being seen. I had the feeling of a member of the I.R.A. in Dublin during the Troubles, and I crouched against the door.

I could now hear the lieutenant's voice: "Of course he's up there! Maddigan'll be here with a warrant any minute now and we'll . . ." His voice faded away.

Behind me, the door suddenly opened and I almost fell. A young student holding some notebooks emerged.

"Sorry," he said, and walked toward the crowd.

The door had not yet closed and I slipped in, with my heart irretrievably contracted to the size of a buckshot. I could just make out in the dim light that I was at the bottom of the fire stairs, so I climbed to the third floor and went into a classroom, then on into an office, somewhat like McGill's, that faced toward the lab building.

From here I had a perfect view of the crowd, the police, the upper façade of the labs, brightly lit by the searchlight and, over all, the spinning papers and dust, which even as I looked began to die down. I was unable to see Molly or McGill and wondered whether they had noticed my absence and were worrying.

I saw a phone on the desk at my side and considered calling up McGill's office, but first I wanted to think over my new idea. I pulled down the shades and turned on the reading lamp, by the light of which I re-examined the fragment I had been carrying around all day. It sparkled brilliantly. On the desk, beside an onyx pen set, a golf trophy and a signed golf ball, was a leather-framed photograph of a blank-faced young woman holding a pudgy little boy. I picked it up and rubbed the glass with the tiny fragment. It left a faint but undeniable scratch. So I was right about one thing.

Then I called McGill's office. In a few moments, I heard the receiver lifted, but no voice. "This is the nucleus," I said, and I heard a sigh of relief from McGill.

"Where in hell are you?"

"Across the way. Look out of your window and I'll turn my light off and on again." I did so.

"You're in Professor Crandal's office. Why did you leave?"

"We'll go into that later. McGill, that fragment is a diamond."

"What!"

"At any rate, it scratches glass."

"Why didn't you tell me that before? And where is it? I couldn't find it anywhere."

"I was sidetracked. I've got it here. Now my idea——"

"A diamond! I begin to see light. Give with the idea, Alec."

"Well, there was all this talk of crystals and then you were telling Molly about carbon and diamonds, and it occurred to me that what we have is something trying to crystallize—something that once *was* a crystal, and got broken up and wants to re-form. It keeps trying with playing cards and pigeons and automobiles, but it's no go. Why don't we give it some carbon to play with, Mc-Gill?"

There was a short silence. I looked across at the office but I couldn't see him. I noticed a piece of dirty newspaper that had fallen out of the maelstrom and had caught on a thick wire that stretched from one of the lab windows to immediately below mine—some kind of aerial, I imagined. Then I saw that the maelstrom, rather than breaking up, as I had thought, was moving over in my direction. I would be pointed out again.

"You mean the graphite, I suppose," McGill said. "Why in hell did you leave and take the fragment with you?"

"I forgot it was in my hand," I said, dodging the first part of the question. "Nobody on the campus recognized me, so I guess I can walk back." Then I remembered the locked basement door and the fact that I could scarcely be let in by McGill, with the cops standing around, but I was feeling lightheaded and damage-proof. It was protecting its nucleus, which, even if I wasn't any more, I had in my hand. My crystalline rabbit's foot.

"Hold on a second," I said. "I've got another idea."

I put down the receiver and picked up the golf ball from the desk and put it on the floor. I stood up and put my right foot on it and, holding my breath, I raised my other foot. In any event, I would not have far to fall—but I did not fall. I remained upright, holding the filter paper and wobbling a little. Then I relaxed and closed my eyes—still I did not fall. The rabbit's foot was working, just as McGill had said. I stepped down two inches and picked up the phone.

"I'm coming across," I said. "That is, if the wire that runs over here from the lab is strong enough to hold me."

"Alec! You're nuts!" McGill said, and I hung up. (Diamonds of the world, unite! You have nothing to lose but your nucleus.)

I took a look over the sill at the wire. It was held by a powerful steel eyebolt, securely attached to the brickwork. Clutching the diamond fragment in its paper, I climbed over the sill and put a foot on the wire and felt immediately seasick. The wire vibrated like a harp string, but did not give noticeably, and I put my other foot on it. Then I almost blacked out and closed my eyes.

When I opened them again I found I had progressed some distance into the void. Nothing was holding me from overbalancing, but my body seemed to right itself automatically, as if I were a veteran tightrope walker.

In a frozen daze, I edged along, keeping my eyes fixed on the distant window in which I could see McGill and Molly watching me with white faces.

When I was about halfway, the crowd caught sight of me and yelled. A man with a broad-brimmed hat ran out from the others and, to my horror, pulled out a gun. Another man picked up a stone, wound himself up like a sand-lot pitcher, and hurled it just before the other pulled his trigger. They were excellent shots: the stone was hit by the bullet and both disintegrated. The man's gun jammed at his second try and the two heroes were grabbed by the police.

With my heart pounding, I kept going, until, about four yards from safety, my foot caught, and I looked down again. There was a splice in the wire, sticking up from which was a sharp end. I staggered and righted myself . . . and let go of the filter paper.

By now, the maelstrom was directly over me and my talisman was caught in the updraft. It did not fall, but I did. After a sickening instant, I was brought up with a jerk that nearly strangled me. The back of my coat had caught on the projecting wire and I swung there like an unused marionette.

The crowd shouted and milled around, and the cops called out directions to each other. One order was to send for the fire department. I found I could breathe, but I could not look down.

The all-important paper was fluttering around near the lab window and McGill was making grabs at it. Then it suddenly blew right in by him. His head reappeared and he shook his clasped hands at me. Molly remained at the window, her eyes round, the fingers of each hand crossed. I essayed a debonair smile, which she tried to answer. In the distance, I heard the owl sound of approaching fire engines.

From behind Molly there suddenly came an intense blue light, which rapidly increased until she became a dark silhouette, and I could just make out McGill looking at the glare, his eyes shielded by what I took to be a deep-blue bottle. His stance suggested elation. There appeared to be a terrific indraft—all the window shades were blowing straight into the lab and Molly's red hair streamed behind her.

In what was actually almost no time I heard the fire department turn into the campus, and one piece of equipment skidded to a stop directly under me. There was the sound of a winch and then I felt something touch my foot. At that moment, my jacket gave way with a tearing sound, Molly closed her eyes, and I landed like an oversize tarantula on top of the fireman's ladder.

Firemen and cops were climbing toward me, alternated like meat and tomatoes on a shish kebab. First to reach me was my friend the lieutenant. He rearrested me and pulled. I shook my head to his earnest entreaties and hung on with the tenacity of the unbrave. It seems to be impossible to detach a determined man from a ladder when you are also on it.

He and his friends gave up finally and ordered the ladder lowered, but one last fluke intervened—if it was a fluke. The machinery refused to work and we drove away, with me swaying grandly on my perch.

The lieutenant had the hook-and-ladder driven to a distant police station, where in due course Vinelli, the lawyer, arrived with his foot in a cast, and I was bailed out. The cops showed me surprising consideration; it turned out they were furious at the irresponsible riding they had been getting from Bill Bart. A scientific big shot that McGill knew, named Joe Stein, convinced them

I was in no way to blame, and the case was dropped. Professor Stein gave a wonderfully incomprehensible but tranquilizing statement to the press, and Molly and I went to Oyster Bay.

"In two weeks everybody'll have forgotten all about it," the lieutenant told us. "You may even be a hero. I don't know."

Before we left, we went with McGill to the lab and saw the diamond. It sat on a bench, gleaming brilliant, smooth-faceted and without a flaw. It was at least two feet across, about the same as the chunk of "glass" on Fifty-first Street.

"The cops never recognized what it was," McGill said, "it being so big."

"Who would?" Molly asked. "McGill, I've got an idea——"

"All I had to do," McGill said, ignoring her, "was to put the graphite on some cinder blocks and the fragment on the graphite. Then I turned a Bunsen flame on it and it caught fire with a terrifically bright flame—very small—I guess you saw it." I nodded. "It didn't give off any heat," he went on. "Adiabatic process. And it got its necessary pressure from the random motions together of the graphite particles. Some random motions! When that was used up, it started on the cinder blocks and then the CO_2 in the air. That's what caused the suction: the blinds were blown straight in. You probably missed that." I shook my head. "Anyway, this thing——"

"McGill," Molly interrupted, "I've got an *idea!*"

"—this thing has got to be dumped out at sea."

"Oh," Molly said, looking crestfallen. "I was just going to say why don't we break a piece off and sell it in Amsterdam?"

"Good God, no! That would only start it up all over again!"

"Just a *little* piece, McGill?"

"NO!"

With Stein's help, McGill convinced the police that the thing had to be dumped, and we dropped it off a police launch beyond Sandy Hook, to their bored perplexity. They would have been still more puzzled if they had known what it was.

McGill came down to Oyster Bay for the weekend and we played a game of gin rummy—a truly memorable game, because the cards behaved and I even lost a little.

He congratulated me in a preoccupied way, which annoyed me. "I should think you'd be gladder than that," I told him.

"I am," he said. "But there's something else——"

"What's that?" asked Molly, worried.

"The schools of fish are traveling head to tail. I'm wondering if that's just the beginning of another mess."

We went back to playing gin rummy, but our minds weren't on what we were doing. They haven't been since. Just yesterday, an ocean liner chased its berthing tugboats away and went sightseeing up the Hudson River.

NAME YOUR SYMPTOM
∞∞∞∞∞∞∞ by Jim Harmon ∞∞∞∞∞∞∞

HENRY INFIELD PLACED THE INSULATED CIRCLET ON
his head gently. The gleaming rod extended above his head about
a foot, the wires from it leading down into his collar, along his
spine and finally out his pants leg to a short metallic strap that
dragged on the floor.

Clyde Morgan regarded his partner. "Suppose—just suppose—
you *were* serious about this, why not just the shoes?"

Infield turned his soft blue eyes to the black and tan ox-
fords with the very thick rubber soles. "They might get soaked
through."

Morgan took his foot off the chair behind the desk and sat down.
"Suppose they were soaked through and you were standing on
a metal plate—steps or a manhole cover—what good would your
lightning rod do you then?"

Infield shrugged slightly. "I suppose a man must take some
chances."

Morgan said, "You can't do it, Henry. You're crossing the line.
The people we treat are on one side of the line and we're on the

other. If you cross that line, you won't be able to treat people again."

The small man looked out the large window, blinking myopically at the brassy sunlight. "That's just it, Clyde. There is a line between us, a wall. How can we really understand the people who come to us, if we hide on our side of the wall?"

Morgan shook his thick head, ruffling his thinning red hair. "I dunno, Henry, but staying on our side is a pretty good way to keep sane and that's quite an accomplishment these days."

Infield whirled and stalked to the desk. "That's the answer! The whole world is going mad and we are just sitting back watching it hike along. Do you know that what we are doing is really the most primitive medicine in the world? We are treating the symptoms and not the disease. One cannibal walking another with sleeping sickness doesn't cure anything. Eventually the savage dies—just as all those sick savages out in the street will die unless we can cure the disease, not only the indications."

Morgan shifted his ponderous weight uneasily. "Now, Henry, it's no good to talk like that. We psychiatrists can't turn back the clock. There just aren't enough of us or enough time to give that old-fashioned *therapy* to all the sick people."

Infield leaned on the desk and glared. "I called myself a psychiatrist once. But now I know we're semi-mechanics, semi-engineers, semi-inventors, semi lots of other things, but certainly not even semi-psychiatrists. A psychiatrist wouldn't give a foetic gyro to a man with claustrophobia."

His mind went back to the first gyro ball he had ever issued; the remembrance of his pride in the thing sickened him. Floating before him in memory was the vertical hoop and the horizontal hoop, both of shining steel-impervium alloy. Transfixed in the twin circles was the face of the patient, slack with smiles and sweat. But his memory was exaggerating the human element. The gyro actually passed over a man's shoulder, through his legs, under his arms. Any time he felt the walls creeping in to crush him, he could withdraw his head and limbs into the circle and feel safe. Steel-impervium alloy could resist even a nuclear explosion. The foetic gyro ball was worn day and night, for life.

The sickness overcame him. He sat down on Morgan's desk. "That's just one thing, the gyro ball. There are so many others, so many."

Morgan smiled. "You know, Henry, not all of our Cures are so —so—not all are like that. Those Cures for mother complexes aren't even obvious. If anybody does see that button in a patient's ear, it looks like a hearing aid. Yet for a nominal sum, the patient is equipped to hear the soothing recorded voice of his mother saying, 'It's all right, everything's all right, Mommy loves you, it's all right . . .'"

"But *is* everything all right?" Infield asked intensely. "Suppose the patient is driving over one hundred on an icy road. He thinks about slowing down, but there's the voice in his ear. Or suppose he's walking down a railroad track and hears a train whistle—if he can hear anything over that verbal Pablum gushing in his ear."

Morgan's face stiffened. "You know as well as I do that those voices are nearly subsonic. They don't cut a sense efficiency more than 23 per cent."

"At first, Clyde—only at first. But what about the severe case where we have to burn a three-dimensional smiling mother image on the eyes of the patient with radiation? With that image over everything he sees and with that insidious voice drumming in his head night and day, do you mean to say that man's senses will only be impaired 23 per cent? Why, he'll turn violently schizophrenic sooner or later—and you know it. The only cure we have for that is still a strait jacket, a padded cell or one of those inhuman lobotomies."

Morgan shrugged helplessly. "You're an idealist."

"You're damned right!" Infield slammed the door behind him. The cool air of the street was a relief. Infield stepped into the main stream of human traffic and tried to adjust to the second change in the air. People didn't bathe very often these days.

He walked along, buffeted by the crowd, carried along in this direction, shoved back in that direction. Most people in the crowd seemed to be Normals, but you couldn't tell. Many "Cures" were not readily apparent.

A young man with black glasses and a radar headset (a photophobe) was unable to keep from being pushed against Infield. He sounded out the lightning rod, his face changing when he realized it must be some kind of Cure. "Pardon me," he said warmly.

"Quite all right."

It was the first time in years that anyone had apologized to Infield for anything. He had been one of those condemned Normals, more to be scorned than pitied. Perhaps he could really get to understand these people, now that he had taken down the wall.

Suddenly something else was pushing against Infield, forcing the air from his lungs. He stared down at the magnetic suction dart clinging leechlike to his chest. Model Acrophobe 101-X, he catalogued immediately. Description: safety belt. But his emotions didn't behave so well. He was thoroughly terrified, heart racing, sweat glands pumping. The impervium cable undulated vulgarly. *Some primitive fear of snake symbols?* his mind wondered while panic crushed him.

"Uncouple that cable!" the shout rang out. It was not his own.

A clean-cut young man with mouse-colored hair was moving toward the stubble-chinned, heavy-shouldered man quivering in the center of a web of impervium cables stuck secure to the walls and windows of buildings facing the street, the sidewalk, a mailbox, the lamppost and Infield.

Mouse-hair yelled hoarsely, "Uncouple it, Davies! Can't you see the guy's got a lightning rod? You're grounding him!"

"I can't," Davies groaned. "I'm scared!"

Halfway down the twenty feet of cable, Mouse-hair grabbed on. "I'm holding it. Release it, you hear?"

Davies fumbled for the broad belt around his thickening middle. He jabbed the button that sent a negative current through the cable. The magnetic suction dart dropped away from Infield like a thing that had been alive and now was killed. He felt an overwhelming sense of relief.

After breathing deeply for a few moments, he looked up to see Davies releasing and drawing all his darts into his belt, making it resemble a Hydra-sized spiked dog collar. Mouse-hair stood by tensely as the crowd disassembled.

"This isn't the first time you've pulled something like this, Davies," he said. "You weren't too scared to release that cable. You just don't care about other people's feelings. This is *official*."

Mouse-hair drove a fast, hard right into the soft blue flesh of Davies' chin. The big man fell silently.

The other turned to Infield. "He was unconscious on his feet," he explained. "He never knew he fell."

"What did you mean by that punch being official?" Infield asked, while trying to arrange his feelings into the comfortable, familiar patterns.

The young man's eyes almost seemed to narrow, although his face didn't move; he merely radiated narrowed eyes. "How long have you been Cured?"

"Not—not long," Infield evaded.

The other glanced around the street. He moistened his lips and spoke slowly. "Do you think you might be interested in joining a fraternal organization of the Cured?"

Infield's pulse raced, trying to get ahead of his thoughts, and losing out. A chance to study a pseudo-culture of the "Cured" developed in isolation! "Yes, I think I might. I owe you a drink for helping me out. How about it?"

The man's face paled so fast, Infield thought for an instant that he was going to faint. "All right. I'll risk it." He touched the side of his face away from the psychiatrist.

Infield shifted around, trying to see that side of his benefactor, but couldn't manage it in good grace. He wondered if the fellow was sporting a Mom-voice hearing aid and was afraid of raising her ire. He cleared his throat, noticing the affectation of it. "My name's Infield."

"Price," the other answered absently. "George Price. I suppose they have liquor at the Club. We can have a *drink* there, I guess."

Price set the direction and Infield fell in at his side. "Look, if you don't drink, I'll buy you a cup of coffee. It was just a suggestion."

Under the mousy hair, Price's strong features were beginning to gleam moistly. "You are lucky in one way, Mr. Infield. People take one look at your Cure and don't ask you to go walking in the rain. But even after seeing *this*, some people still ask me to have a drink." *This* was revealed, as he turned his head, to be a small metal cube above his left ear.

Infield supposed it was a Cure, although he had never issued one like it. He didn't know if it would be good form to inquire what kind it was.

"It's a Cure for alcoholism," Price told him. "It runs a constant blood check to see that the alcohol level doesn't go over the sobriety limit."

"What happens if you take one too many?"

Price looked off as if at something not particularly interesting, but more interesting than what he was saying. "It drives a needle into my temple and kills me."

The psychiatrist felt cold fury rising in him. The Cures were supposed to save lives, not endanger them.

"What kind of irresponsible idiot could have issued such a device?" he demanded angrily.

"I did," Price said. "I used to be a psychiatrist. I was always good in shop. This is a pretty effective mechanism, if I say so myself. It can't be removed without causing my death and it's indestructible. Impervium-shielded, you see."

Price probably would never get crazed enough for liquor to kill himself, Infield knew. The threat of death would keep him constantly shocked sane. Men hide in the comforts of insanity, but when faced with death, they are often forced back to reality. A man can't move his legs; in a fire, though, he may run. His legs were definitely paralyzed before and may be again, but for one moment he would forget the moral defeat of his life and his withdrawal from life and live an enforced sanity. But sometimes the withdrawal was—or could become—too complete.

"We're here."

Infield looked up self-consciously and noticed that they had crossed two streets from his building and were standing in front of what appeared to be a small, dingy café. He followed Price through the screeching screen door.

They seated themselves at a small table with a red-checked cloth. Infield wondered why cheap bars and restaurants always used red-checked cloths. Then he looked closer and discovered the reason. They did a remarkably good job of camouflaging the spots of grease and alcohol.

A fat man who smelled of the grease and alcohol of the tablecloths shuffled up to them with a towel on his arm, staring ahead of him at some point in time rather than space.

Price lit a cigarette with unsteady hands. "Reggie is studying biblical text. Cute gadget. His contact lenses are made up of a lot of layers of polarized glass. Every time he blinks, the amount of polarization changes and a new page appears. His father once told him that if he didn't study his Bible and pray for him, his old dad would die."

The psychiatrist knew the threat on the father's part couldn't create such a fixation by itself. His eyebrows faintly inquired.

Price nodded jerkily. "Twenty years ago, at least."

"What'll you have, Georgie?" Reggie asked.

The young man snubbed out his cigarette viciously. "Bourbon. Straight."

Reggie smiled—a toothy, vacant, comedy-relief smile. "Fine.

The Good Book says a little wine is good for a man, or something like that. I don't remember exactly."

Of course he didn't, Infield knew. Why should he? It was useless to learn his Bible lessons to save his father, because it was obvious his father was dead. He would never succeed because there was no reason to succeed. But he had to try, didn't he, for his father's sake? He didn't hate his father for making him study. He didn't want him to die. He had to prove that.

Infield sighed. At least this device kept the man on his feet, doing some kind of useful work instead of rotting in a padded cell with a probably imaginary Bible. A man could cut his wrists with the edge of a sheet of paper if he tried long enough, so of course the Bible would be imaginary.

"But, Georgie," the waiter complained, "you know you won't drink it. You ask me to bring you drinks and then you just look at them. Boy, do you look funny when you're looking at drinks. Honest, Georgie, I want to laugh when I think of the way you look at a glass with a drink in it." He did laugh.

Price fumbled with the cigarette stub in the black iron ash tray, examining it with the skill of scientific observation. "Mr. Infield is buying me the drink and that makes it different."

Reggie went away. Price kept dissecting the tobacco and paper. Infield cleared his throat and again reminded himself against such obvious affectations. "You were telling me about some organization of the Cured," he said.

Price looked up, no longer interested in the relic of a cigarette. He was suddenly intensely interested and intensely observant of the rest of the café. "Was I? I was? Well, suppose you tell me something. What do you really think of the Incompletes?"

The psychiatrist felt his face frown. "Who?"

"I forgot. You haven't been one of us long. The Incompletes is a truer name for the so-called Normals. Have you ever thought of just how dangerous these people are, Mr. Infield?"

"Frankly, no," Infield said, realizing it was not the right thing to say but tiring of constant pretense.

"You don't understand. Everyone has some little phobia or fixation. Maybe everyone didn't have one once, but after being told they did have them for generations, everyone who didn't have one developed a defense mechanism and an aberration so they would be normal. If that phobia isn't brought to the surface and Cured, it may arise any time and endanger other people. The only safe, good sound citizens are Cured. Those lacking Cures—the Incompletes—*must be dealt with.*"

Infield's throat went dry. "And you're the one to deal with them?"

"It's my destiny." Price quickly added, "And yours, too, of course."

Infield nodded. Price was a demagogue, young, handsome, dynamic, likable, impassioned with his cause, and convinced that it was his divine destiny. He was a psychopathic egotist and a dangerous man. Doubly dangerous to Infield because, even though he was one of the few people who still read enough books from the old days of therapy to recognize Price for what he was, he nevertheless still liked the young man for the intelligence behind the egotism and the courage behind the fanaticism.

"How are we going to deal with the Incompletes?" Infield asked.

Price started to glance around the café, then half shrugged, almost visibly thinking that he shouldn't run that routine into the ground. "We'll Cure them whether they want to be Cured or not —for their own good."

Infield felt cold inside. After a time, he found that the roaring was not just in his head. It was thundering outside. He was getting sick. Price was the type of man who could spread his ideas throughout the ranks of the Cured—if indeed the plot was not already universal, imposed upon many ill minds.

He could picture an entirely Cured world and he didn't like

the view. Every Cure cut down on the mental and physical abilities of the patient as it was, whether Morgan and the others admitted it or not. But if everyone had a crutch to lean on for one phobia, he would develop secondary symptoms.

People would start needing two Cures—perhaps a foetic gyro and a safety belt—then another and another. There would always be a crutch to lean on for one thing and then room enough to develop something else—until everyone would be loaded down with too many Cures to operate.

A Cure was a last resort, dope for a malignancy case, euthanasia for the hopeless. Enforced Cures would be a curse for the individual and the race.

But Infield let himself relax. How could anyone force a mechanical relief for neurotic or psychopathic symptoms on someone who didn't want or need it?

"Perhaps you don't see how it could be done," Price said. "I'll explain."

Reggie's heavy hand set a straight bourbon down before Price and another before Infield. Price stared at the drink almost without comprehension of how it came to be. He started to sweat.

"George, drink it."

The voice belonged to a young woman, a blond girl with pink skin and suave, draped clothes. In this den of the Cured, Infield thought half humorously, it was surprising to see a Normal—an "Incomplete." But then he noticed something about the baby she carried. The Cure had been very simple. It wasn't even a mechanized half-human robot, just a rag doll. She sat down at the table.

"George," she said, "drink it. One drink won't raise your alcohol index to the danger point. You've got to get over this fear of even the sight or smell of liquor."

The girl turned to Infield. "You're one of us, but you're new, so you don't know about George. Maybe you can help if you do. It's all silly. He's not an alcoholic. He didn't need to put that Cure on his head. It's just an excuse for not drinking. All of this is just

because a while back something happened to the baby here"—
she adjusted the doll's blanket—"when he was drinking. Just drinking, not drunk.

"I don't remember what happened to the baby—it wasn't important. But George has been brooding about it ever since. I
guess he thinks something else bad will happen because of liquor.
That's silly. Why don't you tell him it's silly?"

"Maybe it is," Infield said softly. "You could take the shock if
he downed that drink and the shock might do you good."

Price laughed shortly. "I feel like doing something very melodramatic, like throwing my drink—and yours—across the room, but
I haven't got the guts to touch those glasses. Do it for me, will
you? Cauterizing the bite might do me good if I'd been bitten by
a rabid dog, but I don't have the nerve to do it."

Before Infield could move, Reggie came and set both drinks on
a little circular tray. He moved away. "I knew it. That's all he
did, just look at the drink. Makes me laugh."

Price wiped the sweat off his palms. Infield sat and thought.
Mrs. Price cooed to the rag doll, unmindful of either of them now.

"You were explaining," the psychiatrist said. "You were going
to tell me how you were going to Cure the Incompletes."

"I said *we* were going to do it. Actually *you* will play a greater
part than I, *Doctor* Infield."

The psychiatrist sat rigidly.

"You didn't think you could give me your right name in front
of your own office building and that I wouldn't recognize you? I
know some psychiatrists are sensitive about wearing Cures themselves, but it is a mark of honor of the completely sane man. You
should be proud of your Cure and eager to Cure others. *Very*
eager."

"Just what do you mean?" He already suspected Price's
meaning.

Price leaned forward. "There is one phobia that is so wide-
spread, a Cure is not even thought of—hypochondria. Hundreds

of people come to your office for a Cure and you turn them away. Suppose you and the other Cured psychiatrists give *everybody* who comes to you a Cure?"

Infield gestured vaguely. "A psychiatrist wouldn't hand out Cures unless they were absolutely necessary."

"You'll feel differently after you've been Cured for a while yourself. Other psychiatrists have."

Before Infield could speak, a stubble-faced, barrel-chested man moved past their table. He wore a safety belt. It was the man Price had called Davies, the one who had fastened one of his safety lines to Infield in the street.

Davies went to the bar in the back. "Gimme a bottle," he demanded of a vacant-eyed Reggie. He came back toward them, carrying the bottle in one hand, brushing off raindrops with the other. He stopped beside Price and glared. Price leaned back. The chair creaked. Mrs. Price kept cooing to the doll.

"You made me fall," Davies accused.

Price shrugged. "You were unconscious. You never knew it."

Sweat broke out on Davies' forehead. "You broke the Code. Don't you think I can imagine how it was to fall? You louse!"

Suddenly Davies triggered his safety belt. At close range, before the lines could fan out in a radius, all the lines in front attached themselves to Price, the ones at each side clung to their table and the floor, and all the others to the table behind Infield. Davies released all lines except those on Price, and then threw himself backward, dragging Price out of his chair and onto the floor. Davies didn't mind making others fall. They were always trying to make *him* fall just so they could laugh at him or pounce on him; why shouldn't he like to make them fall first?

Expertly, Davies moved forward and looped the loose lines around Price's head and shoulders and then around his feet. He crouched beside Price and shoved the bottle into the gasping mouth and poured.

Price twisted against the binding lines in blind terror, gagging and spouting whisky. Davies laughed and tilted the bottle more.

Mrs. Price screamed. "The Cure! If you get that much liquor in his system, it will kill him!" She rocked the rag doll in her arms, trying to soothe it, and stared in horror.

Infield hit the big man behind the ear. He dropped the bottle and fell over sideways on the floor. Fear and hate mingled in his eyes as he looked up at Infield.

Nonsense, Infield told himself. Eyes can't register emotion.

Davies released his lines and drew them in. He got up precariously. "I'm going to kill you," he said, glaring at Infield. "You made me fall worse than Georgie did. I'm really going to kill you."

Infield wasn't a large man, but he had pressed two hundred and fifty many times in gym. He grabbed Davies' belt with both hands and lifted him about six inches off the floor.

"I could drop you," the psychiatrist said.

"No!" Davies begged weakly. "Please!"

"I'll do it if you cause more trouble." Infield sat down and rubbed his aching forearms.

Davies backed off in terror, right into the arms of Reggie. The waiter closed his huge hands on the acrophobe's shoulders.

"*You* broke the Code all the way," Reggie said. "The Good Book says 'Thou shouldn't kill' or something like that, and so does the Code."

"Let him go, Reggie," Price choked out, getting to his feet. "I'm not dead." He wiped his hand across his mouth.

"No. No, you aren't." Infield felt an excitement pounding through him, same as when he had diagnosed his first case. No, better than that.

"That taste of liquor didn't kill you, Price. Nothing terrible happened. You could find some way to get rid of that Cure."

Price stared at him as if he were a padded-cell case. "That's different. I'd be a hopeless drunk without the Cure. Besides, no one ever gets rid of a Cure."

They were all looking at Infield. Somehow he felt this represented a critical point in history. It was up to him which turn the world took, the world as represented by these four Cured people. "I'm afraid I'm for *less* Cures instead of more, Price. Look, if I can show you that someone can discard a Cure, would you get rid of that—if I may use the word—*monstrous* thing on your head?"

Price grinned. Infield didn't recognize its smugness at the time.

"I'll show you." He took off the circlet with the lightning rod and yanked at the wire running down into his collar. The new-old excitement within was running high. He felt the wire snap and come up easily. He threw the Cure on the floor.

"Now," he said, "I am going out in that rainstorm. There's thunder and lightning out there. I'm afraid, but I can get along without a Cure and so can you."

"You can't! Nobody can!" Price screamed after him. He turned to the others. "If he reveals us, the Cause is lost. We've got to stop him *for good*. We've got to go after him."

"It's slippery," Davies whimpered. "I might fall."

Mrs. Price cuddled her rag doll. "I can't leave the baby and she mustn't get wet."

"Well, there's no liquor out there and you can study your text in the lightning flashes, Reggie. Come on."

Running down the streets that were tunnels of shining tar, running into the knifing ice bristles of the rain, Henry Infield realized that he was very frightened of the lightning.

There is no action without a reason, he knew from the old neglected books. He had had a latent fear of lightning when he chose the lightning-rod Cure. He could have picked a safety belt or foetic gyro just as well.

He sneezed. He was soaked through, but he kept on running. He didn't know what Price and Reggie planned to do when they caught him. He slipped and fell. He would soon find out what they wanted. The excitement was all gone now and it left an empty space into which fear rushed.

Reggie said, "We shall make a sacrifice."

Infield looked up and saw the lightning reflected on the blade of a thin knife. Infield reached toward it more in fascination than fear. He managed to get all his fingers around two of Reggie's. He jerked and the knife fell into Infield's palm. The psychiatrist pulled himself erect by holding to Reggie's arm. Staggering to his feet, he remembered what he must do and slashed at the waiter's head. A gash streaked across the man's brow and blood poured into his eyes. He screamed, "I can't see the words!"

It was his problem. Infield usually solved other people's problems, but now he ran away—he couldn't even solve his own.

Infield realized that he had gone mad as he held the thin blade high overhead, but he did need some kind of lightning rod. Price (who was just behind him, gaining) had been right. No one could discard a Cure. He watched the lightning play its light on the blade of his Cure and he knew that Price was going to kill him in the next moment.

The lightning hit him first.

Reggie squinted under the bandage at the lettering on the door that said INFIELD & MORGAN and opened the door. He ran across the room to the man sitting at the desk, reading by the swivel light.

"Mr. Morgan, your partner, Mr. Infield, he——"

"Just a moment." Morgan switched on the room lights. "What were you saying?"

"Mr. Infield went out without his Cure in a storm and was struck by lightning. We took him to the morgue. He must have been crazy to go out without his Cure."

Morgan stared into his bright desk light without blinking. "This is quite a shock to me. Would you mind leaving? I'll come over to your place and you can tell me about it later."

Reggie went out. "Yes, sir. He was struck by lightning, struck dead. He must have been crazy to leave his Cure . . ." The door closed.

Morgan exhaled. Poor Infield. But it wasn't the lightning that killed him, of course. Morgan adjusted the soundproofing plugs in his ears, thinking that you did have to have quite a bit of light to read lips. The thunder, naturally, was what had killed Infield. Loud noise—any noise—that would do it every time. Too bad Infield had never really stopped being one of the Incompletes. Dangerous people. Morgan would have to deal with them.

HORRER HOWCE
×××××××× by Margaret St. Clair ××××××××

DICKSON-HAWES' FACE HAD TURNED A DELICATE PEA
green. He closed the shutter on the opening very quickly indeed.
Nonetheless, he said in nearly his usual voice, "I'm afraid it's a
trifle literary, Freeman. Reminds of that thing of Yeats'—'What
monstrous beast, Its time come, uh, round again, slouches toward
Bethlehem to be born?' But the people who go to a horror house
for amusement aren't literary. It wouldn't affect them the way it
did me." He giggled nervously.

No answering emotion disturbed the normal sullenness of Freeman's face. "I thought there was a nice feel to it," he said ob-
stinately. "I wouldn't have put so much time in on this stuff
unless I thought you'd be interested. Research is more my line. I
could have made a lot more money working on one of the government projects."

"You didn't have much choice, did you?" Dickson-Hawes said
pleasantly. "A political past is such a handicap, unless one's willing to risk prosecution for perjury."

"I'm as loyal as anybody! For the last five years—eight, ten—

all I've wanted to do was make a little cash. The trouble is, I always have such rotten luck."

"Um." Dickson-Hawes wiped his forehead unobtrusively. "Well, about your little effort. There are some nice touches, certainly. The idea of the monstrous womb, alone on the seashore, slowly swelling, and . . ." In the folds of his handkerchief he stifled a sort of cough. "No, I'm afraid it's too poetic. I can't use it, old chap."

The two men moved away from the shuttered opening. Freeman said, "Then Spring Scene is the only one you're taking?"

"Of those of yours I've seen. It's horrid enough, but not too horrid. Haven't you anything else?" Dickson-Hawes' voice was eager, but eagerness seemed to be mixed with other things—reluctance, perhaps, and the fear of being afraid.

Freeman fingered his lower lip. "There's the Well," he said after a moment. "It needs a little more work done on it, but—I guess you could look at it."

"I'd be delighted to," Dickson-Hawes agreed heartily. "I do hope you understand, old man, that there's quite a lot of *money* involved in this."

"Yeah. You've really got the capital lined up? Twice before, you were sure you had big money interested. But the deals always fell through. I got pretty tired of it."

"This time it's different. The money's already in escrow, not to mention what I'm putting in myself. We intend a coast-to-coast network of horror houses in every gayway, playland and amusement park."

"Yeah. Well, come along."

They went down the corridor to another door. Freeman unlocked it. "By the way," he said, "I'd appreciate it if you'd keep your voice down. Some of the machinery in this stuff's—delicate. Sensitive."

"By all means. Of course."

They entered. To their right was an old brick house, not quite in ruin. To the left, a clump of blackish trees cut off the sky. Just in front of them was the moss-covered coping of an old stone well. The ground around the well was slick with moisture.

Dickson-Hawes sniffed appreciatively. "I must say you've paid wonderful attention to detail. It's exactly like being out of doors. It even smells froggy and damp."

"Thanks," Freeman replied with a small, dour smile.

"What happens next?"

"Look down in the well."

Rather gingerly, Dickson-Hawes approached. He leaned over. From the well came a gurgling splash.

Dickson-Hawes drew back abruptly. Now his face was not quite greenish; it was white. "My word, what a monster!" he gasped. "What is it, anyway?"

"Clockwork," Freeman answered. "It'll writhe for thirty-six hours on one winding. I couldn't use batteries, you know, on account of the water. That greenish flash in the eyes comes from prisms. And the hair is the same thing you get on those expensive fur coats, only longer. I think they call it plasti-mink."

"What happens if I keep leaning over? Or if I drop pebbles down on it?"

"It'll come out at you."

Dickson-Hawes looked disappointed. "Anything else?"

"The sky gets darker and noises come out of the house. Isn't that enough?"

Dickson-Hawes coughed. "Well, of course we'd have to soup it up a bit. Put an electrified rail around the well coping and perhaps make the approach to the well slippery so the customers would have to grasp the hand rail. Install a couple of air jets to blow the girls' dresses up. And naturally make it a good deal darker so couples can neck when the girl gets scared. But it's a nice little effort, Freeman, very nice indeed. I'm almost certain we can use it. Yes, we ought to have your Well in our horror house."

Dickson-Hawes' voice had rung out strongly on the last few

words. Now there came another watery splash from the well. Freeman seemed disturbed.

"I *told* you to keep your voice down," he complained. "The partitions are thin. When you talk that loud, you can be heard all over the place. It isn't good for the—machinery."

"Sorry."

"Don't let it happen again. . . . I don't think the customers ought to neck in here. This isn't the place for it. If they've got to neck, let them do it outside. In the corridor."

"You have no idea, old chap, what people will do in a darkened corridor in a horror house. It seems to stimulate them. But you may be right. Letting them stay here to neck might spoil the illusion. We'll try to get them on out."

"Okay. How much are you paying me for this?"

"Our lawyer will have to discuss the details," said Dickson-Hawes. He gave Freeman a smile reeking with synthetic charm. "I assure you he can draw up a satisfactory contract. I can't be more definite until I know what the copyright or patent situation would be."

"I don't think my Well could be patented," Freeman said. "There are details in the machinery nobody understands but me. I'd have to install each unit in your horror-house network myself. There ought to be a clause in the contract about my per-diem expenses and a traveling allowance."

"I'm sure we can work out something mutually satisfactory."

"Uh . . . let's get out of here. This is an awfully damp place to do much talking in."

They went out into the hall again. Freeman locked the door. "Have you anything else?" Dickson-Hawes asked.

Freeman's eyes moved away. "No."

"Oh, come now, old chap. Don't be coy. As I told you before, there's *money* involved."

"What sort of thing do you want?"

"Well, horrid. Though not quite so poetically horrid as what you have behind the shutter. That's a little too much. Perhaps something with a trifle more action. With more customer participation. Both the Well and Spring Scene are on the static side."

"Uh."

They walked along the corridor. Freeman said slowly, "I've been working on something. There's action and customer participation in it, all right, but I don't know. It's full of bugs. I just haven't had time to work it out yet."

"Let's have it, old man, by all means!"

"Not so loud! You've got to keep your voice down. Otherwise I can't take you in." Freeman himself was speaking almost in a whisper. "All right. Here."

They had stopped before a much more substantial door than the one behind which the Well lay. There was a wide rubber flange all around it, and it was secured at top and bottom by two padlocked hasps. In the top of the door, three or four small holes had been bored, apparently to admit air.

"You must have something pretty hot locked up behind all that," Dickson-Hawes remarked.

"Yeah." Freeman got a key ring out of his pocket and began looking over it. Dickson-Hawes glanced around appraisingly.

"Somebody's been writing on your wall," he observed. "Rotten speller, I must say."

Freeman raised his eyes from the key ring and looked in the direction the other man indicated. On the wall opposite the door, just under the ceiling, somebody had written HORRER HOWCE in what looked like blackish ink.

The effect of the ill-spelled words on Freeman was remarkable. He dropped the key ring with a clatter, and when he straightened from picking it up, his hands were quivering.

"I've changed my mind," he said. He put the key ring back in his pocket. "I always did have the damnedest luck."

Dickson-Hawes leaned back against the wall and crossed his ankles. "How do you get your ideas, Freeman?"

"Oh, all sorts of ways. Things I read, things people tell me, things I see. All sorts of ways." Both men were speaking in low tones.

"They're amazing. And your mechanical effects—I really don't see how you get machinery to do the things you make it do."

Freeman smiled meagerly. "I've always been good at mechanics. Particularly radio and signaling devices. Relays. Communication problems, you might say. I can communicate with anything. Started when I was a kid."

There was a silence. Dickson-Hawes kept leaning against the wall. A close observer, Freeman noticed almost a tic, a fluttering of his left eyelid.

At last Freeman said, "How much are you paying for the Well?"

Dickson-Hawes closed his eyes and opened them again. He may have been reflecting that while a verbal contract is quite as binding as a written one, it is difficult to prove the existence of a verbal contract to which there are no witnesses.

He answered, "Five thousand in a lump sum, I think, and a prorated share of the net admissions for the first three years."

There was an even longer silence. Freeman's face relaxed at the mention of a definite sum. He said, "How are your nerves? I need money so damned bad."

Dickson-Hawes' face went so blank that it would seem the other man had touched a vulnerable spot. "Pretty good, I imagine," he said in a carefully modulated voice. "I saw a good deal of action during the war."

Cupidity and some other emotion contended in Freeman's eyes. He fished out the key ring again. "Look, you must not make a noise. No yelling or anything like that, no matter what you see. They're very—I mean the machinery's delicate. It's full of bugs I haven't got rid of yet. The whole thing will be a lot less ghastly later on. I'm going to keep the basic idea, make it just as exciting as it is now, but tone it down plenty."

"I understand."

Freeman looked at him with a frown. "Don't make a noise," he cautioned again. "Remember, none of this is real." He fitted the key into the first of the padlocks on the stoutly built door.

The second padlock was a little stiff. Freeman had to fidget with it. Finally he got the door open. The two men stepped through it. They were outside.

There is no other way of expressing it: They were outside. If the illusion had been good in the Well, here it was perfect. They stood in a sort of safety island on the edge of a broad freeway, where traffic poured by in an unending rush eight lanes wide. It was the time of day when, though visibility is really better than at noon, a nervous motorist or two has turned on his parking lights. Besides the two men, the safety island held a new, shiny, egg-plant-colored sedan.

Dickson-Hawes turned a bewildered face on his companion. "Freeman," he said in a whisper, "did you *make* all this?"

For the first time, Freeman grinned. "Pretty good, isn't it?" he replied, also in a whisper. He opened the car door and slid into the driver's seat. "Get in. We're going for a ride. Remember, no noise."

The other man obeyed. Freeman started the car—it had a very quiet motor—and watched until a lull in the traffic gave him a chance to swing out from the curb. He stepped on the accelerator. The landscape began to move by.

Cars passed them. They passed some cars. Dickson-Hawes looked for the speedometer on the dashboard and couldn't find it. A garage, a service station, a billboard went by. The sign on the garage read: WE FIX FLATTEDS. The service station had conical pumps. The tomatoes on the billboard were purple and green.

Dickson-Hawes was breathing shallowly. He said, "Freeman—where *are* we?"

Once more, the other man grinned. "You're getting just the effect I mean to give," he retorted in a pleased whisper. "At first, the customer thinks he's on an ordinary freeway, with ordinary people hurrying home to their dinners. Then he begins to notice all sorts of subtle differences. Everything's a little off key. It adds to the uneasiness."

"Yes, but—what's the object of all this? What are we trying to do?"

"Get home to our dinners, like everyone else."

"Where does the—well, difficulty come in?"

"Do you see that car in the outer lane?" They were still conversing in whispers. "Black, bullet shaped, quite small, going very fast?"

"Yes."

"Keep your eye on it."

The black car *was* going very fast. It caught up with a blue sedan in front of it, cut in on it and began to crowd it over to the curb. The blue sedan tried to shake off the black car, but without success. If the driver didn't want to be wrecked, he had to get over.

For a while, the two cars ran parallel. The black car began to slow down and crowd more aggressively than ever. Suddenly it cut obliquely in front of the sedan and stopped.

There was a frenzied scream of brakes from the sedan. It stopped with its left fender almost against the black bullet-shaped car. The bodies were so close, there was no room for the sedan driver to open his door.

Freeman had let the car he was driving slow down, presumably so Dickson-Hawes could see everything.

For a moment there was nothing to see. Only for a moment. Then two—or was it three?—long, blackish, extremely thin arms came out from the black car and fumbled with the glass in the window of the sedan. The glass was forced down. The arms entered the sedan.

From the sedan there came a wild burst of shrieking. It was

like the flopping, horrified squawks of a chicken at the chopping block. The shrieks were still going on when the very thin arms came out with a——

The light hid nothing. The three very thin arms came out with a plucked-off human arm.

They threw it into the interior of the black car. The three arms invaded the sedan once more.

This time, Dickson-Hawes had turned neither white nor greenish, but a blotchy gray. His mouth had come open all around his teeth, in the shape of a rigid oblong with raised, corded edges. It was perfectly plain that if he was not screaming, it was solely because his throat was too paralyzed.

Freeman gave his passenger only a momentary glance. He was looking into the rear-view mirror. He began to frown anxiously.

The shrieking from the blue sedan had stopped. Dickson-Hawes covered his face with his hands while Freeman drove past it and the other car. When the group lay behind them, he asked in a shaking whisper, "Freeman, are there any more of them? The black cars, I mean?"

"Yeah. One of them's coming toward us now."

Dickson-Hawes' head swiveled around. Another of the black cars was hurtling toward them through the traffic, though it was still a long way behind.

Dickson-Hawes licked his lips.

"Is it—after us?"

"I think so."

"But why? Why—us?"

"Part of the game. Wouldn't be horrid otherwise. Hold on. I'm going to try to shake it off."

Freeman stepped down on the accelerator. The eggplant-colored sedan shot ahead. It was a very fast car and Freeman was evidently an expert and nerveless driver. They slid through nonexistent holes in the traffic, glanced off from fenders, slipped crazily from lane to lane, a shuttle in a pattern of speed and escape.

The black car gained on them. No gymnastics. A bulletlike directness. But it was nearer all the time.

Dickson-Hawes gave a sort of whimper.

"No noise," Freeman cautioned in a fierce whisper. "That'll bring them down for sure. *Now!*"

He pressed the accelerator all the way down. The eggplant-colored car bounced and swayed. There was a tinkle of glass from the headlights of the car on the left as the sedan brushed it glancingly. Dickson-Hawes moaned, but realized they had gained the length of several cars. Momentarily, the black pursuer fell behind.

They went through two red lights in a row. So did the black bullet. It began to edge in on them. Closer and closer. Faster and faster.

Dickson-Hawes had slumped forward with his head on his chest. The black car cut toward them immediately.

Freeman snarled. Deliberately, he swung out into the path of the pursuer. For a second, it gave ground.

"Bastards," Freeman said grimly.

The black car cut in on them like the lash of a whip. The sedan slithered. Hub caps grated on concrete. The sedan swayed drunkenly. Brakes howled. Dickson-Hawes, opening his eyes involuntarily for the crash, saw that they were in a safety island. The same safety island, surely, from which they had started out?

The black car went streaking on by.

"I hate those things," Freeman said bitterly. "Damned Voom. If I could— But never mind. We got away. We're safe. We're home."

Dickson-Hawes did not move. "I said we're safe," Freeman repeated. He opened the car door and pushed the other man out through it. Half shoving, half carrying, he led him to the door from which they had entered the freeway. It was still the time of day at which nervous motorists turn on their parking lights.

Freeman maneuvered Dickson-Hawes through the door. He closed it behind them and fastened the padlocks in the hasps. They were out in the corridor again—the corridor on whose wall somebody had written HORRER HOWCE.

Freeman drew a deep breath. "Well. Worked better than I thought it would. I was afraid you'd yell. I thought you were the type that yells. But I guess the third time's the charm."

"What?"

"I mean I guess my goddamn luck has turned at last. Yeah. What did you think of it?"

Dickson-Hawes swallowed, unable to answer.

Freeman regarded him. "Come along to my office and have a drink. You look like you need one. And then you can tell me what you think of this setup."

The office was in the front of the house, down a couple of steps. Dickson-Hawes sank into the chair Freeman pulled out for him. He gulped down Freeman's dubious reddish bourbon gratefully.

After the second drink he was restored enough to ask, "Freeman, was it real?"

"Certainly not," the other man said promptly.

"It looked awfully real," Dickson-Hawes objected. "That arm . . ." He shuddered.

"A dummy," Freeman answered promptly once more. "You didn't see any blood, did you? Of course not. It was a dummy arm."

"I hope so. I don't see how you could have *made* all the stuff we saw. There's a limit to what machinery can do. I'd like another drink."

Freeman poured. "What did you think of it?"

Color was coming back to Dickson-Hawes' cheeks. "It was the most horrible experience I ever had in my life."

Freeman grinned. "Good. People like to be frightened. That's why roller-coaster rides are so popular."

"Not that much, people don't. Nobody would enjoy a roller-coaster ride if he saw cars crashing all around him and people getting killed. You'll have to tone it down a lot. An awful lot."

"But you liked it?"

"On the whole, yes. It's a unique idea. But you'll have to tone it down about 75 per cent."

Freeman grimaced. "It can be done. But I'll have to have a definite commitment from you before I undertake such extensive changes."

"Um."

"There are other places I could sell it, you know," Freeman said pugnaciously. "Jenkins of Amalgamated might be interested. Or Silberstein."

"Jenkins lit out with about six thousand of Amalgamated's dollars a couple of months ago. Nobody's seen him since. And they found Silberstein wandering on the streets last week in a sort of fit. Didn't you know? He's in a mental home. You won't be selling either of *them* much of anything."

Freeman sighed, but made no attempt to dispute these distressing facts. "I'll have to have a definite commitment from you before I make that many major changes," he repeated stubbornly.

"Well . . ." Fright and whisky may have made Dickson-Hawes a little less cautious than usual. "We could pay you fifty a week for a couple of months while you worked on it, as advance against royalties. If we didn't like the final results, you wouldn't have to give back the advance."

"It's robbery. Apprentice mechanics earn more than that. Make it sixty-five."

"I hate haggling. Tell you what. We'll make it sixty."

Freeman shrugged tiredly. "Let's get it down in black and white. I'll just draw up a brief statement of the terms and you can sign it."

"Well, okay."

Freeman stooped and began to rummage in a desk drawer. Once he halted and seemed to listen. He opened another drawer.

"Thought I had some paper. . . . Yeah, here it is." He turned on the desk light and began to write.

Dickson-Hawes leaned back in his chair and sipped at Freeman's whisky. He crossed his legs and recrossed them. He was humming "Lili Marlene" loudly and off pitch. His head rested against the wall.

Freeman's pen moved across the paper. "That's about it," he said at last. He was smiling. "Yeah. I——"

There was a splintering crash, the sound of lath and plaster breaking. Freeman looked up from the unsigned agreement to see the last of his entrepreneurs—the last, the indubitable last—being borne off in the long black arms of the Voom.

It was the first time they had gone through the partitions in search of a victim, but the partitions were thin and the unsuccessful chase on the highway had excited them more than Freeman had realized. There has to be a first time for any entity, even for Voom.

Ten full minutes passed. Dickson-Hawes' shrieks died away. The third episode had ended just as disastrously as the earlier two. There wasn't another entrepreneur in the entire U.S.A. from whom Freeman could hope to realize a cent for the contents of his horror house. He was sunk, finished, washed up.

Freeman remained sitting at his desk, motionless. All his resentment at the bad luck life had saddled him with—loyalty oaths, big deals that fell through, chiselers like Dickson-Hawes, types that yelled when the Voom were after them—had coalesced into an immobilizing rage.

At last he drew a quavering sigh. He went over to the bookcase, took out a book, looked up something. He took out a second book, a third.

He nodded. A gleam of blind, intoxicated vindictiveness had come into his eyes. Just a few minor circuit changes, that was all. He knew the other, more powerful entities were there. It was only a question of changing his signaling devices to get in touch with them.

Freeman put the book back on the shelf. He hesitated. Then he started toward the door. He'd get busy on the circuit changes right away. And while he was making them, he'd be running over plans for the horror house he was going to use the new entities to help him build.

It would be dangerous. So what? Expensive . . . he'd get the money somewhere. But he'd fix them. He'd build a horror house for the beasts that would make them sorry they'd ever existed —A Horrer Howce for the Voom.

MAN OF DISTINCTION
⋙⋙⋙⋙ by Michael Shaara ⋙⋙⋙⋙

THE REMARKABLE DISTINCTION OF THATCHER BLITT
did not come to the attention of a bemused world until late in the
year 2180. Although Thatcher Blitt was, by the standards of his
time, an extremely successful man financially, this was not considered *real* distinction. Unfortunately for Blitt, it never has
been.

The history books do not record the names of the most successful merchants of the past unless they happened by chance to
have been connected with famous men of the time. Thus Croesus
is remembered largely for his contributions to famous Romans
and successful armies. And Haym Solomon, a similarly wealthy
man, would have been long forgotten had he not also been a finan-
cial mainstay of the American Revolution and consorted with famous, if impoverished, statesmen.

So if Thatcher Blitt was distinct among men, the distinction
was not immediately apparent. He was a small, gaunt, fragile man
who had the kind of face and bearing that are perfect for movie
crowd scenes. Absolutely forgettable. Yet Thatcher Blitt was one

of the foremost businessmen of his time. For he was president and founder of that noble institution, Genealogy, Inc.

Thatcher Blitt was not yet twenty-five when he made the discovery which was to make him among the richest men of his time. His discovery was, like all great ones, obvious yet profound. He observed that every person had a father.

Carrying on with this thought, it followed inevitably that every father had a father, and so on. In fact, thought Blitt, when you considered the matter rightly, everyone alive was the direct descendant of untold numbers of fathers, down through the ages, all descending, one after another, father to son. And so backward, unquestionably, into the unrecognizable and perhaps simian fathers of the past.

This thought, on the face of it not particularly startling, hit young Blitt like a blow. He saw that since each man had a father, and so on and so on, it ought to be possible to construct the genealogy of every person now alive. In short, it should be possible to trace your family back, father by father, to the beginning of time.

And of course it was. For that was the era of the time scanner. And with a time scanner, it would be possible to document your family tree with perfect accuracy. You could find out exactly from whom you had sprung.

And so Thatcher Blitt made his fortune. He saw clearly at the beginning what most of us see only now, and he patented it. He was aware not only of the deep-rooted sense of snobbishness that exists in many people, but also of the simple yet profound force of curiosity. Who exactly, one says to oneself, *was* my forty-times-great-great-grandfather? A Roman Legionary? A Viking? A pyramid builder? One of Xenophon's Ten Thousand? Or was he, perhaps (for it is always possible), Alexander the Great?

Thatcher Blitt had a product to sell. And sell he did, for other reasons that he alone had noted at the beginning. The races of mankind have twisted and turned with incredible complexity over the years; the numbers of people have been enormous.

With thirty thousand years in which to work, it was impossible that there was not, somewhere along the line, a famous ancestor for everybody. A minor king would often suffice, or even a general in some forgotten army. And if these direct ancestors were not enough, it was fairly simple to establish close blood kinship with famous men. The bloodlines of man, you see, begin with a very few people. In all of ancient Greece, in the time of Pericles, there were only a few thousand families.

Seeing all this, Thatcher Blitt became a busy man. It was necessary not only to patent his idea, but to produce the enormous capital needed to found a large organization. The cost of the time scanner was at first prohibitive, but gradually that obstacle was overcome, only for Thatcher to find that the government for many years prevented him from using it. Yet Blitt was indomitable. And eventually, after years of heart-rending waiting, Genealogy, Inc., began operations.

It was a tremendous success. Within months, the very name of the company and its taut slogan, "An Ancestor for Everybody," became household words. There was but one immediate drawback. It soon became apparent that, without going back very far into the past, it was sometimes impossible to tell who was really the next father in line. The mothers were certain, but the fathers were something else again. This was a ponderable point.

But Blitt refused to be discouraged. He set various electronic engineers to work on the impasse and a solution was found. An ingenious device which tested blood electronically through the scanner—based on the different sine waves of the blood groups—saved the day. That invention was the last push Genealogy, Inc., was ever to need. It rolled on to become one of the richest and, for a long while, most exclusive corporations in the world.

Yet it was still many years before Thatcher Blitt himself had time to rest. There were patent infringements to be fought, new developments in the labs to be watched, new ways to be found to make the long and arduous task of father-tracing easier and more economical. Hence he was well past sixty when he at last had time to begin considering himself.

He had become by this time a moderately offensive man. Surrounded as he had been all these years by pomp and luxury, by impressive names and extraordinary family trees, he had succumbed at last. He became unbearably name-conscious.

He began by regrouping his friends according to their ancestries. His infrequent parties were characterized by his almost parliamentarian system of seating. No doubt, all this had been in Thatcher Blitt to begin with—it may well be, in perhaps varying quantities, in all of us—but it grew with him, prospered with him. Yet in all those years he never once inspected his own forebears.

You may well ask, was he afraid? One answers, one does not know. But at any rate, the fact remains that Thatcher Blitt, at the age of sixty-seven, was one of the few rich men in the world who did not know who exactly their ancestors had been.

And so, at last, we come to the day when Thatcher Blitt was sitting alone in his office, one languid hand draped vacantly over his brow, listening with deep satisfaction to the hum and click of the enormous operations which were going on in the building around him.

What moved him that day remains uncertain. Perhaps it was that, from where he was sitting, he could see row upon row of action pictures of famous men which had been taken from his time scanners. Or perhaps it was simply that this profound question had been gnawing at him all these years, deeper and deeper, and on this day broke out into the light.

But whatever the reason, at 11:02 that morning, he leaped vitally from his chair. He summoned Cathcart, his chief assistant, and gave him the immortal command.

"Cathcart!" he grated, stung to the core of his being. "Who am I?"

Cathcart rushed off to find out.

There followed some of the most taut and fateful days in the brilliant history of Genealogy, Inc. Father-tracing is, of course, a painstaking business. But it was not long before word had begun to filter out to interested people.

The first interesting discovery made was a man called Blott, in eighteenth-century England. (No explanation was ever given for the name's alteration from Blott to Blitt. Certain snide individuals took this to mean that the name had been changed as a means to avoid prosecution, or some such, and immediately began making light remarks about the Blotts on old Blitt's escutcheon.) This Blott had the distinction of having been a wine seller of considerable funds.

This reputedly did not sit well with Thatcher Blitt. Merchants, he snapped, however successful, are not worthy of note. He wanted empire builders. He wanted, at the very least, a name he had heard about. A name that appeared in the histories.

His workers furiously scanned back into the past.

Months went by before the next name appeared. In ninth-century England, there was a wandering minstrel named John (last name unprintable) who achieved considerable notoriety as a ballad singer, before dying an unnatural death in the boudoir of a lady of high fashion. Although the details of this man's life were of extreme interest, they did not impress the old man. He was, on the contrary, rather shaken. A minstrel. And a rogue to boot.

There were shake-ups in Genealogy, Inc. Cathcart was replaced by a man named Jukes, a highly competent man despite his interesting family name. Jukes forged ahead full steam past the birth of Christ (no relation). But he was well into ancient Egypt before the search began to take on the nature of a crisis.

Up until then, there was simply nobody. Or to be more precise, nobody but *nobodies*. It was incredible, all the laws of chance were against it, but there was, actually, not a single ancestor of note. And no way of faking one, for Thatcher Blitt couldn't be

THE FOURTH GALAXY READER 86

fooled by his own methods. What there was was simply an unending line of peasants, serfs, an occasional foot soldier or leather worker. Past John, the ballad singer, there was no one at all worth reporting to the old man.

This situation would not continue, of course. There were so few families for men to spring from. The entire Gallic nation, for example, a great section of present-day France, sprang from the family of one lone man in the North of France in the days before Christ. Every native Frenchman, therefore, was at least the son of a king. It was impossible for Thatcher Blitt to be less.

So the hunt went on from day to day, past ancient Greece, past Jarmo, past the wheel and metals and farming and on even past all civilization, outward and backward into the cold primordial wastes of northern Germany.

And still there was nothing. Though Jukes lived in daily fear of losing his job, there was nothing to do but press on. In Germany he reduced Blitt's ancestor to a slovenly little man who was one of only three men in the entire tribe, or family, one of three in an area which now contains millions. But Blitt's ancestor, true to form, was simply a member of the tribe. As was his father before him.

Yet onward it went. Westward back into the French caves, southward into Spain and across the unrecognizable Mediterranean into a verdant North Africa, backward in time past even the Cro-Magnons, and yet ever backward, 30,000 years, 35,000, with old Blitt reduced now practically to gibbering and still never an exceptional forebear.

There came a time when Jukes had at last, inevitably, to face the old man. He had scanned back as far as he could. The latest ancestor he had unearthed for Blitt was a hairy creature who did not walk erect. And yet, even here, Blitt refused to concede.

"It may be," he howled, "it *must* be that my ancestor *was* the first man to walk erect or light a fire—to do *something*."

It was not until Jukes pointed out that all those things had been already examined and found hopeless that Blitt finally gave in. Blitt was a relative, of course, of the first man to stand erect, the man with the first human brain. But so was everybody else on the face of the Earth. There was truly nowhere else to explore. What would be found now would be only the common history of mankind.

Blitt retired to his chambers and refused to be seen.

The story went the rounds, as such stories will. And it was then at last, after 40,000 years of insignificance, that the name of Blitt found everlasting distinction. The story was picked up, fully documented, by psychologists and geneticists of the time, and inserted into textbooks as a profound commentary on the forces of heredity. The name of Thatcher Blitt in particular has become famous, has persisted until this day. For he is the only man yet discovered, or ever likely to be discovered, with this particular distinction.

In 40,000 years of scanner-recorded history, the bloodline of Blitt (or Blott) never once produced an exceptional man.

That record is unsurpassed.

THE BOMB IN THE BATHTUB
xxxxxxxx by Thomas N. Scortia xxxxxxxx

THE YOUNG MAN SAID HIS NAME WAS SIDNEY COLE-
man. He looked rather like a smooth-muscled distance swimmer,
lately taken to fat. At the moment, his eyes were sunken and
wild-looking.

"He said my bathroom was the center of a probability nexus,"
the young man wailed. "And now there's an H-bomb in my bathtub."

Caedman Wickes rubbed a lean red hand across the scarred
surface of his desk and winced at the gritty feel of dust under his
palm.

Then he closely inspected the coarse blond bristles on the backs
of his fingers.

"Does it do anything else?" he asked at last with great delibera-
tion. "Tick, for instance?"

"Nothing. It just lies there, eying the hot-water faucet with
that stupid blue eye and mouthing all sorts of platitudes."

"Isn't this all a little ridiculous?" Wickes asked.

"That's what the police thought." Coleman ran blunt fingers
through close-cropped black hair.

"No, I didn't mean that. After all," Wickes pointed out, "if you're going to put anything as big as a bomb in the bathroom, the logical place *is* the bathtub."

"Logical to you, maybe."

Wickes touched his nose reflectively and gestured toward the office door. Its chipped markings spelled in mirrored reverse: *Caedman Wickes, Private Investigator, Specializing in Odd Complaints.*

He said, "In my business I often encounter the unusual. But there's always an internal logic. That's the guiding principle of my success. Always—*always* look for the internal logic. All else follows."

He steepled his fingers reminiscently. "I remember a client who thought he had a Venusian trapped in his washing machine. Very logical, if you stop to think about it. However"—Wickes pursed his lips sorrowfully—"it developed that he was quite mad. A pity, too. Such a lovely idea. Anyway, I meant the idea of using an H-bomb was ridiculous. The best that such a bomb could do would be to vaporize the city and possibly the nearer suburbs. Hardly worth worrying about."

"He didn't actually say it was an H-bomb," Coleman said tiredly. "I just assumed that's what it was. After all, he did say he wanted to destroy this universe."

"Ah!" Wickes's eyes gleamed. "Not the Universe? Just *this* universe?"

"He made a point of that. He said there are an infinite number of probable universes. He just wants to destroy the best of all possible universes—*this* one."

"Undoubtedly paranoid," Wickes commented.

"Of course. This is part of his therapy. He's insane."

"Then this isn't his universe?"

"I should think not. The cure wouldn't be of much use if he destroyed the universe in which he exists, would it?"

Wickes pursed his lips. "That doesn't necessarily follow. Why, I remember——"

Coleman leaped to his feet and leaned forward, bracing his hands on the desk. "Don't! Don't keep on reminiscing! That thing says it's going to detonate this Tuesday. You've got to figure a way to de-fuse it."

"Patience, patience," Wickes chided. "It never pays to lose one's head about these things."

He unfolded his cadaverous six-foot-seven frame from behind the desk, secured a trench coat, black wool scarf and stained snap-brim felt hat from the top of a battered filing cabinet.

"I really should smoke a pipe," he mused as he donned the garments, "but I do think the coat and hat are enough of a concession to convention, don't you?"

"I don't give a damn if you wear pink tights and fly through the air," Coleman snorted. "Just do something about that bomb in my bathtub."

Wickes gestured limply toward the door.

"I can see," he said, as they walked through the hall, their feet evoking protesting squeaks from the curling boards of the floor, "that you don't appreciate the essential beauty of the situation."

"Beauty? How would you like a bomb in *your* bathtub?"

"Not the point at all," Wickes reproved. "Now this much reminds me of the client who had a scheme to psychoanalyze his great-great-great-grandfather. Had a theory that neuroses were transmitted genetically. Well, he wanted me to ascertain the old gentleman's whereabouts on a certain day in the early 1830s and——"

Coleman was looking wildly to the right and left as they descended the stairs. Wickes decided to ignore his distress. Besides, the Adventure of the Retroactive Psychoanalysis, as he was fond of calling it, helped him develop the proper mood.

He was a little annoyed, as they shared a taxi crosstown, that Coleman displayed such a lamentable lack of interest in bearing his proper share of the conversation. He fidgeted continually and evidenced a tendency to start at any loud noise. Once, when an auto backfired, he almost collapsed.

No resiliency, Wickes thought, and clicked his tongue mentally.

The house was a small five-room contemporary in one of the newer developments on the fringe of the city. As Coleman unlocked the front door, Wickes stood looking up and down the block.

"Odd," he said.

"What's that?"

"No television antennae."

"You won't find any in this area," Coleman explained. "We're in a dead spot. Not even radio reception. That's why I got the house so cheaply."

As they entered the house, Wickes became aware of a thin atonal humming in the air. It had an odd musical quality without actually approaching melody.

"Oh, I forgot to tell you," Coleman said. "It sings."

Wickes raised an eyebrow. "The bomb sings? In the bathtub?"

"In the bathtub."

"How appropriate," Wickes said.

While Coleman removed his hat and coat, Wickes crossed the living room, following the sound through a short hall to a large bathroom, done in shades of coral and rose.

There was quite a large bomb in the bathtub.

It had a single vacant-looking blue eye. It was staring at the hot-water faucet and singing.

"You see?" Coleman said from behind him. "The police wouldn't believe me." His voice was shrill and hysterical.

"This is the best of all possible worlds," the bomb said. "But tomorrow will be better."

"Interesting," Wickes said.

"What am I going to do?" Coleman wailed.

"Every day, in every way, things are getting better and better," the bomb intoned. Its humming rose in pitch a fraction of an octave.

"Incurable optimist," Wickes observed.

"You!" Coleman sobbed. "Get out of my bathtub!"

"Can't," the bomb said, interrupting its singing. "No legs. No arms. I won't," it added after a moment.

It started to sing again. The music was oddly regular, with an internal consistency that Wickes found vaguely familiar.

"What are you singing?" he asked.

"'Frankie and Johnny,'" the bomb said. For the first time, the blue eye moved from the faucet to stare at Wickes. "Like it?"

"Well," Wickes said, considering, "it doesn't sound much like 'Frankie and Johnny.'"

"It is, though," the bomb said. "I'm coding it."

"It's giving me a headache," Coleman complained.

"Philistine," the bomb sneered, but the singing rose in pitch and quickly became inaudible. The eye returned to its fixed stare. This time, it chose the cold-water faucet.

"You'd better lie down," Wickes advised Coleman.

He pulled a tape measure from his pocket and began to measure the relationship of the fixtures in the bathroom to each other. Occasionally he clicked his tongue and made quick notes in a brown leatherette notebook.

Coleman watched him silently.

The bomb continued its idiot stare at the water faucet.

Wickes mumbled something.

"What's that?" Coleman asked.

"Like Count Buffon's needle problem," Wickes said. "The ratio of the bathtub width to the width of the room."

"What about it?"

"Three point one four one six," Wickes intoned. "Pi, that is."

He nodded and pushed the bath mat up against the stool. Thoughtfully, he produced a pair of dice from his pocket. He began to roll them on the floor, bouncing them against the tiled base of the tub.

The dice repeatedly came up seven.

"My advice," Wickes said slowly.

"Yes?" Coleman urged.

"When this is all over——"

"Yes?"

"I'd tear out the bathtub and install a dice table. Of course, you'd have to change the house rules somewhat, since each throw would be a seven, but——"

He was speaking to an empty doorway. Coleman had stumbled weakly down the hall to collapse in a chair in the living room. From the bathroom Wickes heard him groan softly.

"This is the best of all possible worlds," the bomb said in a dogmatic tone.

"Is it?" Wickes asked.

"Oh, yes, indeed. It has to be. Betcha," it challenged smugly. Then it began to sing again.

"Can't you sing anything but 'Frankie and Johnny'?" Wickes asked.

"That was 'Down by the Old Mill Stream.'"

"It sounded like 'Frankie and Johnny.'"

"No breeding," the bomb sniffed. "This is undoubtedly the best of all possible worlds," it added after a moment.

"Why?" Wickes demanded.

"Oh, it just is."

"That's not true, you know. Actually it's a pretty inferior world."

"It is not! It *has* to be the best!"

"I'm afraid it's not."

"Lies, lies!" the bomb exclaimed passionately. "I'll give you odds—any odds."

"You mean bet?"

"Of course! Afraid?"

"Why does it have to be the best of possible worlds?"

"Put up or shut up."

"Why the best of possible worlds?" Wickes insisted.

The bomb was silent. Then it began to hum in a rising crescendo. Wickes walked to the living room. Coleman was sitting in a chair, his head in his hands.

"'Frankie and Johnny'?" he asked wanly.

"'Down by the Old Mill Stream,'" Wickes told him.

"'Mairzy Doats,'" the bomb corrected from the bathroom.

"You know," Wickes said, "this could get quite maddening."

"Why didn't you take the bet?" Coleman asked sarcastically.

"No need to be snide. Besides, I never bet. Still, that bit is significant."

"How so?"

"Well, you can infer certain things about a society whose machines like to gamble."

"Yeah," Coleman said. "Maybe that universe has been conquered by a race of one-armed bandits from Las Vegas."

"Not in the least unlikely," Wickes said. "Except that this one has no arms. Anyway, the world of the bomb certainly knows more about probability than we do."

"'Find the internal logic'?" Coleman quoted.

"Exactly," Wickes said, with surprised approval. "I couldn't have put it more succinctly myself."

Wickes seated himself in a barrel chair and looked fixedly at the tips of his black shoes. Finally, he rose and walked to the phone on the table by Coleman's chair.

"It's about time," Coleman remarked acidly.

"Tush," Wickes said.

He dialed a number and spoke for a few moments. Then he dialed another number. After a short, low conversation, he replaced the phone triumphantly.

"Hah," he said.

"Hah?" Coleman queried. "Hah?"

"Yes, hah. That was the program director of WWVI. They have a disk jockey on now."

"With a bomb ready to explode," Coleman cried, "he phones requests to disk jockeys. What did you ask for? 'Mairzy Doats'?"

"That wasn't necessary. They've just played it. And before that, 'Down by the Old Mill Stream.' And before that——"

"'Frankie and Johnny'?"

"Precisely. I see you understand my methods."

"Yes," Coleman said weakly and sank back into his chair.

"Now I must leave," Wickes said.

"With that still in there? What about me?"

"Well, you could read to it," Wickes suggested.

Coleman stared as Wickes walked to a bookcase by the door and scanned the titles. He selected a book and handed it to Coleman.

"This," he said.

"Crime and Punishment?"

"A delightful book," Wickes said. "So full of—of——" He waved his hand uncertainly. "Of *Weltschmerz*. Oh, yes," he said at the door. "If you get bored with that, try *The Seven Who Were Hanged.* A little healthy morbidity will do worlds of good—even for a bomb."

And he closed the door with appropriate consideration.

After leaving Coleman, Wickes walked for several blocks, lost in thought. The situation, he decided, did have its intriguing points. The particular problem was the point of contact. Obviously nothing would be gained by merely de-fusing the bomb. The alien organization of therapists who had placed it there would simply try again, perhaps with more success.

But how to move against those unpredictable minds in the unguessable gamble? Rather like the great-to-the-fourth-power-grandfather acting against Wickes's own psychoanalysis-bent client.

The lever—if only there were some lever. But there was only

the bomb with its insane optimism and wild gambling fever and equally insane habit of encoding popular songs.

He stopped in the middle of the sidewalk, heedless of the glares of passers-by. In seconds, his head was wreathed in a thick tobacco smoke of concentration. He became aware of his surroundings again only when the pipestem grew too hot.

He hailed a cab and gave directions to the local branch library. There he spent some time among the math shelves, selecting first one volume on statistics and probability and then another. Finally he found what he wanted, a long table of random numbers used in setting up random sequences in physical experiments. When the librarian wasn't looking he stealthily tore out the two pages of the table and left.

Then he went to a magic store, where he bought a deck of marked cards, a pair of trick dice and a book on roulette systems. In the taxi he read through the opening chapters of the roulette book and finally tossed it from the window when the cab stopped for a red light.

At his office he made two phone calls, one to a friend who was an electronics engineer, the other to a friend who played the bassoon. Then he scrambled beneath his filing cabinet until he found a battered tape recorder that he used as a dictaphone, drew on the trench coat and battered hat, and headed for the street.

After spending three hours with his bassoon-playing friend, he dropped by his engineer friend's house to pick up the pieces of equipment that his friend had assembled for him. He stopped at a drugstore for a quick snack and arrived at Coleman's house at seven-forty.

"It's about time," the young man said. "I'm absolutely hoarse." He was carrying the copy of *Crime and Punishment*, his thumb inserted in a place about a third of the way through. As he closed the door, Wickes heard a faint muttering from the bathroom.

"Lies, lies," the bomb was saying.

"It doesn't like Dostoevsky." Coleman sighed.

"*De gustibus non est disputandum,*" Wickes airily explained.

"Yeah," Coleman said uncertainly.

"I," Wickes announced grandly as he removed his coat with a flourish, "have been learning to compose for the bassoon."

He gestured toward the peeling leather case of the tape recorder, which he had placed next to a featureless black suitcase.

Coleman stared at him with lips compressed.

"Oh, hand me my coat a minute," Wickes said. "That's a good fellow."

He extracted several rolled newspapers, which he proceeded to unroll. Several items on the front pages were outlined in black.

"Dostoevsky is all very well," Wickes said, "but we mustn't neglect current events." He smirked knowingly.

Coleman's lips became even whiter.

"Here," Wickes said, handing Coleman a small package.

"What is it?" Coleman asked hopefully.

"Dice. We may want to get up a crap game."

"Have you gone——"

"Mad? Oh, no. At least, not in the usual sense. Now let me see how this operates."

"This" was the enigmatic black suitcase from which Wickes extracted a bewildering assortment of electronic parts. Following a diagram he took from his pocket, he began to connect the several units together. Eventually, he ran a long wire across the room, hanging it over the doorway and the living-room drapes.

"Antenna," he explained.

He found a wall plug and connected the device. Then he began to assemble the tape recorder.

"Wait till you hear this," he said. "Bassoon solo."

"The man has gone batty," Coleman glumly told the walls.

Wickes twisted several dials on the recorder and flipped a toggle on the other device. The room suddenly filled with the low-register grunts of a bassoon. The notes were long and anguished and made absolutely no melody.

Coleman slapped his hands to his ears as the discordance was echoed by a sudden blast of sound from the bathroom.

"You see," Wickes yelled above the maddening cacophony, "the bomb is in constant communication with its makers. It uses the radio waves that are absorbed in this dead space. That's why you can't get reception in this area. A natural consequence of the probability nexus in the bathroom is to shunt all radiation into the universe from which the bomb comes."

"Yes, but——"

"So we feed it random radio impulses—my bassoon solo composed from a table of random numbers. It can't code a random sequence. Ergo, it can't communicate."

At this point, the bomb made a loud groaning noise.

"Now!" Wickes cried with a wild gleam in his eyes. He charged for the bathroom, a rolled newspaper outthrust before him like a lance.

The bomb lay in the bathtub, moaning softly. Coleman halted behind Wickes as he held up the newspaper and began to read.

" 'Father Slays Family of Five,' " Wickes intoned.

The quivering bomb screamed piercingly.

" 'Thousands Die in Wake of Eruption,' " he read.

"Lies, lies, lies, lies!"

" 'Indian Plague Takes Million Lives.' "

The bomb began to howl, its voice rising to an earsplitting pitch.

"Here! You stop that!"

Wickes turned to the gleaming machine that occupied the space where one wall of the bathroom had been.

"I said stop that," the dark little man in the machine said.

"It's him, it's him," Coleman bleated. "The man I told you about when I came to your office."

"Interesting," Wickes said. He pointed toward the machine's lower quarter, where a small metallic sign glowed. The sign said: "Paranoids Anonymous. 'You, too, can destroy a universe.' "

"Stop it, I say!" the little man yelled, waving what was obviously a weapon.

"Turn off the tape recorder," Wickes told Coleman.

Coleman headed toward the living room.

"What's the big idea?" the man demanded as he descended from the machine. His swarthy face was stormy under thick brows. He was dressed in a pair of shorts and singlet tailored from some metallic material. Calf-length boots encased his feet. A harness of some type encircled his waist and shoulders, and from this harness, various unknown pieces of apparatus dangled.

"This is the best of all possible worlds," the bomb said with the suspicion of a sniffle.

"Of course it is," the man said soothingly. "Don't you let anyone tell you it isn't."

"Any odds it isn't?" Wickes offered.

"Huh!" the man said. But he looked interested.

"Afraid of losing your—ah—shirt?" Wickes demanded.

"Won't do you any good," the man said darkly. "Got to destroy a universe. The best one. This is it."

A small box that depended from the harness buzzed softly. The man removed it, pressed it to his lips and spoke a few incomprehensible words.

"Look," Wickes said, "this has to be the best of all possible universes, doesn't it?"

"It is," the man said smugly. "They planned it that way."

"They?"

"My psychometricians. It wouldn't do to destroy just any universe. It has to be the best."

"I must say you're remarkably objective about it."

"Why not? It's *my* neurosis, isn't it?"

"Maybe this isn't the best of all possible worlds."

"Ridiculous," mumbled the bomb from the bathtub.

"Best for whom?" Wickes demanded. "By whose standards? Yours?"

"Naturally."

"Want to bet?"

The man licked his lips. "Nobody ever accused me of being a con."

"If it's the best possible world for you," Wickes said, "you should win."

"True, true," said the bomb.

Coleman had returned to the room. He was eying the dark man with something akin to horror.

"The dice, please," Wickes said to Coleman.

"What's the idea?" the man demanded.

"I'll prove my point."

The dark man smiled shrewdly. "There's something you should know."

"Never mind."

"Don't say I didn't try to warn you."

"Let's make this interesting," Wickes said. "A little side bet?"

"Done." The man pulled filmy currency from one pocket.

"I can't spend your money," Wickes pointed out.

"You can't win anyway."

"How about something more tangible?" Wickes asked. "One of those gadgets, for instance." He pointed to the harness.

"Roll them from the wall," the man said, extracting one of the instruments.

Wickes sank to one knee and rolled the dice. They came up double fours.

"Hah!" Wickes said.

He rolled three more times. On the fourth roll, the dice came up six and two.

Half an hour later, Wickes had stripped the visitor to his shorts. The man jumped angrily to his feet. "You switched dice!"

"Prove it."

"I quit."

"Coward! I mean con!"

"That does it. You!" the man yelled at the bomb. "Forget about Tuesday! Detonate in one hour!"

Then he leaped into the machine and it flickered from view.

"Now you've done it," Coleman moaned.

"Today is the finest day of all," the bomb said.

"Hm-m-m," Wickes mused, inspecting the pile of loot at his feet. Finally he selected the boxlike communicator that the man had used and inspected it closely.

Coleman sank to the floor and began to roll the abandoned dice dispiritedly. After a moment, he picked them up and examined them closely.

"Hey!" he exclaimed. "These dice don't have any ones, threes or fives!"

"That's right," Wickes said.

"Then how can you throw sevens?"

"You can't."

"But that's dishonest."

"Why? He was trying to cheat me."

As Coleman pondered the question, Wickes began to speak earnestly into the communicator. Before long, he seemed satisfied.

"Well, now," he said, "let's relax. Can you make some coffee?"

"That thing is ready to go off in an hour," Coleman protested. "Do something!"

"Patience, patience. All that can be done has been done."

He walked down the hall to the living room, Coleman trailing him dejectedly.

"At least call the bomb squad," Coleman said.

"Hardly necessary."

"You blasted crackpot!"

"There's no need to be abusive," Wickes said. "If you'll only apply logic, you'll see that certain features of this other universe may be——"

"Peace, my children," said a voice from the bathroom.

Standing in the doorway was the majestic figure of a man. He was tall and very fair, with a light crown of blond hair. His eyes were expressive and ethereal.

"Well," Wickes said, "you certainly didn't waste time."

"I am always ready for a suffering universe," the man said, lifting his eyes unto the ceiling.

"It's in the bathroom," Wickes said.

"I have already taken care of it," the man replied, "while you two were having your childish tiff."

"Childish!" Coleman cried. "If you think——"

"Peace, brotherhood," the man said. "We must all live in perfect love."

He turned and walked back toward the bathroom.

"Wait," Wickes called and hurried after him. Coleman followed awkwardly, his eyes wide and unbelieving. In the bathroom, the tub was quite empty.

"Love is all-powerful," the saintlike man said. For the first time, Wickes noticed the faint halo flickering above his head.

The man began to mount a machine in the wall.

"Alas," he sighed, "other worlds, other needs. Busy, busy."

Before the machine flickered from sight, Wickes saw the flickering metal sign on the machine.

It said: "Messiahs, Incorporated. 'You, too, can save a universe.'"

Later, in the living room, Coleman sprawled limply on the divan while Wickes leaned on the mantel and stared dreamily into the dead fireplace, sucking on his unlit pipe.

"I can see how you cut off the bomb's communication," Coleman said, "but why the newspapers?"

"Well," Wickes explained, "it wouldn't have done our paranoid friend to destroy just any universe. It couldn't be one that was better off obliterated or there would be no point to the therapy. Hence Dostoevsky and the newspapers. I had to demonstrate the world was better off destroyed. That's the only way I could pry the paranoid from his vantage point in his world. Destroy the bomb's conviction that this was the best universe, but prevent the bomb's getting the complete story back to him."

"But that rigged crap game?"

"Well, it was obvious that they set great store by gambling. Moreover, I was certain the box he used kept him in contact with his world. I had only to win the communicator. All else followed."

"By internal logic?"

"Of course."

"Like Venusians in washing machines."

"Naturally."

"Forgive me for being stupid," Coleman said ironically.

"You're just not used to thinking in these terms," Wickes said. "Surely it must be obvious that if there is an organization that aids paranoids by allowing them to destroy a universe, there must be some counterorganization for those poor fellows who want to save a universe."

"Messiahs, Incorporated?"

"Exactly. The internal logic of the situation demanded it. I had only to contact them. The job was made to order—a universe that needed saving."

Coleman struggled to his feet. "I think I need an aspirin," he said weakly. He stumbled down the hall to the bathroom.

Wickes heard his sudden cry of alarm. He ran toward the bathroom. Coleman had collapsed into the bathtub.

The little man in the scarlet-edged toga was waving a dagger wildly. He stopped when he saw Wickes and smiled apologetically.

"Oh, my," he said. "You *aren't* Julius Caesar, are you?"

He moved swiftly toward his machine in the wall.

Before it disappeared, Wickes managed to decipher the flickering sign on its frame.

It read: "Hindsight, Unlimited. 'You, too, can change a universe.'"

Wickes clasped his hands together ecstatically.

"Lovely," he murmured. "Simply lovely."

In the bathtub, Coleman only whimpered.

YOU WERE RIGHT, JOE
∞∞∞∞∞∞ by J. T. McIntosh ∞∞∞∞∞∞

I CAN'T BE SURE YOU'RE GETTING THIS, JOE, BUT you've been right about so many of the other things, I guess you're very likely right about that, too.

You remember you figured that I wouldn't just materialize naked in the middle of a city street. You said I'd be a genuine human being of the time, correctly dressed and with some kind of personal history. But you warned me—and I appreciate this, Joe; you didn't have to warn me, but you did it—you warned me that there was no telling I'd be like *me*.

I may as well admit now I wasn't happy about that. I never was much to look at and there wasn't any danger of my becoming the heavyweight champion of the world. But I'd got used to being the way I was, and I didn't altogether like the idea of seeing a stranger's face every time I looked in the mirror.

If I'd known what I was going to be like, I'd never have done it. I'm sorry, Joe, but even for you I couldn't have faced it. Now that I'm here, though, I'll just have to make the best of it.

You were right, Joe, all along the line. Nobody ran screaming when I got here and I haven't been arrested. I was fitted into a spot that was made for me, dressed in the right clothes, able to speak the right language. I've got a name. And just as you said, I'm different. *Different?* That's like saying Gina Lollobrigida isn't like Aunt Phoebe!

When I first got here I looked around, of course. I saw people walking about and colored buildings with hardly any straight lines in them. It took no more than a glance to show me this was a pretty advanced civilization, many centuries ahead of our time.

Before I did any more looking around, I did the second obvious thing. I looked down at what I could see of me.

I nearly jumped out of my skin, Joe. You know those ads: *You can have a body like mine?* Well, that was me—golden tan, rippling muscles, chest a mile wide. Yeah, me Tarzan. I wore very short, tight trunks and shoes, that was all, and believe me, I was scared stiff of myself.

Well, you warned me, Joe. Funny, I was prepared to find myself very young. I even took the risk of finding myself very old. But I never saw myself as Superman. I can't seem to get used to the idea at all.

It wasn't that everybody around here was like this. Far from it. They all seemed young and fit and good-looking, but not big and not strong. I could see right away by the attention I got that I was something special.

And it scared the life out of me. Some people wouldn't mind finding themselves looking like a Greek god. Me, I'm not the type. I've spent my life not being noticed—you know that, Joe—and I wasn't cut out to be a symbol of manhood. I don't think I'll ever get used to it.

Anyway, Joe, apart from this, everything seems to be all right. And I'd like to say right away that I think it's safe for you to come along, too, if you want to. You never said you were sending me as a guinea pig, to see whether it was safe to go yourself, but I'm not completely dumb. I was ready to take the gamble just the same.

If you come, you'll probably also find yourself a gorgeous hunk of man. You'll be able to figure it out better than me, but I guess maybe it's because the world we live in makes us tougher than the people living in *this* world have to be. When we show up here, we come out a lot bigger and stronger than we ever dreamed we were.

Well, maybe you won't mind being Superman, Joe. Come to think of it, I guess it'll suit you fine.

It's difficult to explain what I know and don't know about this world. My name's Elan Rock, by the way. I know *that*. I know the language, and though I haven't used it yet, I'm sure that when I do it'll come out just right. I know how to open doors and operate what they use instead of phones here and what to say instead of "Good morning" and how to do what they call reading and where I can get their idea of a drink.

I know everything like that. But what kind of society this is and how it's governed and what year it is and why there are no square buildings and why everybody walks instead of using cars, I don't know.

Now I'll have to break off for a while, Joe. When I'm used to this, I'll be able to talk to you no matter what I'm doing. Meantime, I don't want to make any big mistakes in my first few minutes here in the future.

I'll call you again soon.

I know a lot more now, Joe. I've seen myself in a mirror and it's just as I thought, only worse. I've got the face of Apollo to go with the figure of Charles Atlas. I'd tell you more about how I look, but you wouldn't believe it.

The way I figure it, I couldn't just jump into the future and be somebody who'd never existed before. Elan Rock had to half exist for twenty-five years so that I could come shooting up from the Dark Ages and *be* him.

I think you said something like that once, Joe, only I couldn't digest all you were telling me in such a short time before I got started.

You were right, too, about my reaching a place which was just within my limit of comprehension, a place just short of an environment that would make me go crazy.

And yet it's a lot simpler than ours. I know the whole code of laws, for example. I happened to see them a few minutes ago, over the door of what passes here for a Department of Justice. Translated, they go something like this:

You mustn't annoy other people. And if you're other people, you mustn't allow yourself to be annoyed too easily.

That's all there is to it. That code is taken to cover murder and stealing and other things like that, which most people would agree are crimes. You can kill yourself if you like—that's no crime. The only sex crimes are acts that would break one of these two laws. And notice that it's a crime to be annoyed too easily.

You know, I got a respect for these people when I realized these were the only laws they needed. It wouldn't be any good trying to run *our* society under a pair of laws like that. Herb Jones would prove in court that he was annoyed by long underwear hanging out in Homer Smith's back yard. And a smart lawyer would prove that Herb Jones hadn't been too easily annoyed. So, according to the law, Herb Jones would get heavy damages.

You can give people a tremendous amount of freedom if you know they won't abuse it. That's how things must be here.

I was just beginning to get used to the idea of being Apollo when I hit snag number two.

I'm trying to suspend judgment about this, Joe. Naturally, morals differ in different societies. All the same, it gave me my second shock when a little dark girl, pretty as anything, took my hand and—well, gave me to understand that she expected me to go up to her apartment and make love to her.

I smiled and shook my head, and she was obviously surprised and hurt, but what could I do? It's bad enough suddenly becoming a beefcake king without being in a place where sex is so free and open that—hell, you remember how I used to get all red and stutter when I had to talk to a girl!

It was only after the little brunette had gone on, her lovely straight back a living exclamation point, that I realized I could have politely thanked her and explained that I kept getting such propositions and a man can spread himself only so far and—you know what I mean.

I'll try that next time. I'm uneasily convinced that there's going to be a next time, maybe in five minutes. When it happens, I'll . . .

Sorry I broke off like that, Joe.

Before we go any further, we'd better have an understanding about the power over me that you say you have. You told me that if you didn't hear from me, if I held out on you, you could do something and I'd die. Frankly, I don't believe it, Joe. I think you said that just to keep me in line.

I don't think you can do anything to me now any more than you can talk to me. You explained why I could communicate with you and why you couldn't communicate with me. I didn't understand what you said, but you were very convincing, anyway.

You weren't very convincing, though, when you said you could still control me while I'm here and you're still there. Didn't you know, Joe, that people can sometimes tell the truth from a lie, even when they don't understand either of them?

But all the same, Joe, I'm not running out on you. I'm going to keep reporting to you honestly what's going on.

Only if I'm wrong and you *can* reach clear up to here, Lord knows how many hundred years in the future, don't put the bite on me simply because I cut off for a few minutes. I may have a good reason.

Like just then. You can't blame me for cutting off that way. Something so screwy just happened that, for a moment, I thought the time jump had driven me nuts.

Along the street came a half dozen savages in animal skins. I looked at the other people around for my cue. They seemed surprised but not frightened. So I guessed it was just an act, some stunt or other, maybe part of a parade, and tried to look surprised but not frightened, like everybody else.

It was the savages who were frightened. They were yelling and running and glancing behind them. One carrying a stone club stopped in front of a woman a few yards from me, said something and raised his club.

Sooner or later, I had to find out if I was as strong as I looked. I stepped in and let the caveman have it on the chin. At the last second I realized that if I gave him all I had, I'd probably break his neck, so I pulled the punch.

What do you know, Joe—I knocked a caveman twenty-five yards! It must have been all of that before he stopped staggering back and went down. He was plenty tough, because even after that, he wasn't out.

On the other hand, neither he nor his companions seemed to have any urge to come at me with their stone clubs.

"Oh, you wonderful man!" said the girl I'd saved from a fatal headache. I'd give her a better line if I could, but that's the only way I can translate it without the various suggestions which accompanied it.

Other people in the street were hurrying over. The savages exchanged quick glances, turned tail and ran. The man I'd floored was last in line for a while, but before they disappeared from sight, he had pushed past the others and was in front again. That's leadership for you.

I shrugged and walked on, pretending this sort of thing happened every day. Nobody stopped me, though there was excited conversation behind me. I didn't look back.

I don't know what that incident was all about. I'd have stopped and talked about it, only I didn't dare.

Maybe not everybody is as civilized as the people in this city.

There's no law that children should go to school, for instance, so maybe the morons and drones of this community go outside and live as savages. Maybe there are people who don't believe in civilization. Maybe . . .

Your guess is as good as mine, Joe. Probably better.

There's a park beside me now, and I'd go inside and stop to consider things, if not for one thing.

It seems very likely to me that if girls make advances in the open street here, the parks must really be something for shy young guys like me. Flustering, to say the least.

I've got a lot of things to find out, and sooner or later I've got to take the risk of talking to people. The trouble is, how can I be natural when I feel as unnatural as a kitten laying eggs? Can I go up to the first pretty girl I see and say, "Take my hand, I'm a stranger in paradise"?

I can't. She would.

Nevertheless, I'll have to talk to somebody the first time I see an opportunity.

There must be some kind of festival going on. Here's another procession—about twenty people, coming along the side of the park. I can't make out what they're supposed to be, but they're quite a sight. Like how Hollywood in our time would represent the people of the future. The women in brass bikinis and the men carrying enormous ray guns. And all as clean as if they'd been washed in the newest detergent. They look a bit puzzled. Maybe they've lost their way.

I'm slipping into the park in case they ask me. If I keep moving, the local talent won't get a chance to take a good look at me and decide I'm just what they always wanted.

Looks like I was right about the parks. It shouldn't be so unexpected, I guess. It was in our time that necking in public came in. This is only a step further.

Now what in hell's this?

Believe it or not, Joe, I just killed a saber-toothed tiger!

I know that's hard to swallow, Joe. There were three of them, worse than anything you ever saw in a book or movie. They weren't really saber-toothed tigers—they were something there isn't a name for. Perhaps nobody yet dug up a skeleton of one of these things.

There were these three tigers and half a dozen couples and me within thirty yards or so. I didn't have much time to take a good squint at the beasts. The biggest of them came at me. I guess he figured that once I was out of the way, the other twelve packed lunches could be picked up without any argument. He was right at that.

I'm not boasting, Joe—I stood where I was because I was too scared to run. I told you I'm big, but not compared with a saber-toothed tiger.

He leaped at me, and I remembered how Tarzan used to throw himself on tigers' backs and get a half-Nelson grip on them. It didn't seem too practical, however.

I dodged the first rush. Somebody threw a knife at the tiger and nearly hit me. I got hold of it and faced the beast again. I didn't think for a moment that I was going to be able to do anything with the knife, which was a little folding one with a three-inch blade, but when you're practically naked and have to defend yourself against a wild animal, you use a wooden sword if that's the only thing available.

The other specimens held off, waiting to see what happened. All the women were screaming, which helped, I guess. These creatures didn't seem to know any more about human beings than human beings knew about them.

The next time the tiger came at me, I ripped his side open as he passed, and from the roars he let loose, I began to think for the first time that maybe I *would* be alive in five minutes' time, after all.

It was that knife. I don't know yet whether it was just sharp or if it had some other quality about it, but it cut through the beast's flesh like water. And though a two-inch-deep cut all along his side didn't by any means put him out of action, he didn't like it.

Why I had a chance, Joe, was because the poor ugly tiger, with all his strength, didn't have reaction time worth a damn. I could run around him like a speedboat circling a scow. Talk about telegraphing punches—this creature didn't telegraph them, he sent long letters about them by pony express.

I slashed the tendons about his neck and it was no more dangerous than crossing a busy street at midday—less, probably. He struggled a lot and he took a long time to die, but in the end he did die.

I turned to the other tigers. They had seen what had happened, however, and showed unexpected intelligence by running as hard as they could go for a clump of trees two hundred yards away. The beasts disappeared among them and no one was sorry.

The six couples who were still around rushed up to congratulate me, pat me on the back and say I was wonderful. Two of the girls kissed me, and their escorts (I guess that's the word) didn't seem to mind. I didn't mind too much myself. In time, I think I could get used to this world.

But not to the sudden appearance of three unfriendly prehistoric monsters.

We got out of the park without wasting any time about it, just in case what had happened before might happen again.

I found myself walking with a man and girl who talked so easily that I couldn't let the chance slip. There's no reserve among these people, Joe, and if they're surprised at the things you ask, they hide it politely.

It seemed that the arrival of the three tigers in the park had been as big a shock to them as it was to me. They weren't used to things like that. None of them showed any desire to become used to them, either.

So the sudden arrival of three prehistoric monsters wasn't a normal hazard of living in this world.

The couple I talked to had been as frightened as the rest, but they got over it pretty quickly. They're not nervous, these people. Put them in danger and they're frightened; remove the danger and they shrug and say they're glad that's over.

Maybe that means there isn't much mental illness about. So why the savages?

These two people were soon willing to talk about anything at all, and a casual remark by the girl about my being alone gave me a chance to find out about the sex setup here.

Seems what they've done is separate love and sex. If you want someone, you don't have to pretend to yourself and her and everybody else that you're in love with her. On the other hand, if you're in love with a girl, you aren't necessarily limited to her and her only.

It's not so very different from things in our time, except they don't kid themselves and each other about it here. There's still love and there's still marriage, of course, but whether you're in love or not, or married or not, the usual thing is to have a fairly full sex life. Unless you don't want to.

And all I have to do if I want to be left alone—which I do, at least meantime—is wear a silver bracelet on my right arm. Which I'm now doing. One of my new friends gave it to me.

I didn't stay with the people I'd met in the park; I slipped away from them as soon as I could. It seems to me the best way of gaining information is getting a little at a time from different people. That way I won't reveal the full extent of my ignorance to anybody, just little bits of it.

I'm out of the park now and back on the main streets. There shouldn't be any saber-toothed tigers roaming around loose out here.

These don't look like main streets. I haven't seen a car or plane or truck or bicycle or wheelbarrow. Everything that moves on wheels does so in special underground lanes.

That's the solution to the traffic problem—no traffic, no problem.

I don't precisely know how you get to the underground lanes. That, however, is a question which can wait.

Already I'm getting used to the style of architecture. I think I like it.

Smooth curves have always been more beautiful than straight lines. We built in stone and in straight lines because we didn't know any better.

Here most of the material is plastic of some kind—buildings, windows, pavement, everything. A moment ago I bent to feel the pavement when no one was looking. It's perfectly smooth, unblemished, something between stone and rubber, but it's too soft for stone and too hard for rubber. It's obviously molded and it wears well. I couldn't leave any marks on it with my fingernail, though it gave when I pressed it.

In the streets there's nothing but people walking. People not in any hurry, all very young-looking (maybe the older people use the public transportation). Friendly people, happy people.

I know what you're thinking, Joe—there must be a catch somewhere.

All I know is, so far I haven't seen it. Unless it's the saber-toothed tigers.

This is getting beyond a joke. The cavemen didn't give me much trouble, I dodged the men with the ray guns and the prehistoric monsters, and I managed to handle the saber-toothed tigers. But if this sort of thing goes on much longer, communication from me is going to stop very suddenly.

You won't like that, Joe, because you'll never know what happened to me. I won't like it myself. I like this place, except the hazards. I'd like to stay in it.

All in one piece, though.

This time it was men in red coats with the most primitive-

looking muskets I ever saw. They were firing them, too. I didn't
see anybody hit, but that doesn't mean these men weren't shooting
to kill. The guns they were using didn't seem to be accurate to
much closer than ninety degrees, which was just as well.

Perhaps somebody mopped them up. I didn't wait to see.
Neither did anyone else. We didn't exactly stampede in panic,
but we didn't waste any time getting out of range of those
muskets.

This wasn't part of any game, Joe. I'm beginning to get ideas
about this.

Suppose they do time experiments here. Suppose there's a sort
of cowcatcher to brush off people and things who wander across
the track. Or suppose there's a sort of time magnetism which pulls
all time travelers in here.

How the saber-toothed tigers and the savages with stone clubs
could be time travelers, I don't know, but any theory's better than
none.

Only how come I landed up just as you said I would, a duly
accepted member of this world, dressed in the right clothes and
twice the man I was before, while all the others appear exactly as
they were in their own time?

I guess you've got an answer, Joe, as usual. Wish you could pass
it on to me.

Here's something else. About a dozen people, men and women,
in ball dress. Seventeenth century, I guess. They're blinking and
staring around.

Gosh, I thought *we* invented the low-cut dress. The dress that
redhead's wearing wouldn't get past the Hays Office if it was
three inches higher. No, that's an exaggeration. It wouldn't get
past the Hays Office if it was *four* inches higher.

You probably got some of that, Joe.

It was awkward. These refugees from the seventeenth century
picked me to talk to. The redhead came straight to me. Her manner was prim and correct, which showed she was a lady, but her

eyes were no lady's. They were even more inviting than curious.

I treated her like a sister.

The trouble was, I could understand what these people were saying and no one else who was around could. I found it hard to make up my mind whether to pretend not to understand them or not.

I guessed from the way they blinked and shaded their eyes that it had been night where they came from. As a matter of fact, they'd been at a ball.

Naturally they wanted to know what it was all about. Before I'd really made up my mind whether to admit I could understand them or not, I found myself answering their questions.

Since this group, unlike the redcoats, was obviously puzzled rather than hostile, they were soon in the center of an excited crowd, chattering away but unable to understand a word.

I kept saying a word or two to the people beside me as well as talking to the strangers, to make it clear which side I was on. People offered me suggestions about what to tell the visitors and I did as they said. No one seemed much surprised that only I could talk to them. Everybody assumed, I guess, that I was a history student or something.

This went on for about ten minutes. Then the strangers winked out like a light and we were left staring stupidly at each other.

I didn't draw attention to myself this time by being the first to go on my way. But when it was clear that nobody suspected I knew any more about the incident than they did, I made my escape as soon as I decently could.

One side issue I'd like to mention is this, Joe. Humanity really is on the upgrade. Looking at these people from the seventeenth century and comparing them with the people here, I couldn't doubt that there had been a big advance in intelligence, looks, poise and everything else that counts. It was like seeing a mongrel beside a pedigree pup.

Even the redhead, who obviously regarded herself as a beauty, was nothing special compared with any girl in the crowd.

I'd hardly got away from that when, in the very next street, I saw a bullfight, of all things. At first the bull and the matador didn't seem to be aware that things weren't what they'd been a few minutes before.

Then the matador looked up and stared, petrified. The bull nearly got him. He turned just in time, but his mind was no longer on the job. I don't blame him.

The bull and the matador didn't last as long as the visitors from the seventeenth century. They couldn't have been here more than a couple of minutes.

I hope all these people got back where they came from. I liked that redhead, despite her gap teeth. I didn't care for the matador and the bull, but I don't wish them any harm.

Joe, I don't know how to say this.

I've been picked up. It wasn't an arrest—they made that clear from the start. In fact, they're very interested in me and it looks as if I'm going to have a great time here as the Hercules from the Past.

There were three men and two women, and they apologized for interfering with my liberty. Seems I have the same rights as everybody else here.

But there was desperate urgency, they said. They promised to explain everything later. Meanwhile, they had to insist on taking me somewhere in a hurry.

They knew my name and all about me. They even knew I wasn't the same as I'd been in my own time, because though nothing like this has ever happened, once it had happened it took them less than half an hour to figure out exactly what *had* happened.

Joe, I feel like a heel. But they told me to tell you this. They told me they felt worse about it than I do.

You see, if I'd simply landed up here and made no attempt to get in touch with you, they might never have known what had happened. But this link with you is the thing that's caused all the trouble.

We're holding open a hole in time, Joe. And as long as it's open, anything, anywhere, anytime, can fall right through the hole.

They told me there's a sort of dimensional elastic stretched all through time because of you and me. They can't leave it like that any longer. It could pull time itself apart.

Joe, you always said it was up to everybody to look out for himself. That's what they're doing, so you were right about that, too.

I mean you've been right about so many things that I got them to let me explain what will happen so you'll have a chance to figure a way out.

You see, they're cutting the elastic, Joe. And you know what's going to happen? They say I'll be all right because I'm here and they're going to cut it on my side.

But when it comes shooting back through time, it's going to pack one hell of a wallop.

You've got a few minutes to work it out. You can do it, Joe. After all, look how often you were right.

Good luck, Joe—and take care of yourself.

WHAT'S HE DOING IN THERE?

~~~~~~~~~~ by Fritz Leiber ~~~~~~~~~~

THE PROFESSOR WAS CONGRATULATING EARTH'S
first visitor from another planet on his wisdom in getting in touch
with a cultural anthropologist before contacting any other scientists (or governments, God forbid!), and in learning English from
radio and TV before landing from his orbit-parked rocket, when
the Martian stood up and said hesitantly, "Excuse me, please, but
where is it?"

That baffled the Professor and the Martian seemed to grow
anxious—at least his long mouth curved upward, and he had
earlier explained that its curling downward was his smile—and he
repeated, "Please, where is it?"

He was surprisingly humanoid in most respects, but his complexion was textured so like the rich dark armchair he'd just been
occupying that the Professor's pin-striped gray suit, which he had
eagerly consented to wear, seemed an arbitrary interruption between him and the chair—a sort of Mother Hubbard dress on a
phantom conjured from its leather.

The Professor's Wife, always a perceptive hostess, came to her husband's rescue by saying with equal rapidity, "Top of the stairs, end of the hall, last door."

The Martian's mouth curled happily downward and he said, "Thank you very much," and was off.

Comprehension burst on the Professor. He caught up with his guest at the foot of the stairs.

"Here, I'll show you the way," he said.

"No, I can find it myself, thank you," the Martian assured him.

Something rather final in the Martian's tone made the Professor desist, and after watching his visitor sway up the stairs with an almost hypnotic softly jogging movement, he rejoined his wife in the study, saying wonderingly, "Who'd have thought it, by George! Function taboos as strict as our own!"

"I'm glad some of your professional visitors maintain 'em," his wife said darkly.

"But this one's from Mars, darling, and to find out he's—well, similar in an aspect of his life is as thrilling as the discovery that water is burned hydrogen. When I think of the day not far distant when I'll put his entries in the crosscultural index . . ."

He was still rhapsodizing when the Professor's Little Son raced in.

"Pop, the Martian's gone to the bathroom!"

"Hush, dear. Manners."

"Now it's perfectly natural, darling, that the boy should notice and be excited. Yes, son, the Martian's not so very different from us."

"Oh, certainly," the Professor's Wife said with a trace of bitterness. "I don't imagine his turquoise complexion will cause any comment at all when you bring him to a faculty reception. They'll just figure he's had a hard night—and that he got that baby-elephant nose sniffing around for assistant professorships."

"Really, darling! He probably thinks of our noses as disagreeably amputated and paralyzed."

"Well, anyway, Pop, he's in the bathroom. I followed him when he squiggled upstairs."

"Now, son, you shouldn't have done that. He's on a strange planet and it might make him nervous if he thought he was being spied on. We must show him every courtesy. By George, I can't wait to discuss these things with Ackerly-Ramsbottom! When I think of how much more this encounter has to give the anthropologist than even the physicist or astronomer . . ."

He was still going strong on his second rhapsody when he was interrupted by another high-speed entrance. It was the Professor's Coltish Daughter.

"Mom, Pop, the Martian's——"

"Hush, dear. We know."

The Professor's Coltish Daughter regained her adolescent poise, which was considerable. "Well, he's still in there," she said. "I just tried the door and it was locked."

"I'm glad it was!" the Professor said while his wife added, "Yes, you can't be sure what——" and caught herself. "Really, dear, that was very bad manners."

"I thought he'd come downstairs long ago," her daughter explained. "He's been in there an awfully long time. It must have been a half hour ago that I saw him gyre and gimble upstairs in that real gone way he has, with Nosy here following him." The Professor's Coltish Daughter was currently soaking up both jive and *Alice*.

When the Professor checked his wrist watch, his expression grew troubled. "By George, he is taking his time! Though, of course, we don't know how much time Martians . . . I wonder."

"I listened for a while, Pop," his son volunteered. "He was running the water a lot."

"Running the water, eh? We know Mars is a water-starved planet. I suppose that in the presence of unlimited water, he might be seized by a kind of madness and . . . But he seemed so well adjusted."

Then his wife spoke, voicing all their thoughts. Her outlook on life gave her a naturally sepulchral voice.

"*What's he doing in there?*"

Twenty minutes and at least as many fantastic suggestions later, the Professor glanced again at his watch and nerved himself for action. Motioning his family aside, he mounted the stairs and tiptoed down the hall.

He paused only once to shake his head and mutter under his breath, "By George, I wish I had Fenchurch or von Gottschalk here. They're a shade better than I am on intercultural contracts, especially taboo-breakings and affronts. . . ."

His family followed him at a short distance.

The Professor stopped in front of the bathroom door. Everything was quiet as death.

He listened for a minute and than rapped measuredly, steadying his hand by clutching its wrist with the other. There was a faint splashing, but no other sound.

Another minute passed. The Professor rapped again. Now there was no response at all. He very gingerly tried the knob. The door was still locked.

When they had retreated to the stairs, it was the Professor's Wife who once more voiced their thoughts. This time her voice carried overtones of supernatural horror.

"*What's he doing in there?*"

"He may be dead or dying," the Professor's Coltish Daughter suggested briskly. "Maybe we ought to call the fire department, like they did for old Mrs. Frisbee."

The Professor winced. "I'm afraid you haven't visualized the complications, dear," he said gently. "No one but ourselves knows that the Martian is on Earth, or has even the slightest inkling that interplanetary travel has been achieved. Whatever we do, it will have to be on our own. But to break in on a creature engaged in —well, we don't know what primal private activity—is against all anthropological practice. Still——"

"Dying's a primal activity," his daughter said crisply.

"So's ritual bathing before mass murder," his wife added.

"Please! Still, as I was about to say, we do have the moral duty to succor him if, as you all too reasonably suggest, he has been incapacitated by a germ or virus or, more likely, by some simple environmental factor such as Earth's greater gravity."

"Tell you what, Pop—I can look in the bathroom window and see what he's doing. All I have to do is crawl out my bedroom window and along the gutter a little ways. It's safe as houses."

The Professor's question beginning with, "Son, how do you know——" died unuttered and he refused to notice the words his daughter was voicing silently at her brother. He glanced at his wife's sardonically composed face, thought once more of the fire department and of other and larger and even more jealous—or would it be skeptical?—government agencies, and clutched at the straw offered him.

Ten minutes later, he was quite unnecessarily assisting his son back through the bedroom window.

"Gee, Pop, I couldn't see a sign of him. That's why I took so long. Hey, Pop, don't look so scared. He's in there, sure enough. It's just that the bathtub's under the window and you have to get real close up to see into it."

"The Martian's taking a bath?"

"Yep. Got it full up and just the end of his little old schnozzle sticking out. Your suit, Pop, was hanging on the door."

The one word the Professor's Wife spoke was like a death knell. *"Drowned!"*

"No, Ma, I don't think so. His schnozzle was opening and closing regular-like."

"Maybe he's a shape changer," the Professor's Coltish Daughter said in a burst of evil fantasy. "Maybe he softens in water and thins out after a while until he's like an eel and then he'll go exploring through the sewer pipes. Wouldn't it be funny if he went under the street and knocked on the stopper from underneath and crawled into the bathtub with President Rexford, or Mrs. President Rexford, or maybe right into the middle of one of Janey Rexford's Oh-I'm-so-sexy bubble baths?"

"Please!" The Professor put his hand to his eyebrows and kept it there, cuddling the elbow in his other hand.

"Well, have you thought of something?" the Professor's Wife asked him after a bit. "What are you going to do?"

The Professor dropped his hand and blinked his eyes hard and took a deep breath.

"Telegraph Fenchurch and Ackerly-Ramsbottom and then break in," he said in a resigned voice, into which, nevertheless, a note of hope seemed also to have come. "First, however, I'm going to wait until morning."

And he sat down cross-legged in the hall a few yards from the bathroom door and folded his arms.

So the long vigil commenced. The Professor's family shared it and he offered no objection. Other and sterner men, he told himself, might claim to be able successfully to order their children to go to bed when there was a Martian locked in the bathroom, but he would like to see them faced with the situation.

Finally dawn began to seep from the bedrooms. When the bulb in the hall had grown quite dim the Professor unfolded his arms.

Just then, there was a loud splashing in the bathroom. The Professor's family looked toward the door. The splashing stopped and they heard the Martian moving around. Then the door opened and the Martian appeared in the Professor's gray pin-striped suit. His mouth curled sharply downward in a broad alien smile as he saw the Professor.

"Good morning!" the Martian said happily. "I never slept better in my life, even in my own little wet bed back on Mars."

He looked around more closely and his mouth straightened. "But where did you all sleep?" he asked. "Don't tell me you stayed dry all night! You *didn't* give up your only bed to me?"

His mouth curled upward in misery. "Oh, dear," he said, "I'm afraid I've made a mistake somehow. Yet I don't understand how. Before I studied you, I didn't know what your sleeping habits would be, but that question was answered for me—in fact, it looked so reassuringly homelike—when I saw those brief TV scenes of your females ready for sleep in their little tubs. Of course, on Mars, only the fortunate can always be sure of sleeping wet, but here, with your abundance of water, I thought there would be wet beds for all."

He paused. "It's true I had some doubts last night, wondering if I'd used the right words and all, but then when you rapped 'Good night' to me, I splashed the sentiment back at you and went to sleep in a wink. But I'm afraid that somewhere I've blundered and——"

"No, no, dear chap," the Professor managed to say. He had been waving his hand in a gentle circle for some time in token that he wanted to interrupt. "Everything is quite all right. It's true we stayed up all night, but please consider that as a watch—an honor guard, by George!—which we kept to indicate our esteem."

THE GENTLEST UNPEOPLE
⋙⋙⋙⋙⋘ by Frederik Pohl ⋙⋙⋙⋙⋘

I

POPAGATOR AND THE SLIDE STOPPED AT THE SEV-
enth square and rested under a tinkleberry tree. They were nearly
equal in points, but Popagator's time was already several seconds
faster than The Slide's.

Popagator flung himself gleefully on a hummock of damp green
sand and cried: "Concede the game, friend, concede it! I've as
good as won. And I will now lead you in our lifetime series by
eight hundred and six games to seven fifty-nine!" He spoke in
English; it was all the fashion that year.

The Slide snarled: "Shut up and throw."

Popagator merely smiled—well, no. He didn't *smile*. He
couldn't; he had no lips to smile with, being only a Venusian and
a scrawny, shrunken one at that. But he indicated polite amusement. He toyed idly with the gem-encrusted hilt of his whirlarang
and made a courteous observation.

"I see," he said, diplomatically changing the subject, "that the
monster has been this way." He sat up and sniffed. That was not
necessary; both of them had long ago detected the rancid reek of
the monster.

The Slide said moodily: "I wish that fellow ahead of us would play through so we could get on with our game." The fruit of the tree overhead tinkled merrily in the soggy wind.

Popagator stood up and made a couple of practice tosses, whishing air noisily through his bony mouth cavity. It was the equivalent of a nonchalant whistle. The whirlarang spun up into the cloudy air, hovered, sailed high, dipped and returned to his hands.

He caught The Slide's eye and said apologetically: "A little sloppy on the backspin, I'm afraid."

The Slide grumbled unwillingly: "No, it would have been a ten-pointer at least. You're at the top of your form today, Popagator. I wish we could get this game over with."

The Venusian ahead of them, it was true, was taking an ungodly length of time to play the eighth square. He was slumped against a dike that held a water trap, in the middle of the looped grove of twiny trees that made the eighth square such a tricky over-and-under shot. His head was down, as though he were asleep, and his whirlarang was not in his hand.

"Inconsiderate," growled The Slide.

In truth, it was. No doubt the fellow was taking a little rest, too, just as they were, but, all the same, it was very far from being sportsmanlike.

Popagator frowned—well, no. He couldn't frown any more than he could smile, for much the same reasons. It takes loose folds of flesh either to smile or to frown. There are no loose folds on a Venusian's face; in fact, there is no external flesh at all, or none to speak of, since they are arthropods.

Popagator caught another whiff of the sour monster odor and coughed chokingly. To take his mind off it, he clattered his whirlarang noisily from "hand" to "hand," admiring the play of light from the sparkling facets set into the hilt.

Venusians are all great admirers of point sources of light, since the clouds of their atmosphere make such common objects as sun and stars completely unknown to them. And Popagator's whirlarang, gemmed like a Pharaoh, was a particularly noble instrument. It had been in his family for one hundred and nine generations.

Popagator stroked the worn hilt reminiscently, thinking of the splendid comeback he had made on square five when, trailing by a point and a half, he had thrown a perfect triple reverse to catch up in points and lead in time.

All Venusians are skilled in the use of the whirlarang; Popagator could not remember a day, since his first dim memories as a tiny imago, when it had not been an obsession with him—first as a matter of theory, then, as he passed the larval and soft-bodied stages and developed the hard limbs that came with adult life, as a matter of hourly, daily and incessant practice. It was a major fact in the life of every Venusian. They had very little else to do.

The whirlarang itself was basically the same instrument that Australian bushmen, forty million miles away, had themselves developed in the dawn of their crude culture. But where loinclothed savages had found only a hunting instrument and a weapon of war, Popagator's enormously cultured race had refined it, had redesigned and rebuilt it out of a complex assortment of materials far beyond the resources of a savage, and had surrounded it with a code of behavior and rules that turned a whirlarang round into a contest as complicated and as absorbing as chess or contract bridge, with the added requirements of strength and enormous physical skill.

"I am tired," rasped The Slide, "of waiting for that fellow to play through! They shouldn't allow singles anyway."

Popagator soothed: "Let us walk forward to the next square. That is polite, not ill-mannered. And perhaps it will remind him that we are waiting."

He moved forward over the sandy, spongy ground with a clickety-click of his bony members, The Slide click-scratching moodily along behind. The closer they got to the silent Venusian on square eight, the stronger the fetid, repulsive monster stench became.

"Whew," choked The Slide. "If I had known it was going to be this bad, I never would have——"

He stopped.

Both stopped, not only speech but movement.

There was a reason why the idle Venusian on square eight was not playing through, and the reason was this:

He was dead.

His hand member was split open, and so was his lolling head. Bluish tricklings of brain and nervous tissue leaked nastily out. His whirlarang was missing.

Dead.

Murdered.

Popagator looked at The Slide, and The Slide stared with all of his eyes at Popagator.

"Murder," said Popagator at last. "It's a case for the Justice Machines."

The Slide nodded—well, no. But he gave assent, in the way customary to Venusians.

"It is murder," he echoed. "We must report this with all possible haste."

"Right," Popagator agreed. "Well, play, friend! We've got fourteen squares to go and we must hurry. We must notify the Justice Machines the very moment we finish!"

II

The monster sat on the tail strut of his rocket, whistling. He turned over the whirlarang he had taken from the Venusian, admiring the play of light on the rubies and diamonds set into its handle.

"Son of a gun," he said aloud, hiccuping. "This sure beats working for a living!" He tilted a stainless-steel flask to his lips and belched happily.

The monster's name was David T. Jiminez, and he was a certified space explorer in the employ of the I.G.Y. He tossed the whirlarang into the air and clumsily caught it. He was forty-nine years old, and for the first time in his life he was sublimely happy.

Jiminez emptied the flask and tossed it away. "Hi-diddle-de-dee," he sang. "The spaceman's life for me!"

He banged the whirlarang against the side of his rocket, hiccuped, frowned and thought for a second. That wasn't such a good idea. Jiminez had no very good idea of just how fragile the hull of a rocketship was—"I don't dig that science jazz," he had told the I.G.Y. personnel office disarmingly—but, you never know, maybe he might knock a hole in it. Why take a chance? There was plenty of junk around.

He prowled through a heap of parts, tools and instruments that were tossed rusting on the sea-green moss. There was a black box, forearm length, with a hinged lid; on it was stenciled:

CAUTION

CONTENTS FRAGILE. STOW IN PADDED LOCKER.
PROTECT AGAINST JOLTS AND JARS.

He opened the lid, hefted the silvery tube inside thoughtfully, nodded and began to bang it against the whirlarang, trying to loosen the gems from their setting.

A clicking, rasping voice from behind him said inquiringly: "O Monster?"

Jiminez turned around belligerently. It was one of the damned bugs—naturally; there weren't any other human beings in this part of Venus. That was what made it so nice.

Jiminez disliked people, but he couldn't stand the bugs. It wasn't so bad that they were more or less the shape of a human being, or even that they lived in houses like human beings, used tools like human beings, even operated machinery like human beings—and kinds of machinery that, in some cases, humans couldn't quite match, or even understand.

What was really bad was that they *talked* like human beings. That, in Dirty Davey Jiminez's opinion, was pretty gaw-dam uppity of them, giving themselves airs. He had no idea that the Venusians did it from motives of purest politeness, since humans had shown themselves unable to grasp the barest fundamentals of the Venusian tongue.

He snarled, "Beat it, you."

Delicately turning away from Jiminez's breath, the Venusian said apologetically, "O Monster, I am Popagator. Isn't that the whirlarang of Wnotagashti the Drum?"

"You bugs gimme a pain," Jiminez said impatiently. "How'm I supposed to know?"

"Wnotagashti the Drum has been killed," the Venusian explained helpfully. "His head was split open. You were in the area just before it happened."

Jiminez thought for a moment, weaving slightly. "Oh, yeah, that. I tell you what happened, buster. I took it off him and he give me an argument. Well, I lost my temper. I mean it was a gaw-dam case of deliberate and insupportable rudeness, and if there's one thing I can't stand, it's a lot of gaw-dam rudeness. You know how it is. So I bashed him."

The Venusian moved inconspicuously to windward. He said compassionately: "A terrible ordeal, O Monster. Wnotagashti the Drum must have been deranged."

"That's what I thought," Jiminez agreed. "Now why don't you beat it so I can get a little work done around here?"

"Certainly. But—O Monster, there is one thing."

"Now what? Ain't you got any consideration? I got plenty on my mind already, you know."

"The Justice Machines," said Popagator apologetically. "My whirlarang companion, The Slide, has notified them of the accident to Wnotagashti the Drum. They will surely investigate you, O Monster."

Jiminez straightened up with faint alarm. "What the devil you talking about?" he demanded.

Popagator whished air noisily through his mouth cavity for a second in a disarming way. He said: "It is their function, O Monster. They are devices, like those which you call 'harness bulls.' One will come to interview you in this matter, perhaps quite soon."

"But the little rat gimme a hard time!" Jiminez protested, his stomach moving queasily. What was wrong here? Had he made a mistake of some sort? He said: "Dint you hear me? I only took the stinking thing away from him. And right away he *argues* with me! Talk about bad manners, bub, I tell you this was the *worst*."

"I understand," Popagator sympathized. "It is very clear, O Monster. You need only tell this to the Justice Machine, that is all. But I wished to notify you that it was coming, as an act of courtesy."

"Sure," said Jiminez, ungraciously, but feeling slightly more relaxed. "All right now, would you do me a favor and get lost? I got things to do, Charley. I can't spend the whole day talking to every lousy bug that comes along, understand?"

"I understand, O Monster," Popagator said in grave apology. "Good-by."

Jiminez pawed around the junk on the ground until he found another flask and took a long pull on it.

Confidence flowed back into him. He wiped his lips and sat down for a moment to rest—well, no. He sat down to finish the jug.

Jiminez had not always been a paid space traveler for the International Geophysical Year (as it was still quaintly called). For thirty-five years of his life, in fact, he had been a jockey.

That was all behind him now—mostly because of the trouble the State Board gave him in New York over the 1983 running of the Belmont 'Cap. The nag involved was named Heuristic Harry, and when he beat the finest three-year-olds of his day by six lengths, naturally there were questions. The benzedrine sulfate they found in Heuristic Harry's saliva provided some of the answers, and that was the end of the line for Jiminez's career as a jockey, at least in that part of the world.

A set-down jockey pushing fifty doesn't have many chances to make a living. And even somebody like Jiminez doesn't like to resign himself to starving to death.

He tried Mexico for a while, but there were all too many set-down jocks fighting for mounts there, and not much money anyway. Jiminez had got used to a lot of money.

And then, when he saw the ad, he had drifted toward the I.G.Y. district office. It seemed that fewer than one man in ten thousand had the peculiar genetic constitution that made it possible for him to endure the cosmic radiation that killed off most humans. It seemed further that small men—ex-jocks, for example—were particularly useful for space travel, since they didn't take as much room.

Jiminez still laughed out loud when he remembered the personnel officer's face. The man had stared silently at a blank wall for nearly five minutes, his mouth working soundlessly, with Jiminez's completed test forms in front of him. But finally he had signed them, stamped them "Approved" and turned his back until Jiminez was out of the room. It looked, thought Jiminez, as though they were having real trouble finding the kind of men they needed.

So—well, first he had tried to hold them up for double the usual pay, and failed; he had listened to an appeal to his sense of altruism and dedication to human progress from another I.G.Y. man, laughed in the man's face and drifted away.

But there wasn't much else to do, and that was a fact.

And then he had been stuck in a hotel room, wondering how to get out without paying the rent. And there had been a magazine. Jiminez wasn't much of a reader, but it was a long wait until the night desk clerk would sneak out for a quick beer, so he painfully spelled out the article on the first Venusian exploration parties.

And then Jiminez realized just what opportunities were open to him under the auspices of the I.G.Y.'s space-exploration program.

Hurling the second empty flask away, Jiminez stood up, wobbling.

He picked up the whirlarang from the ground and, still carrying it, lurched over to the vats he had scrabbled out of the soggy Venusian soil. It was a ritual with him; nearly every time he finished a flask, he inspected the progress of his mash, to make sure that there would be more when that was gone.

The mash had stopped bubbling. Nearly all the fermentation was over; it was almost time to dip out the sour juice and distill it. There would be, he calculated with difficulty, somewhere upward of fifty gallons of what you could call either beer or wine, as you chose, for him to push through the still.

It was a good little still. It had been designed by some very high-priced talent to meet the needs of explorers for safe, potable water, and it worked just as well for Jiminez's purposes. It would give a high, powerful yield. Call it ten gallons of approximately hundred-proof brandy—if you wanted to call it brandy. Sometimes he thought of it as whisky, sometimes as gin; it didn't really resemble anything on Earth. But it would be ten gallons of something.

At a quart a day—and he could make do with that—it would carry him through another month and leave a two-week supply, or nearly, for the return flight to Earth.

That was very good. In another month it would be just about time to take off for Earth again, according to the pre-set flight patterns built into the rocket's controls. And by then he would be ready.

Grinning happily, Jiminez lurched back to the ship and tossed the whirlarang into the open hatch. It landed with a splintering crash—some metal-and-glass object had been in the way and was now a thousand fragments—and one of the sparkling jewels was dislodged.

It rolled away under the sturdy legs of the tripod that held the silent pressure-temperature-humidity recorder. But that didn't matter; he would find the jewel before he took off. Because then he would take out that recorder—along with a lot of other junk the I.G.Y. people had installed—and leave it to rust on the soil of Venus.

He had already tossed out about half the stuff; there was plenty of time to get rid of the rest. Those things weighed plenty. What Jiminez wanted was to get rid of them. In the first place, all those clever and expensive little devices would be of no use at all to the I.G.Y.—because Jiminez's landing plan did not involve a return to the Yuma, Arizona, base where he was expected. It was his notion to land in either New Zealand or the Belgian Congo. And in the second place, he needed all the weight he could save.

The glittering facets of the whirlarang were diamonds and rubies. The whirlarang itself was hollow platinum.

He had already acquired nearly six hundred pounds of assorted gems and precious metals, and it was necessary to balance that weight, now tossed carelessly into the ship, by an equal weight of unnecessary junk removed.

It was all easy, amazingly easy. These funny-looking bugs that were the dominant race on Venus were just too polite to refuse anything. They never said no. They never stopped him, no matter what he did.

Jiminez began ladling fermentation liquor into the pot of the still. He was sweating profusely in the warm, wet air, but he didn't mind, not at all. The bugs lived in a sort of tin-plate Utopia; all their major needs were cared for by machines, running soundlessly out of sight and providing food, power, clothes, homes. According to the magazine article, they had lived that way for a thousand generations, since the time they nearly destroyed their planet in a war and substituted a code of politeness and a driving interest in games for more dangerous ways of life.

It worked out very nicely, whatever the reason. He walked into their houses and took away their very cooking utensils, and they didn't do a thing. The cook pots were spun platinum.

He shinnied up the side of the largest structure in their town— a triangular tower four stories high; embedded zircons and topaz were his footholds and grips, and at the top were fourteen diamonds of a hundred carats and up. He pried them from their settings and the bugs didn't do a thing.

He pulled two hundred meters of silver wire out of the municipal power plant—that was before he caught onto the fact that silver was a waste of time—and for five days the town was without electricity, until the automatic machines were able to replace it. And the Venusians still didn't do a thing.

Only the bug this morning, the one he'd taken the whirlarang away from, *he* had acted up.

Jiminez rested from his labors. He poured himself a shot of his last batch of brew, held his nose, threw it down, retched briefly and felt it take hold. He pondered cloudily: Would there be any trouble about that?

Probably not, he thought. Let the Justice Machine come. As the other bug had said, he had an ironclad case.

Anyway, he thought belligerently, let them try! It was plain self-defense, because how did he know what the bug was trying to do? Those whirlarang gadgets could kill somebody, couldn't they? And the bugs were pretty good with them. And——

Well, anyway. If the Justice Machine did come—and he was pretty sure it never would; it was just a bug bluff—he would outline the situation in a few simple words and it would go away again. That was all there was to it. The bug had, surprisingly, refused to yield the whirlarang—apparently it was only in the games that they acted normally selfish, greedy and competitive. So naturally he had hit the bug. He had to admit that maybe he wouldn't have done it if it hadn't been for a certain hangover. But he hadn't realized that the bugs could be killed quite so easily.

It was a plain accident, of course.

Besides, it was self-defense.

Furthermore, they wouldn't do anything about it.

He was very sure of that, right up to the moment when he heard the clattering and clanking of something big and mechanical coming out of the charred second-growth vines that were already springing up around his rocket, and an enormous metallic creation on wheels, with about a million waving arms and limbs, rolled dangerously up to him. And, wham, zowie, the limbs were all around him.

Dirty Davey Jiminez whooped and screamed and fought, but it didn't do a bit of good. The Justice Machine wasn't listening. It carried him away. He was caught, fair and square.

III

The monster named Jiminez howled to the unfeeling machine: "You can't do this to me! I demand a mouthpiece. I'm practically an ambassador, don't you know that? I work for the gaw-dam International Geofistical Year! Ever hear of it, damn you? Sure you have! That's an official government thing in the United Nations, buster, and they got lots of moxie back on Earth. They'll have a fleet of warships down here so fast, it'll make your head spin! I mean——" He stopped, confused. The machine had no head.

Jiminez sat down and tried to think. He had a hangover that was getting worse with every minute, but it was time to do some thinking.

The machine had carried him, hollering and wriggling as much as he could, but whatever he did, it was no use; the machine was built to handle adult Venusians, and it managed a mere monster without effort or strain. It had taken him to the triangular tower.

A door he had never suspected had opened and he had found himself in jail.

Anyway, he thought it was a jail because he was locked in, and because the machine stayed with him as a warden. There was a whole world under the gay, gem-studded homes of the Venusians that appeared on the surface, so Jiminez discovered. The Justice Machine bore him through corridors, past a dreadfully odorous place where filth-stained walls hinted at unpleasant events, into a narrow cell. There was a constant thrumming in the walls and floor. Machines were nearby, the machines, no doubt, on which the Venusians depended for all their goods.

The Justice Machine set him down and retreated to a post by the door.

Jiminez wiped his lips on the back of his hand, glowered at the silent machine and considered his position.

He admitted to himself through a pounding headache that it was a rough spot. He had been in rougher, perhaps, but he couldn't think when.

There was a sound from the door and a clicking, rasping voice inquired: "O Monster?"

It was the bug named—named—Jiminez managed to recall it: Popagator.

"Hah!" cried Jiminez, at once again enraged. "You, Popagator! I thought you told me the Justice Machine wouldn't bother me!"

"An error, O Monster," Popagator apologized.

"Error, hah? You bet it was an error. Popagator, I'm telling you, you better get me out of here! You hear me? Don't you know I got the whole United Nations behind me? You know what that means, don't you? One bleat from me and, wham, zowie, the great white fathers from far off in space will come blazing and shooting down with their devil birds. Man, I'm warning you!"

Popagator stepped nimbly out of range of the monster's breath. He said ruefully: "The thing is, Monster, the deed is a terrible one. You killed one of our people——"

"But he gimme a rough time!"

"—while he was playing the whirlarang game. It is not the killing, Monster. It is interrupting the game. Wnotagashti the Drum may have been deranged, but he was entitled to throw his whirlarang."

"It was a accident!" roared Jiminez. "Self-defense, see? I only touched the gaw-dam bug, that's all. He split wide open. How was I supposed to know he was so——"

"Peace, O Monster," Popagator said with warm sympathy. "Now I understand your position. It was an accident?"

"Gaw-dam *right!*"

"Then," said Popagator with great assurance, "you need not worry. The Justice Machine will shortly examine you, when witnesses are found."

"Witnesses? What kind of witnesses?"

"Those who may know something to your benefit, Monster. For be assured, all of our people love you monsters very much. We wish to help you."

"The best way to help me," Jiminez snarled, "is to get me out of this stinking joint."

"Of course, Monster. It is only necessary to go through the formality before the Justice Machine." He shrugged—well, no. But he achieved the same effect.

Jiminez took a deep breath and sat down, grumbling. The crime, he began to understand, was not so much murder, or insecticide, but interfering with someone playing a game. That was a *definite* breach of regulations.

"But I didn't know!" Jiminez cried hoarsely. "Our customs are all different, and besides he gave me a hard time."

"Of course, O Monster," soothed Popagator. "I understand. Believe me, I shall see that the Justice Machine takes that into account at the hearing. And surely you will be released. Have no doubt of it."

"That's better," grunted Jiminez, slightly appeased.

"Of course," said the Venusian delicately, "if by any unforeseen chance——"

"Hey, wait!" squawked Jiminez. "What chance?"

"O Monster," said Popagator gravely, "there is always the theoretical and hardly to be considered possibility that the Justice Machine will make a mistake."

"*Now* you tell me! Listen, buster, I'm practically an ambassador, get that through your thick head! If anything hap——"

"But in that event," the Venusian interrupted quickly, "there remains the Appeals Panel. You see? Our machines are arranged so that even the hardly possible chance of error can still be corrected."

"It damn better be," said Jiminez in a surly tone. He slumped back against the wall. "Jeez," he groaned, "what a head. Say, listen. It looks like I'm going to be here for a while. I want you to do something for me."

"Command me, O Monster."

"You take a hike down by my ship, okay? There's a rack of steel bottles marked 'Emergency Water Supply.' Some of them are sealed tight. Don't pay any attention to those—they've got water in them—but bring me one of the others."

"Certainly, O Monster." Popagator turned to go.

He was halted by the Earthman. "Wait a minute! Come to think of it, better bring me two!"

The trial didn't take very long. The Justice Machine waved its ropy steel tentacles and cascades of flickering lights flashed up and down its sides as it weighed the evidence of the eight Venusians. Nobody asked Jiminez to testify, but that was just as well. He wasn't paying much attention anyway. He caroled:

> "*The wind blew through the old man's whiskers.*
> *His heart was filled with joy and song.*"

The Justice Machine squatted on its metal wheels, its innards clicking. No sound came out of the Justice Machine—it only received information; it did not broadcast any. The witnesses were brief and explicit. There was a lot of talk about the lifetime Total Aggregate Whirlarang Weighted Score of the deceased Wnotagashti the Drum. Jiminez couldn't make much sense of it and didn't much try.

"He never had to wear pajamas——"

The Justice Machine's lights flickered incandescently and then, suddenly, all went out at once.

Three of the machine's tentacles made a gesture toward Jiminez. The Venusians chattered excitedly among themselves.

"Because his whiskers were so long!"

Jiminez, heedless, sang drunkenly on, waving the stainless steel flask of home-stilled popskull in time with the clicking of the machine. At last he noticed that the small-bodied Venusian named Popagator was standing before him, humbly awaiting his attention.

"O Monster?" said Popagator.

"Well, now what?" Jiminez demanded belligerently, hiccuping.

"The trial is over, O Monster. The Justice Machine has reached its decision."

"It has, has it?" panted Jiminez, standing up with some difficulty. "Aha. Oho. And just a-*bout* bloody time, if you ask me. Well, I guess I'm about ready to shake the dust of this crummy planet off my feet anyhow. So long, bugs! So long, suckers! Here goes Jiminez for the Belgian Congo and a lifetime of luxury!" He laughed raucously, disregarding the fact that he could not take off for another three and a half weeks, and started for the door.

But he didn't make it. The Justice Machine flared in blinding colors and spun swiftly to come between him and the door.

"Hey!" cried Jiminez, more surprised than angry. "What's matter?"

Popagator came up behind him and coughed apologetically—well, no. What he did was to contract his dorsal chitin with a faint popping sound, but it was the equivalent of a cough.

He said regretfully: "O Monster, don't worry, but there has been some mistake. The Justice Machine found you guilty."

IV

The Slide spun around three times, and on the third turn released the hilt of his whirlarang with that slippy-slidy motion that was the hallmark of his entire family. The whirlarang shot out straight and true for the grove of tinkleberry trees that indicated the target area of the eighth square. It circled the grove twice, flipflopped, described a lazy S and returned to its owner.

He caught it triumphantly. "A six-pointer!" he crowed. "Top that, Popagator!"

"I don't know if I can," Popagator confessed moodily. "I'm off my form today."

"You certainly are," jeered the larger Venusian. "It isn't often I take three straight games from you. What's bothering you? The Monster?"

Popagator nodded—well, no.

The Slide said sympathetically: "I know how you feel. It presses on your mind, thinking of him sitting in that cell and waiting for the Justice Machine to report on the decision of the Appeals Panel. I feel it myself."

"We've got to help him!"

"Of course, Popagator. It's cruel to worry another being—and Earth monsters are considered to be beings in spite of everything."

"I hate to think of him worrying, as he must be."

"Me, too."

Popagator said seriously: "I want to do something about it right away. I propose that we both visit him to cheer him up—the sooner, the better."

"Agreed!" cried The Slide. "Come, let's hurry! We'll finish this game and then—no more than two more, eh? And then we'll race to his side!"

But it was a long time for Dave Jiminez. With a full flask by his side, he was cold sober. That had never happened before in his life.

The Justice Machine was silent and motionless by the door; it never moved, never made a sound except once when, driven by desperation, he approached it. And then it was all sudden movement and threatening lashings of the arms, and he retreated and never approached it again.

But now it moved.

It rolled aside. The door opened and two Venusians clattered in—that Popagator and another one who had testified at the crazy mockery they called a trial. The Slide, his name was.

"This is a friend, O Monster," said Popagator. "He is on your side, just as I am. You mustn't worry. We'll see that you get out of here."

"Damn better," snarled Jiminez. "What's holding things up?"

"The Appeals Panel," said The Slide. "It is considering your case. Naturally, it will reverse the Justice Machine's decision."

"Naturally," growled Jiminez. "How long does *that* take?"

Both Venusians hesitated and looked at each other.

"It doesn't take long, O Monster," said Popagator at last.

"Better not." Jiminez looked at his visitors and made a repelled face. Still, even cockroach-shaped visitors were better than no visitors at all. Anyway, he felt slightly better. He felt good enough, in fact, to bend down for the ignored stainless-steel flask. He took a long pull, moaned as his throat constricted, stood rigid for a moment and then relaxed.

"Zowie," he said hoarsely. "Say, just out of curiosity—what would happen if the Appeals Panel ruled against me?"

"Why," said Popagator, "the penalty for interference with the game is death, of course."

"D——" Jiminez paused, the flask half-tilted in his hand, his sallow face turning a dirty gray. "D——"

"Death," the Venusian finished for him. But he added, in a warmly sympathetic tone: "There's nothing to worry about, O Monster. We are on your side. We'll see that no harm comes to you."

"You will? *How* will you? What happens if you don't?"

"O Monster," said Popagator apologetically, "then the Justice Machine will exterminate you. But don't worry. It is nearly certain that the Appeals Panel will correct the error."

Jiminez slowly set the flask down and began loosening his collar.

He stared at the Justice Machine. Like all the Venusian gadgets, it seemed to be built to last. He could just imagine those ropy metal limbs wrapping around a Venusian and cracking the shell, wrenching the limbs off, ending life in a matter of seconds. With a mammalian Earthman, all flesh and fat and fluids surrounding a frame of bone, it would be squishier. But no less final.

He swallowed, and found his throat was dry.

"That room——" He coughed. "That room I passed on the way in."

"The Room of Reckoning, O Monster?"

"If that's what you call the one that looks like a slaughterhouse, yeah. Is that the place where——"

"That is the place, O Monster," said Popagator gravely.

There was a clicking from the Justice Machine and lights flashed up and down its sides.

Jiminez jumped, kicking the flask at his feet clattering against the wall. He hesitated, torn between basic urges; he glanced frantically at the Justice Machine, then dropped to his knees, scrabbling for the flask and stopper.

He heard a sorrowful voice say: "Oh, my. This is very strange."

He looked up, apprehensive. Popagator and The Slide were clacking at each other in a low tone.

"What happened?" Jiminez bleated in fright.

Popagator looked at the other Venusian, and then spoke. "The Appeals Panel, O Monster. It has acted in your case."

"And?"

The Venusian's embarrassment was almost human. "Don't worry, O Monster. But they, too, found you guilty."

Jiminez fell back against the wall.

Then he surged forward, furious. "Now wait!" he bawled. "I took enough from you guys! I demand you get me out of this place right *now*. This damn thing has gone far enough and it isn't going any further, you hear? I'm *warning* you. Do you want the great white godlings from the sky coming down here shooting and stomping and——"

"Oh, no, O Monster," interrupted The Slide. "Of course not."

"*Well*, then! Then you damn better smarten up. I tell you there's going to be one terrible mess here on Venus if I don't get back. The I.G.Y. don't like it when us emissaries get knocked off, you know! And what the I.G.Y. says *goes*."

"That is true, O Monster," The Slide admitted. "It is known to all of us. The I.G.Y. is in charge of Venus."

"So you better get me out of here!"

The Venusians whispered fleetingly to one another.

"Speak up!" Jiminez cried. "Talk English!"

"We were only discussing how we could best help you," apologized Popagator. Then, in a voice as warm as toast, he added: "O Monster, there is a way. It is clear that our machines are not equipped to deal with Earth persons. We must act against the machines."

"Meaning what?"

"Meaning, O Monster, that Venusians such as we cannot permit you to suffer unjustly. It is against our code of behavior." Popagator looked gravely at Jiminez with all of his eyes and said: "We are going to help you escape!"

Jiminez, alone in the cell, waited, drinking heavily. It was a searing torment to him, to think that he was trusting the word of the lousy bugs. Bugs were to be stepped on or sprayed with D.D.T. Bugs were to furnish him with the good things of life, such as jewels and gold, that would finance a happy and dissolute old age back on Earth. Bugs were not to be *trusted*.

But he had no choice.

And then, at last, there was a scratching at the door.

It was Popagator, The Slide and four other Venusians.

Jiminez froze, watching. Two of the Venusians stepped up to the quietly menacing Justice Machine and did something he couldn't follow to the arrays of lights and glittering projections on its sides.

There was a series of clicks and a flash of muted lights. And then the Justice Machine rolled quietly out into the corridor and away.

"We relieved it of duty, O Monster," said Popagator proudly. "It is a thing which is seldom done."

"Is it a thing that'll get me out of here?" Jiminez demanded.

"Oh, beyond doubt. Monster," Popagator added politely, "permit me to introduce you to our colleagues in this venture of rescuing you. Reading from left to right, these are Xxil the Predestinarian, Klamagog, Small Wnotagashti and Susternong. The Slide you already know."

"Pleased to meet you," Jiminez said absently. "Now let's get the—— Hey. Small who?"

"Small Wnotagashti, O Monster."

"Any relation to——"

"Oh, yes. His son, O Monster."

Jiminez swallowed. "You mean this character's the son of the bug I knocked off and he's still willing to help me get out of this place?"

"We Venusians are extremely helpful and polite," Popagator explained. "Now we must go. We have to walk down this corridor, past the machine areas, into the Room of Reckoning. There——"

"Oh, no, you don't!" Jiminez cried. "I'm not going in that place! What is this, a double cross?"

"It is necessary, O Monster," Popagator said patiently. "There is a chute in the Room of Reckoning which is used for removing the"—he hesitated—"which leads to a way out."

"There isn't any other way, O Monster."

Jiminez, carrying the last few drops of precious numbwit in the stainless-steel flask, shambled after the little posse of Venusians. They went down the long corridor past the shuddering chambers of the machines, and no one was to be seen.

"We are here, O Monster," said one of them.

"Where?" asked Jiminez suspiciously.

"The Room of Reckoning, the avenue of your escape," Popagator said in a voice as sweet as honey and as warm as toast. "Open that door, O Monster, and walk in."

Jiminez, his hand on the door, turned, suddenly afraid, but they were crowding in on him, all six of them. The door was borne open and he was thrust inside.

And there was the Justice Machine, its ropy arms a-swing, in the room with the moldering spatters of green and blue, that now added a new range of colors to its scheme.

Outside, in the soggy evening air, the Venusians congratulated each other on the tact and delicacy with which they had handled the matter.

"It would have been cruel to let him suffer," said Small Wnota-gashti solemnly. "My father would have wanted it this way."

"We have done well," agreed Popagator, and the others went about their errands, leaving him with The Slide.

The Slide stretched and yawned—well, no. But he relaxed. "We

Venusians," he commented, "are polite and thoughtful to a fault. Tell me, do you think we can get another game in before dark?"

"If not," twinkled Popagator, "we can always play under the lights. *I* don't have any trouble with nighttime rules!"

The Slide excused himself: "This has been a strain, you know."

"Of course. It is well known that monsters require even more politeness and patience than our own race. It is the least we can do for them." They started off toward the first square. After a moment, Popagator added absently: "You know, in one way we have failed the monsters even yet."

"Failed them? What are you talking about, Popagator?"

"The ship," Popagator explained. "They expect it to be returned. Perhaps we should return it as a matter of common politeness, with a few of us aboard?"

He hefted his whirlarang and tossed it in a slow curve, following it with his eye.

"I am sure," he said thoughtfully, "that there would be many acts of politeness we could perform on their own planet."

THE HATED
~~~~~~~~~~~~ by Paul Flehr ~~~~~~~~~~~~

THE BAR DIDN'T HAVE A NAME. NO NAME OF ANY
kind. Not even an indication that it had ever had one. All it said
on the outside was:

Café
EAT
Cocktails

which doesn't make a lot of sense. But it was a bar. It had a big
TV set going ya-ta-ta ya-ta-ta in three glorious colors, and a juke
box that tried to drown out the TV with that lousy music they
play. Anyway, it wasn't a kid hangout. I kind of like it. But I
wasn't supposed to be there at all; it's in the contract. I was supposed to stay in New York and the New England states.

Café-EAT-*Cocktails* was right across the river. I think the name
of the place was Hoboken, but I'm not sure. It all had a kind of
dreamy feeling to it. I was——

Well, I couldn't even remember going there. I remembered

THE FOURTH GALAXY READER

one minute I was in downtown New York, looking across the river. I did that a lot. And then I was there. I don't remember crossing the river at all.

I was drunk, you know.

You know how it is? Double bourbons and keep them coming. And after a while the bartender stops bringing me the ginger ale because gradually I forget to mix them. I got pretty loaded long before I left New York. I realize that. I guess I had to get pretty loaded to risk the pension and all.

Used to be I didn't drink much, but now, I don't know, when I have one drink, I get to thinking about Sam and Wally and Chowderhead and Gilvey and the captain. If I don't drink, I think about them, too, and then I take a drink. And that leads to another drink, and it all comes out to the same thing. Well, I guess I said it already, I drink a pretty good amount, but you can't blame me.

There was a girl.

I always get a girl someplace. Usually they aren't much and this one wasn't either. I mean she was probably somebody's mother. She was around thirty-five and not so bad, though she had a long scar under her ear down along her throat to the little round spot where her larynx was. It wasn't ugly. She smelled nice —while I could still smell, you know—and she didn't talk much. I liked that. Only——

Well, did you ever meet somebody with a nervous cough? Like when you say something funny—a little funny, not a big yock— they don't laugh and they don't stop with just smiling, but they sort of cough? She did that. I began to itch. I couldn't help it. I asked her to stop it.

She spilled her drink and looked at me almost as though she was scared—and I had tried to say it quietly, too.

"Sorry," she said, a little angry, a little scared. "*Sorry*. But you don't have to——"

"Forget it."

"Sure. But you asked me to sit down here with you, remember? If you're going to——"

"*Forget it!*" I nodded at the bartender and held up two fingers. "You need another drink," I said. "The thing is," I said, "Gilvey used to do that."

"What?"

"That cough."

She looked puzzled. "You mean like this?"

"*Goddamn it, stop it!*" Even the bartender looked over at me that time. Now she was really mad, but I didn't want her to go away. I said, "Gilvey was a fellow who went to Mars with me. Pat Gilvey."

"*Oh.*" She sat down again and leaned across the table, low. "*Mars.*"

The bartender brought our drinks and looked at me suspiciously. I said, "Say, Mac, would you turn down the air conditioning?"

"My name isn't Mac. No."

"Have a heart. It's too cold in here."

"Sorry." He didn't sound sorry.

I was cold. I mean that kind of weather, it's always cold in those places. You know around New York in August? It hits eighty, eighty-five, ninety. All the places have air conditioning and what they really want is for you to wear a shirt and tie.

But I like to walk a lot. You would, too, you know. And you can't walk around much in long pants and a suit coat and all that stuff. Not around there. Not in August. And so then, when I went into a bar, it'd have one of those built-in freezers for the used-car salesmen with their dates, or maybe their wives, all dressed up. For what? But I froze.

"*Mars,*" the girl breathed. "*Mars.*"

I began to itch again. "Want to dance?"

"They don't have a license," she said. "Byron, *I* didn't know you'd been to *Mars!* Please *tell* me about it."

"It was all right," I said.

That was a lie.

She was interested. She forgot to smile. It made her look nicer. She said, "I knew a man—my brother-in-law—he was my husband's brother—I mean my ex-husband——"

"I get the idea."

"He worked for General Atomic. In Rockford, Illinois. You know where that is?"

"Sure." I couldn't go there, but I knew where Illinois was.

"He worked on the first Mars ship. Oh, fifteen years ago, wasn't it? He always wanted to go himself, but he couldn't pass the tests." She stopped and looked at me.

I knew what she was thinking. But I didn't always look this way, you know. Not that there's anything wrong with me now, I mean, but I couldn't pass the tests any more. Nobody can. That's why we're all one-trippers.

I said, "The only reason I'm shaking like this is because I'm cold."

It wasn't true, of course. It was that cough of Gilvey's. I didn't like to think about Gilvey, or Sam or Chowderhead or Wally or the captain. I didn't like to think about any of them. It made me shake.

You see, we couldn't kill each other. They wouldn't let us do that. Before we took off, they did something to our minds to make sure. What they did, it doesn't last forever. It lasts for two years and then it wears off. That's long enough, you see, because that gets you to Mars and back; and it's plenty long enough, in another way, because it's like a strait jacket.

You know how to make a baby cry? Hold his hands. It's the most basic thing there is. What they did to us so we couldn't kill each other, it was like being tied up, like having our hands held so we couldn't get free. Well. But two years was long enough. Too long.

The bartender came over and said, "Pal, I'm sorry. See, I turned the air conditioning down. You all right? You look so——"

I said, "Sure, I'm all right."

He sounded worried. I hadn't even heard him come back. The girl was looking worried, too, I guess because I was shaking so hard I was spilling my drink. I put some money on the table without even counting it.

"It's all right," I said. "We were just going."

"We were?" She looked confused. But she came along with me. They always do, once they find out you've been to Mars.

In the next place, she said, between trips to the powder room, "It must take a lot of courage to sign up for something like that. Were you scientifically inclined in school? Don't you have to know an awful lot to be a space flyer? Did you ever see any of those little monkey characters they say live on Mars? I read an article about how they lived in little cities of pup tents or something like that—only they didn't make them, they grew them. Funny! Ever see those? That trip must have been a real drag, I bet. What is it, nine months? You could've had a baby! Excuse me—— Say, tell me. All that time, how'd you—well, manage things? I mean didn't you ever have to go to the you-know or anything?"

"We managed," I said.

She giggled, and that reminded her, so she went to the powder room again. I thought about getting up and leaving while she was gone, but what was the use of that? I'd only pick up somebody else.

It was nearly midnight. A couple of minutes wouldn't hurt. I reached in my pocket for the little box of pills they give us—it isn't refillable, but we get a new prescription in the mail every month, along with the pension check. The label on the box said:

CAUTION

Use only as directed by physician. Not to be taken by persons suffering heart condition, digestive upset or circulatory disease. Not to be used in conjunction with alcoholic beverages.

I took three of them. I don't like to start them before midnight, but anyway I stopped shaking.

I closed my eyes, and then I was on the ship again. The noise in the bar became the noise of the rockets and the air washers and the sludge sluicers. I began to sweat, although this place was air conditioned, too.

I could hear Wally whistling to himself the way he did, the sound muffled by his oxygen mask and drowned in the rocket noise, but still perfectly audible. The tune was "Sophisticated Lady." Sometimes it was "Easy to Love" and sometimes "Chasing Shadows," but mostly "Sophisticated Lady." He was from Juilliard.

Somebody sneezed, and it sounded just like Chowderhead sneezing. You know how everybody sneezes according to his own individual style? Chowderhead had a ladylike little sneeze; it went *hutta*, real quick, all through the mouth, no nose involved. The captain went *Hrasssh;* Wally was Ashoo, ashoo, *ashoo*. Gilvey was *Hutch*-uh. Sam didn't sneeze much, but he sort of coughed and sprayed, and that was worse.

Sometimes I used to think about killing Sam by tying him down and having Wally and the captain sneeze him to death. But that was a kind of a joke, naturally, when I was feeling good. Or pretty good. Usually I thought about a knife for Sam. For Chowderhead it was a gun, right in the belly, one shot. For Wally it was a Tommy gun—just stitching him up and down, you know, back and forth. The captain I would put in a cage with hungry lions, and Gilvey I'd strangle with my bare hands. That was probably because of the cough, I guess.

She was back. "Please tell me about it," she begged. "I'm *so* curious."

I opened my eyes. "You want me to tell you about it?"

"Oh, please!"

"About what it's like to fly to Mars on a rocket?"

"Yes!"

"All right," I said.

It's wonderful what three little white pills will do. I wasn't even shaking.

"There's six men, see? In a space the size of a Buick, and that's all the room there is. Two of us in the bunks all the time, four of us on watch. Maybe you want to stay in the sack an extra ten minutes—because it's the only place on the ship where you can stretch out, you know, the only place where you can rest without somebody's elbow in your side. But you can't. Because by then it's the next man's turn.

"And maybe you don't have elbows in your side while it's your turn off watch, but in the starboard bunk there's the air-regenerator master valve—I bet I could still show you the bruises right around my kidneys—and in the port bunk there's the emergency-escape-hatch handle. That gets you right in the temple if you turn your head too fast.

"And you can't really sleep, I mean not soundly, because of the noise. That is, when the rockets are going. When they aren't going, then you're in free fall, and that's bad, too, because you dream about falling. But when they're going, I don't know, I think it's worse. It's pretty loud.

"And even if it weren't for the noise, if you sleep too soundly you might roll over on your oxygen line. Then you dream about drowning. Ever do that? You're strangling and choking and you can't get any air? It isn't dangerous, I guess. Anyway, it always woke me up in time. Though I heard about a fellow in a flight six years ago——

"Well. So you've always got this oxygen mask on, all the time, except if you take it off for a second to talk to somebody. You don't do that very often, because what is there to say? Oh, maybe the first couple of weeks, sure—everybody's friends then. You don't even need the mask, for that matter. Or not very much. Everybody's still pretty clean. The place smells—oh, let's see— about like the locker room in a gym. You know? You can stand

it. That's if nobody's got space sickness, of course. We were lucky
that way.

"But that's about how it's going to get anyway, you know. Outside the masks, it's soup. It isn't that you smell it so much. You
kind of *taste* it, in the back of your mouth, and your eyes sting.
That's after the first two or three months. Later on, it gets worse.

"And with the mask on, of course, the oxygen mixture is coming in under pressure. That's funny if you're not used to it. Your
lungs have to work a little bit harder to get rid of it, especially
when you're asleep, so after a while the muscles get sore. And
then they get sorer. And then——

"Well.

"Before we take off, the psych people give us a long doo-da
that keeps us from killing each other. But they can't stop us from
thinking about it. And afterward, after we're back on Earth—this
is what you won't read about in the articles—they keep us apart.
You know how they work it? We get a pension, naturally. I mean
there's got to be a pension, otherwise there isn't enough money in
the world to make anybody go. But in the contract, it says to get
the pension we have to stay in our own area.

"The whole country's marked off. Six sections. Each has at least
one big city in it. I was lucky, I got a lot of them. They try to
keep it so every man's home town is in his own section, but—well,
like with us. Chowderhead and the captain both happened to
come from Santa Monica. I think it was Chowderhead that got
California, Nevada, all that Southwest area. It was the luck of
the draw. God knows what the captain got.

"Maybe New Jersey," I said, and took another white pill.

We went on to another place and she said suddenly, "I figured
something out. The way you keep looking around."

"What did you figure out?"

"Well, part of it was what you said about the other fellow getting New Jersey. This is New Jersey. You don't belong in this section, right?"

"Right," I said after a minute.

"So why are you here? I know why. You're here because you're looking for somebody."

"That's right."

She said triumphantly, "You want to find that other fellow from your crew! You want to fight him!"

I couldn't help shaking, white pills or no white pills. But I had to correct her.

"No. I want to kill him."

"How do you know he's here? He's got a lot of states to roam around in, too, doesn't he?"

"Six. New Jersey, Pennsylvania, Delaware, Maryland—all the way down to Washington."

"Then how do you know——"

"He'll be here." I didn't have to tell her how I knew. But I knew.

I wasn't the only one who spent his time at the border of his assigned area, looking across the river or staring across a state line, knowing that somebody was on the other side. I knew. You fight a war and you don't have to guess that the enemy might have his troops a thousand miles away from the battle line. You know where his troops will be. You know he wants to fight, too.

Hutta. Hutta.

I spilled my drink.

I looked at her. "You—you didn't——"

She looked frightened. "What's the matter?"

"Did you just sneeze?"

"Sneeze? Me? Did I——"

I said something quick and nasty, I don't know what. No! It hadn't been her. I knew it.

It was Chowderhead's sneeze.

Chowderhead. Marvin T. Roebuck, his name was. Five feet eight inches tall. Dark-complected, with a cast in one eye. Spoke with a Midwest kind of accent, even though he came from Cali-

fornia—"shrick" for "shriek," "hawror" for "horror," like that. It
drove me crazy after a while. Maybe that gives you an idea what
he talked about mostly. A skunk. A thoroughgoing, deep-rooted,
mother-murdering skunk.

I kicked over my chair and roared, "Roebuck! Where are you,
damn you?"

The bar was all at once silent. Only the juke box kept going.

"I know you're here!" I screamed. "Come out and get it! You
louse, I told you I'd get you for calling me a liar the day Wally
sneaked a smoke!"

Silence, everybody looking at me.

Then the door of the men's room opened.

He came out.

He looked *lousy.* Eyes all red-rimmed and his hair falling out—
the poor crumb couldn't have been over twenty-nine. He shrieked,
"You!" He called me a million names. He said, "You thieving rat,
I'll teach you to try to cheat me out of my candy ration!"

He had a knife.

I didn't care. I didn't have anything and that was stupid, but
it didn't matter. I got a bottle of beer from the next table and
smashed it against the back of a chair. It made a good weapon,
you know; I'd take that against a knife any time.

I ran toward him, and he came all staggering and lurching toward me, looking crazy and desperate, mumbling and raving—I
could hardly hear him, because I was talking, too. Nobody tried
to stop us. Somebody went out the door and I figured it was to
call the cops, but that was all right. Once I took care of Chowderhead, I didn't care what the cops did.

I went for the face.

He cut me first. I felt the knife slide up along my left arm but,
you know, it didn't even hurt, only kind of stung a little. I didn't
care about that. I got him in the face, and the bottle came away,
and it was all like gray and white jelly, and then blood began to
spring out. He screamed. Oh, that scream! I never heard anything

like that scream. It was what I had been waiting all my life for.

I kicked him as he staggered back, and he fell. And I was on top of him, with the bottle, and I was careful to stay away from the heart or the throat, because that was too quick, but I worked over the face, and I felt his knife get me a couple times more, and—

And—

And I woke up, you know. And there was Dr. Santly over me with a hypodermic needle that he'd just taken out of my arm, and four male nurses in fatigues holding me down. And I was drenched with sweat.

For a minute, I didn't know where I was. It was a horrible queasy falling sensation, as though the bar and the fight and the world were all dissolving into smoke around me.

Then I knew where I was.

It was almost worse.

I stopped yelling and just lay there, looking up at them.

Dr. Santly said, trying to keep his face friendly and noncommittal, "You're doing much better, Byron, boy. *Much* better."

I didn't say anything.

He said, "You worked through the whole thing in two hours and eight minutes. Remember the first time? You were sixteen hours killing him. Captain Van Wyck it was that time, remember? Who was it this time?"

"Chowderhead." I looked at the male nurses. Doubtfully, they let go of my arms and legs.

"Chowderhead," said Dr. Santly. "Oh—Roebuck. That boy," he said mournfully, his expression saddened, "he's not coming along nearly as well as you. *Nearly*. He can't run through a cycle in less than five hours. And, that's peculiar, it's usually you he—— Well, I better not say that, shall I? No sense setting up a counterimpression when your pores are all open, so to speak?" He smiled at me, but he was a little worried in back of the smile.

I sat up. "Anybody got a cigarette?"

"Give him a cigarette, Johnson," the doctor ordered the male nurse standing alongside my right foot.

Johnson did. I fired up.

"You're coming along *splendidly*," Dr. Santly said. He was one of these psych guys that thinks if you say it's so, it makes it so. You know that kind? "We'll have you down under an hour before the end of the week. That's *marvelous* progress. Then we can work on the conscious level! You're doing extremely well, whether you know it or not. Why, in six months—say in eight months, because I like to be conservative"—he twinkled at me—"we'll have you out of here! You'll be the first of your crew to be discharged, you know that?"

"That's nice," I said. "The others aren't doing so well?"

"No. Not at all well, most of them. Particularly Dr. Gilvey. The run-throughs leave him in terrible shape. I don't mind admitting I'm worried about him.

"That's nice," I said, and this time I meant it.

He looked at me thoughtfully, but all he did was say to the male nurses, "He's all right now. Help him off the table."

It was hard standing up. I had to hold onto the rail around the table for a minute. I said my set little speech: "Dr. Santly, I want to tell you again how grateful I am for this. I was reconciled to living the rest of my life confined to one part of the country, the way the other crews always did. But this is much better. I appreciate it. I'm sure the others do too."

"Of course, boy. Of course." He took out a fountain pen and made a note on my chart; I couldn't see what it was, but he looked gratified. "It's no more than you have coming to you, Byron," he said. "I'm grateful that I could be the one to make it come to pass."

He glanced conspiratorially at the male nurses. "You know how important this is to me. It's the triumph of a whole new approach to psychic rehabilitation. I mean to say our heroes of space travel are entitled to freedom when they come back home to Earth, aren't they?"

"Definitely," I said, scrubbing some of the sweat off my face onto my sleeve.

"So we've got to end this system of designated areas. We can't avoid the tensions that accompany space travel, no. But if we can help you eliminate harmful tensions with a few run-throughs, why, it's not too high a price to pay, is it?"

"Not a bit."

"I mean to say," he said, warming up, "you can look forward to the time when you'll be able to mingle with your old friends from the rocket, free and easy, without any need for restraint. That's a lot to look forward to, isn't it?"

"It is," I said. "I look forward to it very much," I said. "And I know exactly what I'm going to do the first time I meet one—I mean without any restraints, as you say," I said. And it was true; I did. Only it wouldn't be a broken beer bottle that I would do it with.

I had much more elaborate ideas than that.

KILL ME WITH KINDNESS

~~~~~~~~ by Richard Wilson ~~~~~~~~

I WOKE UP AT NOON AFTER A BLURRED NIGHT BEFORE and padded around in my bare feet. Even the bathroom had inch-thick carpet. I showered and brushed my teeth, but put off shaving.

Back in bed—it was eight feet long, six wide and had a contraption that kept the weight of the blanket off my toes—I ordered breakfast.

"Eggs McCutchen, *café au lait*, pumpernickel bread with Wisconsin butter and—oh, orange juice," I said. "*Fresh* orange juice."

"Yes, sir," said a voice.

Simple fare was what I needed. I'd had flaming bananas the previous day, but that's too rich for breakfast. And canned orange juice is always terrible, even here in Paradise.

I hummed a bit of "The Prisoner's Song," but forgot just how it went. "Play Bunny Berrigan doing that number, will you?" I asked.

During the second chorus, my tray came out of the headboard.

I'd have preferred eating at the table, but for a while I was making myself enjoy some of my enforced luxuries. Breakfast in bed was one of them.

"Tray away," I said when I'd finished. The day before, I'd said, "Fast broken." They always understood my meaning (I'd been experimenting with that) and the tray vanished into the headboard. Another day was off and running, however slowly.

"Play 'Nothin' to Do and All Day to Do It In,'" I said. That should have been a stumper. Years ago, I'd remembered the tune and tried half a dozen record specialists, but none had it. It was a cut-out, long gone from the catalogues.

But *they* had it. Erskine Butterfield sang and his piano tinkled and it was like old times, only I wasn't as poor. Now I had everything I wanted, sort of. I roused myself and went in to shave.

"What'll it be today?" I asked the Ear. "Dry, safety, straight or depil?"

"You haven't tried electrolysis, sir," the pleasant neuter voice said. "That would eliminate the daily chore."

"No, no," I sang, "you can't take that away from me."

"Shall I play that?"

"No, no," I said, not singing. "Let me try the electric shaver with the Rotary Action."

It popped out of the chute under the mirror. I dabbed on green pre-shave gunk and went to work.

"No Razor Pull," I said. "But slow. And it doesn't get the Hidden Hair."

No comment from the Ear. I wasn't always favored with a reply to my witticisms.

Dropping the shaver down the chute, I mulled the uniform of the day. Yesterday I'd worn a Tarzan-style leopard skin with a special pouch for cigarettes. The day before, it had been a midnight-blue dinner jacket (shawl lapels) and scarlet cummerbund. What the hell.

"Attention to costume," I said. "Today the well-dressed guinea pig will wear, from the feet up, in order: desert boots, soft wool knee socks, khaki shorts, short-sleeve khaki shirt (*two* pockets, please) and sun helmet."

"Yes, sir."

The clothing came out of a wall chute. The sun helmet reminded me of Fredric March in *Trade Winds* (Joan Bennett), and that reminded me of March and Carole Lombard in *Nothing Sacred*.

"This morning I will see some movie excerpts," I told the Ear. "I will see the scene in *Nothing Sacred* where Fred clips Carole on the jaw. Then I will see the bit in *City Lights* where Chaplin swallows the whistle, and the business in that Marx Brothers picture where a hundred people crowd into the stateroom. I forget the name of it."

"At once, Mr. Bland," the voice said. I went down the hall to the projection room. My unseen friend could have hoked it up by saying "Immediate seating on all floors" or "Smoking in the balcony only," but their sense of humor isn't broad. This is probably just as well for me, their subject. They take pretty good care of me, everything considered.

On my way down the hall, I remembered another bit. "I also want to see Groucho do *Hurray for Captain Spaulding*"—the sun helmet again—"and the one where he's on the couch with Thelma Todd and Chico keeps coming through the window with the ice."

"Yes, sir."

It was better than the film library at the Museum of Modern Art. I kept remembering other classic bits and asking for them and then it was lunch time.

But what I really wanted to see was a new movie—to go to it with my own critical faculties all sharpened up after reading Zinsser's caustic comments in the *Herald Tribune* and Zunser's kinder ones in *Cue*. (But nuts to those wise guys in *Time* and *The New Yorker*.)

I knew, though, that the Ear and his buddies would never allow that. They never let me see anything current. Maybe it was impossible for them to get it, or maybe it was part of their experiment to keep me ignorant of everything that had happened since the day of my capture.

Whatever the reason, the result was the same. I'd never see a new Hitchcock movie, or read a new novel by Marquand, or find out if the Democrats got the White House back in 1960.

Zinsser and Zunser, I thought, tasting the syllables. Many of the things I liked to read, or look at, came in pairs. Crane and Cain were in my library. Hoppers and Groppers were on my walls. But nothing new.

I sighed and got up, the pleasure I'd had from Groucho and Chico and Thelma almost forgotten.

"I'll have lunch at the swimming pool," I said. (I had nearly everything.)

"Certainly, sir."

"Stuffed celery (cottage cheese, I think) with a sprinkling of paprika. Carrot strips, chilled. Half an avocado. Ry-krisp; no butter. A bottle of Tuborg beer and a packet of Senior Service." I try to keep it light at lunch, especially after a late breakfast. It's my own fault, but I don't get much exercise.

"Yes, sir."

"Oh—and have Esther Williams swim in waltz time as I lunch."

The voice became reproving, though polite. "We must reiterate with regret, sir, that requests concerning live human beings cannot be granted. However, if you desire it, a film excerpt of an Esther Williams water ballet is available."

"Never mind," I said. "Just needling you." I like to remind them every once in a while that I know their limitations. The trouble, though, was that it also reminded me of my isolation.

After lunch I wandered into the gun room and whanged away at tin cans with a 12-gauge shotgun. The slam against my shoulder was satisfying and the ruination of an off-target wall still more so. But I knew it would be refinished the next time I went in—even if it were only five minutes later. They have almost infinite resources.

Still feeling combative, I went to the billiard room and smacked the balls around. This reminded me that my next movie session would have to include W. C. Fields' business with the bent cue and, by association, his segment of *If I Had a Million* with Alison Skipworth and their junk-car vengeance on reckless drivers.

But not today. The trick was not to overindulge or I'd always be in the movies, or drinking before lunch, or lying in bed all day.

"Ha, ha!" I said.

"Sir?"

"Nothing. Point for my side, that's all. You wouldn't understand."

"We endeavor to. Will you explain?"

"No."

"As you wish." The voice sounded disappointed, as if it had missed a trick.

I haven't a clue to the identity of my captors. I use the plural because it obviously takes more than one to operate this elaborate supercage I'm forced to call home. There would have to be a whole flock of them to supply my peculiar demands, and a gaggle of others to study me at all hours and keep tabs on my reactions.

Gaggle and flock weren't the words, I thought. Gaggle is for geese and flock is for sheep. I amused myself for a while by adapting words to groups of captors, species unknown. Were they from Saturn?

"A dour of Saturnians," I said aloud to the ever-listening Ear.

"I beg your pardon?"

"I'm classifying you. If you're from Saturn, I dub a group of you dour. Are you from Saturn?"

"No comment, Mr. Bland." I hadn't expected any.

"A dour of Saturnians," I said, enjoying the sound of it, "would be comparable, philologically speaking, to a pride of lions or a crash of rhinoceros."

"I follow you," the Ear said. "Or a murmuring of starlings. There is poetry in your language, Mr. Bland."

"Thank you," I said. "Jupiter?"

"No comment. But I'm listening."

"Aren't you always? Jupiter. Let's see. That would make you Jovians. How about a jubilation of Jovians?"

"Not bad." He was beginning to unbend. I almost liked him for it.

"I didn't think so, either. Pluto, maybe? How about a splash of Plutonians? That's a bit obscure, I admit—Pluto water—whisky and splash?"

"I liked your first better."

"So did I, frankly. But you're only as good as your last one, as they say in Filmland. Let's press on. Venus? A miasma of Venusians?"

"No comment," said the Ear.

"You're hard to please."

"I've got one for you."

"For me?" I was surprised. The Ear almost never volunteered anything.

"For your people. A tintinnabulation of Terrans."

"Bravo!" I said, really admiring it. "We *can* be a noisy bunch—with bells on. I suppose I do give you a lot of trouble, Jeeves, old man—always ringing for some crazy thing."

"Not at all, sir. Merely playing your game."

"You've inspired me. I've got one for Mercury. An instability of Mercurians. How's that?"

"Rather good. How about Mars—to complete the inner planets?"

But nothing occurred to me except a phalanx of Martians, which was hardly worth uttering. "I'm getting bored with the game."

"As you like."

At the library I spent an hour with Mark Twain and E. B. White and Richard Bissell, then, my eyes tiring, demanded talking books.

I listened to some Dylan Thomas, and Charles Laughton reading the Bible, and Laurence Olivier and Churchill and F.D.R., and Edith Sitwell and a bit of Al Smith, and fell asleep during some dedication speech.

"Cocktail time," I said, waking up thirsty. "Attention to orders."

"Yes, sir." The voice was attentive, as always.

"No martini today. No gibson. Nor screwdriver nor bronx. A paratroop plunge."

"A paratroop plunge?" This was beyond their ken, as I had hoped. They couldn't know everything. The fact that they couldn't read my mind helped considerably in enduring my prisonership.

"Brandy, cointreau, champagne and club soda are the ingredients," I said.

"Yes, sir," the voice acknowledged, back on familiar ground. "Ingredients noted."

I gave the proportions and the tall, potent drink appeared at my elbow. It was really an elongated Sidecar, but it was as heady as a drop from five thousand feet. I had another and thought about dinner.

I remembered Bemelmans and considered an elephant cutlet, but I was afraid that, unlike Bemelmans' chef, they *would* cut up an elephant for only one customer. So I ordered a simple steak, a baked potato, mixed greens, bread sticks and a decent red wine.

The trick now was to occupy myself till bedtime. The nights were the worst. Last night I'd overdone it, drinking Chivas Regal straight, out of a brandy snifter, and had got to bed rather non compos. That had been a point for their side.

"This is do-it-yourself night," I decided. "Bring me the makings of a crystal set."

They had it all set up for me when I got to the hobby room—and they'd goofed. They didn't often make mistakes, but this one was a pip. Instead of the components of a primitive radio receiver, they'd provided a glass-blowing outfit, complete with furnace, that would have passed muster at Steuben.

I laughed, a little more contemptuously than was warranted, and loftily explained their mistake. I could tell they didn't like my rubbing their noses in it (if they have noses), but there wasn't much they could do about it.

The section of the floor where they'd set up the miniature glassworks dropped and I had a glimpse of violet mist down below before the floor came up again, this time with a workbench and the makings of a crystal set on it.

It was the first time I'd seen how they materialized things, except for my sliding-panel meals, and I was disappointed in them. Trap doors. It reminded me of the time I was one of the kids who rushed to the stage when Blackstone the Magician asked for volunteers. Blackstone was getting old then and maybe he was careless, but I had a revealing glimpse of a piece of his sleight of hand that took all the magic out of it.

But there was still a difference. I had known Blackstone was human and merely a skilled illusionist. I didn't know what these people were. I didn't even know if they were people.

I suddenly felt like shouting at them: "Who are you? What are you doing to me?" But that would have given them too much satisfaction. I knew in essence who they were and what I was to them, and my self-imposed duty on behalf of humanity was to maintain my composure, refuse to be goaded into excesses. It was obvious that they were looking for my weaknesses and I had to display as few as possible, however inviting it might seem at the moment to indulge myself in their virtually unlimited largesse.

I've never had a scientific mind. Fortunately the crystal-set kit had detailed instructions and I was able to absorb myself in assembling it without frustration.

I had some vague hope that when I got it working I'd be able to hear a live, uncensored broadcast, but, of course, they'd foreseen that possibility. All I heard were harmless canned broadcasts. They'd taped these, eliminating newscasts and anything else that might have given me a clue to what was happening in the real world. I might as well have saved myself the trouble and turned on the blond mahogany Magnavox in my bedroom or the limed-oak Capehart in the living room.

They did leave some timeless commercials; for authenticity's sake, I suppose. But I wonder whether it was entirely by accident that the one the prisoner in their Paradise heard through the earphones of the crystal set that night was about new, improved Joy.

It was the same with the television set. Everything was kinescope. They allowed me no newspapers or magazines and the books in the library had all been published before my capture.

I probably should put down a few facts for posterity. I don't know who will read them—they promise they won't, as long as I live, and I halfway believe them.

Now that I've written it down, I wonder how long I'll live. How long do you keep a guinea pig? As long as it's useful to you. If it dies, or if you drive it crazy, you dispose of it and get yourself another one. Guinea pigs have to be expendable or they aren't guinea pigs.

But I mustn't be pessimistic, even here in the supposed secrecy of my journal. Let's get on to the facts for you people in posterity.

Name: Oliver T. Bland—known as Ollie to my erstwhile friends. (*They* always call me Mr. Bland or Sir.)

Age: 34.

Occupation: guinea pig. All right, seriously: I used to be a copyreader on a big daily newspaper here in New York—one of those unromantic people who sees to the grammar and spelling and guards against libel and constructs the headlines.

"Here in New York" is, of course, a phrase my respect for fact will not allow. I was captured in the city. That much I know. I've since been transferred, transported—whatever—to this seeming mansion which could be anywhere. On Earth, suspended above it, on the Moon—on Mars, for all I know.

What I call my mansion—thinking of a big dog I once kept in a long enclosure—is Man-run 2. Nobody starts counting with 2, so there's another one, obviously, but they haven't told me yet who's in it. I'd like to think it's another Earthman—misery loving company—but this could be a sort of interplanetary zoo.

But back to the known facts.

Length of sentence: indefinite. I've been here months, I imagine. There are no calendars and I've been careless about this journal, not writing in it every day, as I should. I distrusted them at first (I still do, but not as much) and shied away from giving them anything they seemed to want. I've become more philosophical in recent weeks—you might say more self-indulgent—though I think I'm honoring my pledge to resist them in anything that really matters.

What else? Does it matter that I'm divorced? (I wonder if they think that's typical of our species.) She has custody of our son (Jason Robinson Bland) and has remarried. I thought of remarrying, too, but with alimony and support payments, it was sort of impossible—except to a rich girl who wouldn't have to live on the remnants of my salary. Of course there was always Betty Forsythe —an amiable, understanding homebody type, still living with her mother. Betty would have had me. She'd have scrimped along with me and loved it, poor kid.

I wonder what my wife—ex-wife—thinks has become of me? Probably that I've chucked it and gone off to Tahiti or Alaska as I sometimes threatened. And Jace (Jason Robinson, aged three)? Does he still remember me? Or is he calling his stepfather Daddy now?

No more tonight, journal mine. I'm depressed and I mustn't be, if I'm to keep up my morale and resist *them*.

I'll order a nightcap and go to bed. What shall it be? Scotch is best, but I've drunk the best scotch and I want a change. . . .

No, you devils, I won't indulge myself too far. I'll have a sensible glass of warm milk. Yes, damn you, milk. Then I'll sleep, and tomorrow will be another day.

I brush my teeth religiously and avoid sweets, to prevent developing a cavity. But suppose I did get one? A painful one? Would they let me suffer and study my reactions (God forbid they should take a clinical interest in human pain) or would they fill the tooth? And to fill it, would someone come? Or could they do it all by remote control?

They could put me to sleep and I'd never see the dentist.

Anyhow, I brush my teeth religiously and I use dental floss.

June 25

That's an arbitrary date. It could be right because they captured me on February 17 and I think it's about four months. I picked it because June 25 is my birthday and I felt like a party.

I ordered *café au lait* for breakfast, and a brioche. I don't have breakfast in bed any more. Too damn inconvenient.

I ate on the terrace overlooking the photomural of the meadow. As I drank my second cup and smoked a Murad (desiring nonchalance), I told the Ear it was my birthday and I wanted a present suitable for a thirty-five-year-old boy.

That give him pause, as I hoped it would. I'm becoming an accomplished Ear-baiter.

"A thirty-five-year-old is not a boy," he said finally.

"This one is," I told him. "And this one wants a birthday present."

"Certainly, sir. What would you like?"

"I want a surprise, so the choice is up to you. You should know me well enough now to pick something appropriate."

I guess he went away. At least he was silent for an hour while I got ready for my day. I soaked in the tub, shaved (safety razor, close), trimmed my fingernails, combed my hair (four months long) and dressed in a Scarlet Pimpernel outfit. It went with the hair. I ordered the costume complete with snuffbox, whose dubious delights I postponed.

I was in the library having elevenses (scones and butter, Ceylon tea with milk) when the Ear announced his presence.

"Sir, we have decided on your birthday present."

I put down my cup and said, "Yes?"

"We have carefully considered and have come to the conclusion that the present which would give you the most pleasure would be to acquaint you with—to employ your terminology—the inhabitant of Man-run 1."

"Oh?" I said. I was doing my best to suppress my excitement. "And what manner of creature might that be?"

"A person of your species," the Ear said, "but of the opposite sex."

I don't remember what I said to that, but I do know I realized I had to get out of the ruffles and velvet. She couldn't see me that way, whoever she was. And I ordered my first haircut.

I was directed to the hobby room, where I found a barber chair set up. I sat down and scissors and comb came out of the back of the chair at the ends of metallic tentacles and went to work. (The same procedure, modified, would have filled a cavity, I realized.)

As I was being barbered, I decided what to wear. White-on-white shirt. Solid blue knitted tie. Light gray flannel slacks. Dark gray Harris tweed jacket. Black Italianate shoes. Blue anklet socks. Pack of Tareytons in the jacket pocket for her. (I always considered Tareytons a woman's cigarette, no doubt because of their ads.)

As I retied my tie, having got it uneven the first time, I asked the Ear: "How old is she?"

"Twenty-three."

"Fine! Is she pretty?"

"By your standards, yes."

"Good enough. Does she know it's my birthday?"

"Yes."

"Does she know which birthday?"

"No."

"No? Then do me a favor. When you materialize the cake, have thirty candles on it instead of thirty-five, will you?"

"Certainly." There was a definite tinge of amusement in the voice.

"No, make it twenty-nine. I don't look thirty-five, do I?"

"My dear Mr. Bland, a man is as old as he feels."

If that was true, I wasn't very old. I felt like any kid who was going to have a birthday party given for him.

She came in through a door in the living room which had always been locked before. I was standing nervously by the sideboard, on which cocktail things had been set up, fingering my tie and wondering what I was going to say. Dance music came softly from the Capehart.

She certainly was pretty. Blond, just a bit under average height, wearing a short dinner gown that accentuated her slim waist and showed her shapely legs.

"Please come in," I said. "My name is Bland, Oliver Bland. Ollie to my friends."

The door remained open behind her and I saw a section of what I supposed was her living room. It seemed identical with mine.

"How do you do," she said.

She walked toward me slowly, looking around. "My name is Margaret Purvis—Peggy for short." She held out her hand and I took it briefly.

"Very glad to know you," I said, shaking a little, but managing to control my voice. Not only another human being after all those months, but a pretty girl! "Can I make you a drink? I have just about everything."

"I know." She smiled. "Everything and nothing. I think I'll have a whisky sour, if that's not too complicated."

"Not at all." I made two of them.

She raised her glass to me and said, "Happy birthday, Ollie. May your next one be happier."

"Thank you. But this one is admirable, thanks to you."

We finished our drinks and danced to the canned hi-fi and talked, trading backgrounds.

Peggy had been captured one morning on her way to work in the insurance office where she'd been a secretary. She'd got into a bus which had drawn up to the curb as usual, and not until she'd sat down in the rear did she stop to think that the bus should have been crowded.

By then, it was too late. The bus went into a tunnel (where no tunnel should have been) and in the darkness she went to sleep, or was put to sleep, with no recollection of how. She woke up in Man-run 1.

"What part of the city was it?" I asked.

"The near North Side," she said, and only then did I realize she wasn't from New York.

"Chicago?" I said.

"Yes. Isn't this Chicago?"

I gathered that Peggy's impression was that our luxurious prison was some underground experimental laboratory in or near her former city.

"Who do you think the Ear is?" I asked her.

"The Ear? Oh, you must mean the one I call Uncle. Well, I don't really know. Some rich old kindly mad scientist, I guess."

I made fresh drinks and told her about my capture. I'd been coming back from lunch and was alone in the elevator except for the operator. I'd said "Six" as usual, and when the car stopped, I automatically stepped out into the hall. Only it wasn't the sixth floor. The elevator door slid closed behind me and I blanked out as I was reaching for the button. I woke up in Man-run 2.

July 4, 9 A.M.

Peggy and I have been getting along famously, considering that she has a mind of her own and our courtship hasn't been exactly smooth. My long isolation evidently made me forget how irritating women can sometimes be.

Whoever said men were the practical ones and women the romantics didn't know Peggy and me. *I* was the romantic. Here we were, my thoughts ran, to all intents and purposes the last man and the last woman. (Or the first?) Obviously the thing to do then, since escape was impossible, was to settle down and perpetuate the race.

I didn't look at it quite so coldly, of course, but that's what it amounted to.

Peggy wouldn't admit there was no way out. And she made it clear that she'd have nothing to do with a man who did. All too often, when I'd arranged a romantic atmosphere with soft lights and music, she'd sit up straight with some practical thought, like breaking through the ceiling to see what was up there. I'd explain that I'd tried all the possibilities long ago. But she had to see for herself.

So I'd break through the ceiling again and show her the big impenetrable metallic dome above, which sealed in the man-runs and the acre or so of recreation space beyond them. Then I'd break through a wall, exposing the wiring and plumbing and air-conditioning pipes—and the same metal barrier.

And the Ear patiently cleaned up after me.

Finally I proved to Peggy's satisfaction not only that there was no way out, but that, by looking for one, I'd been willing to lose the creature comforts of captivity. Now we could be married.

I pictured a simple little ceremony, Peggy and I reading aloud the words of a civil wedding ceremony—or a religious service, if she wanted one—and exchanging rings and vows.

"I want a church wedding," Peggy announced.

"But, Peggy——"

"With organ music and a choir. *And* a minister," she said. "It has to be legal."

I groaned. "What you're saying, then, is that you won't marry me."

"Ollie Bland, I said no such thing. But a wedding is what a girl dreams of and plans for years. It's no good being the best-dressed woman if there's nobody to look at me."

"I'll look at you."

"That's not enough, Ollie. I want to be shown off to others—and I want to go places. Havana, New Orleans, Paris . . ."

She went on like that for quite a while. Then the Ear spoke up. It was a relief to hear another voice.

"I can arrange a church wedding," he said.

The Ear had a white satin wedding gown whisked out and laid at Peggy's feet. That shut her up while he turned the hobby room into a chapel whose construction blended in exactly with a projection on the wall of a filmed marriage service, with organ, choir and all.

The film clip was beautifully edited so Peggy and I could make the responses to the projected minister's questions. The Ear assured us it was a film of an actual wedding and that the minister was genuine, not a Hollywood actor.

But as we were running through the rehearsal, Peggy said: "Where's the marriage license? I'd like to see you fake *that!*"

I blew up then and Peggy fled in tears to Man-run 1.

Later

That was yesterday. Peggy locked her door last night and I haven't seen her all morning.

I was enjoying my solitary lunch—a strictly nonfeminine hero sandwich and a quart of beer—when the Ear announced his presence.

"I have a present for you, Mr. Bland."

"I haven't recovered from the last one yet," I said, meaning Peggy.

"The present is your freedom. Your term is up."

It took a while to sink in. While it was sinking, the Ear explained that both Peggy and I would be set down on Earth anywhere we chose, with a pleasant amount of money (genuine) to reimburse us for the loss of our time.

I knocked on Peggy's door. She'd already heard the news.

"Will you go to New York with me, Peggy?" I asked.

She laughed. "I will not. A girl doesn't want to marry the first man who asks her. I want to look around. I'm going back to Chicago."

I must admit I wasn't too terribly crushed.

The Ear had me set down in my old office building late in the day. There were few people around, it being the Fourth of July —Independence Day. I could imagine the Ear enjoying his pleasant little joke.

I went through the file of back copies of the newspaper to see what had been happening in the world in the past several months. Same old thing—alarms, excursions, crises and a few governments changing hands. I hadn't really missed anything in that department. What I had missed was human companionship, female and of my own choice. *This* world, at least, was full of girls. And my pockets were full of money. I went out on the town.

Two weeks later my pockets were considerably emptier and my hunger for female companionship considerably abated. I'd had a wow of a time—one wow after another—but now that my fling was over, I realized that this wasn't my idea of living. Maybe I was getting old, but what I really wanted was not women, but one woman with whom I could enjoy the pleasures of quiet domesticity. A complaisant old-fashioned girl whose chief interest was pleasing her husband. I thought of Betty Forsythe. I guess she'd always been in the back of my mind. I looked her up.

"Betty," I said one evening as we sat on the couch at her place (a homebody, my Betty was, bless her), "would you go to the ends of the Earth with me?"

"Even beyond, Oliver," said the complaisant Betty. This was the girl for me.

"Do you hear that, Ear?" I asked. He'd told me he would be within earshot, so to speak, for a while.

"I heard, Mr. Bland," his voice said.

"I'll sign up for that second term now," I told him.

"Excellent," the Ear said. "But I must remind you that the second term will be considerably longer. Unfortunately, I can't give you the reasons."

"Say no more." I could imagine there might be a long spaceship journey, or an upcoming kink in communications between our worlds. "Who could weary of Paradise?"

Betty had said nothing, waiting patiently for me to explain when I saw fit. I'd never told her about the Ear, but she didn't require a long explanation. She had supreme faith in me.

"Whatever you say, Oliver dear," Betty assured me, and the next day we went to City Hall and got the marriage license.

January 27

Well, here we are back at the old stand, journal mine.

I've arranged with the Ear to enlarge Man-run 2 for me right to the edge of the dome. Now it includes a bit of synthetic insectless outdoors—a stream gurgling through a grove of quite realistic trees and compliant fish that bite at anything.

Indoors, I have an office to go to, nine to five, five days a week (sometimes six or seven). I have a salary and I get raises periodically and once I went on strike for a pension plan. The Ear is a good boss. He praises me when I've done a particularly fine piece of work (I'm cataloguing the characters in Dickens' novels). A man likes to be told when he's doing a good job.

Betty (I almost wrote "Peggy") and I have our separate bedrooms. It seems to be better that way. In fact, she has all of Manrun 1 to retire to when she sees fit. She often does.

Here she comes now. I've asked her not to interrupt me when I'm working. Listen to my automatic answers, dear posterity. They may come in handy.

"Well, what is it now?

"Oh, you're all dressed up and have no place to go? How originally you put it, darling.

"And it's no good being the best-dressed woman if there's nobody to look at you? *I* look at you, don't I?

"That's not enough, eh? You want to be shown off to others? Now where have I heard that before?

"Oh, I'm hateful, am I? Go *ahead* and cry. . . . Well, frankly, *I* wish you could go home to Mother, too."

Me, I'm going fishing.

OR ALL THE SEAS WITH OYSTERS

∿∿∿∿∿∿ by Avram Davidson ∿∿∿∿∿∿

WHEN THE MAN CAME INTO THE F & O BIKE SHOP, Oscar greeted him with a hearty "Hi, there!" Then, as he looked closer at the middle-aged visitor with the eyeglasses and business suit, his forehead creased and he began to snap his thick fingers.

"Oh, say, I know you," he muttered. "Mr.—um—name's on the tip of my tongue, doggone it . . ." Oscar was a barrel-chested fellow. He had orange hair.

"Why, sure you do," the man said. There was a Lion's emblem in his lapel. "Remember, you sold me a girl's bicycle with gears, for my daughter? We got to talking about that red French racing bike your partner was working on——"

Oscar slapped his big hand down on the cash register. He raised his head and rolled his eyes up. "Mr. Whatney!" Mr. Whatney beamed. "Oh, *sure*. Gee, how could I forget? And we went across the street afterward and had a couple a beers. Well, how you *been*, Mr. Whatney? I guess the bike—it was an English model, wasn't it? Yeah. It must of given satisfaction or you would of been back, huh?"

Mr. Whatney said the bicycle was fine, just fine. Then he said, "I understand there's been a change, though. You're all by yourself now. Your partner . . ."

Oscar looked down, pushed his lower lip out, nodded. "You heard, huh? Ee-up. I'm all by myself now. Over three months now."

The partnership had come to an end three months ago, but it had been faltering long before then. Ferd liked books, long-playing records and high-level conversation. Oscar liked beer, bowling and women. Any women. Any time.

The shop was located near the park; it did a big trade in renting bicycles to picnickers. If a woman was barely old enough to be *called* a woman, and not quite old enough to be called an *old* woman, or if she was anywhere in between, and if she was alone, Oscar would ask, "How does that machine feel to you? All right?"

"Why . . . I guess so."

Taking another bicycle, Oscar would say, "Well, I'll just ride along a little bit with you, to make sure. Be right back, Ferd." Ferd always nodded gloomily. He knew that Oscar would not be right back. Later, Oscar would say, "Hope you made out in the shop as good as I did in the park."

"Leaving me all alone here all that time," Ferd grumbled.

And Oscar usually flared up. "Okay, then, next time *you* go and leave *me* stay here. See if I begrudge you a little fun." But he knew, of course, that Ferd—tall, thin, popeyed Ferd—would never go. "Do you good," Oscar said, slapping his sternum. "Put hair on your chest."

Ferd muttered that he had all the hair on his chest that he needed. He would glance down covertly at his lower arms; they were thick with long black hair, though his upper arms were slick and white. It was already like that when he was in high school, and some of the others would laugh at him—call him "Ferdie the Birdie." They knew it bothered him, but they did it anyway. How was it possible—he wondered then; he still did now—for people deliberately to hurt someone else who hadn't hurt them? How was it possible?

He worried over other things. All the time.

"The Communists——" He shook his head over the newspaper. Oscar offered an advice about the Communists in two short words. Or it might be capital punishment. "Oh, what a terrible thing if an innocent man was to be executed," Ferd moaned. Oscar said that was the guy's tough luck.

"Hand me that tire iron," Oscar said.

And Ferd worried even about other people's minor concerns. Like the time the couple came in with the tandem and the baby basket on it. Free air was all they took; then the woman decided to change the diaper and one of the safety pins broke.

"Why are there never any safety pins?" the woman fretted, rummaging here and rummaging there. "There are *never* any safety pins."

Ferd made sympathetic noises, went to see if he had any; but, though he was sure there'd been some in the office, he couldn't find them. So they drove off with one side of the diaper tied in a clumsy knot.

At lunch, Ferd said it was too bad about the safety pins. Oscar dug his teeth into a sandwich, tugged, tore, chewed, swallowed. Ferd liked to experiment with sandwich spreads—the one he liked most was cream-cheese, olives, anchovy and avocado, mashed up with a little mayonnaise—but Oscar always had the same pink luncheon-meat.

"It must be difficult with a baby." Ferd nibbled. "Not just traveling, but raising it."

Oscar said, "Jeez, there's drugstores in every block, and if you can't read, you can at least reckernize them."

"Drugstores? Oh, to buy safety pins, you mean."

"Yeah. Safety pins."

"But . . . you know . . . it's true . . . there's never any safety pins when you look."

Oscar uncapped his beer, rinsed the first mouthful around. "Aha! Always plenny of clothes hangers, though. Throw 'em out every month, next month same closet's full of 'em again. Now whatcha wanna do in your spare time, you invent a device which it'll make safety pins outa clothes hangers."

Ferd nodded abstractedly. "But in my spare time I'm working on the French racer. . . ." It was a beautiful machine, light, low-slung, swift, red and shining. You felt like a bird when you rode it. But, good as it was, Ferd knew he could make it better. He showed it to everybody who came in the place until his interest slackened.

Nature was his latest hobby, or, rather, reading about Nature. Some kids had wandered by from the park one day with tin cans in which they had put salamanders and toads, and they proudly showed them to Ferd. After that, the work on the red racer slowed down and he spent his spare time on natural-history books.

"Mimicry!" he cried to Oscar. "A wonderful thing!"

Oscar looked up interestedly from the bowling scores in the paper. "I seen Edie Adams on TV the other night, doing her imitation of Marilyn Monroe. Boy, oh, boy."

Ferd was irritated, shook his head. "Not that kind of mimicry. I mean how insects and arachnids will mimic the shapes of leaves and twigs and so on, to escape being eaten by birds or other insects and arachnids."

A scowl of disbelief passed over Oscar's heavy face. "You mean they change their *shapes?* What you giving me?"

"Oh, it's true. Sometimes the mimicry is for aggressive purposes, though—like a South African turtle that looks like a rock and so the fish swim up to it and then it catches them. Or that spider in Sumatra. When it lies on its back, it looks like a bird dropping. Catches butterflies that way."

Oscar laughed, a disgusted and incredulous noise. It died away as he turned back to the bowling scores. One hand groped at his

pocket, came away, scratched absently at the orange thicket under the shirt, then went patting his hip pocket.

"Where's that pencil?" he muttered, got up, stomped into the
office, pulled open drawers. His loud cry of "Hey!" brought Ferd
into the tiny room.

"What's the matter?" Ferd asked.

Oscar pointed to a drawer. "Remember that time you claimed
there were no safety pins here? Look—whole gahdamn drawer is
full of 'em."

Ferd stared, scratched his head, said feebly that he was certain
he'd looked there before. . . .

A contralto voice from outside asked, "Anybody here?"

Oscar at once forgot the desk and its contents, called, "Be right
with you," and was gone. Ferd followed him slowly.

There was a young woman in the shop, a rather massively built
young woman, with muscular calves and a deep chest. She was
pointing out the seat of her bicycle to Oscar, who was saying
"Uh-huh" and looking more at her than at anything else. "It's just
a little too far forward ("Uh-huh"), as you can see. A wrench
is all I need ("Uh-huh"). It was silly of me to forget my tools."

Oscar repeated, "Uh-huh" automatically, then snapped to. "Fix
it in a jiffy," he said, and—despite her insistence that she could do
it herself—he did fix it. Though not quite in a jiffy. He refused
money. He prolonged the conversation as long as he could.

"Well, thank *you*," the young woman said. "And now I've got
to go."

"That machine feel all right to you now?"

"Perfectly. Thanks——"

"Tell you what, I'll just ride along with you a little bit, just——"

Pear-shaped notes of laughter lifted the young woman's bosom.
"Oh, you couldn't keep up with me! My machine is a *racer!*"

The moment he saw Oscar's eye flit to the corner, Ferd knew
what he had in mind. He stepped forward. His cry of "No" was

drowned out by his partner's loud, "Well, I guess this racer here can keep up with yours!"

The young woman giggled richly, said, well, they would see about that, and was off. Oscar, ignoring Ferd's outstretched hand, jumped on the French bike and was gone. Ferd stood in the doorway, watching the two figures, hunched over their handlebars, vanish down the road into the park. He went slowly back inside.

It was almost evening before Oscar returned, sweaty but smiling. Smiling broadly. "Hey, what a babe!" he cried. He wagged his head, he whistled, he made gestures, noises like escaping steam. "Boy, oh, boy, what an afternoon!"

"Give me the bike," Ferd demanded.

Oscar said, yeah, sure; turned it over to him and went to wash. Ferd looked at the machine. The red enamel was covered with dust; there was mud spattered and dirt and bits of dried grass. It seemed soiled—degraded. He had felt like a swift bird when he rode it. . . .

Oscar came out wet and beaming. He gave a cry of dismay, ran over.

"Stand away," said Ferd, gesturing with the knife. He slashed the tires, the seat and seat cover, again and again.

"You crazy?" Oscar yelled. "You outa your mind? Ferd, no, don't, Ferd——"

Ferd cut the spokes, bent them, twisted them. He took the heaviest hammer and pounded the frame into shapelessness, and then he kept on pounding till his breath was gasping.

"You're not only crazy," Oscar said bitterly, "you're rotten jealous. You can go to hell." He stomped away.

Ferd, feeling sick and stiff, locked up, went slowly home. He had no taste for reading, turned out the light and fell into bed, where he lay awake for hours, listening to the rustling noises of the night and thinking hot, twisted thoughts.

They didn't speak to each other for days after that, except for the necessities of the work. The wreckage of the French racer lay behind the shop. For about two weeks, neither wanted to go out back where he'd have to see it.

One morning Ferd arrived to be greeted by his partner, who began to shake his head in astonishment even before he started speaking. "How did you *do* it, how did you *do* it, Ferd? Jeez, what a beautiful job—I gotta hand it to you—no more hard feelings, huh, Ferd?"

Ferd took his hand. "Sure, sure. But what are you talking about?"

Oscar led him out back. There was the red racer, all in one piece, not a mark or scratch on it, its enamel bright as ever. Ferd gaped. He squatted down and examined it. It *was* his machine. Every change, every improvement he had made, was there.

He straightened up slowly. "Regeneration . . ."

"Huh? What say?" Oscar asked. Then, "Hey, kiddo, you're all white. Whad you do, stay up all night and didn't get no sleep? Come on in and siddown. But I still don't see how you done it."

Inside, Ferd sat down. He wet his lips. He said, "Oscar—listen——"

"Yeah?"

"Oscar. You know what regeneration is? No? Listen. Some kinds of lizards, you grab them by the tail, the tail breaks off and they grow a new one. If a lobster loses a claw, it regenerates another one. Some kinds of worms—and hydras and starfish—you cut them into pieces, each piece will grow back the missing parts. Salamanders can regenerate lost hands, and frogs can grow legs back."

"No kidding, Ferd. But, uh, I mean: Nature. Very interesting. But to get back to the bike now—how'd you manage to fix it so good?"

"I never touched it. It regenerated. Like a newt. Or a lobster."

Oscar considered this. He lowered his head, looked up at Ferd from under his eyebrows. "Well, now, Ferd . . . Look . . . How come all broke bikes don't do that?"

"This isn't an ordinary bike. I mean it isn't a real bike." Catching Oscar's look, he shouted, "Well, it's *true!*"

The shout changed Oscar's attitude from bafflement to incredulity. He got up. "So for the sake of argument, let's say all that stuff about the bugs and the eels or whatever the hell you were talking about is true. But they're alive. A bike ain't." He looked down triumphantly.

Ferd shook his leg from side to side, looked at it. "A crystal isn't, either, but a broken crystal can regenerate itself if the conditions are right. Oscar, go see if the safety pins are still in the desk. Please, Oscar?"

He listened as Oscar, muttering, pulled the desk drawers out, rummaged in them, slammed them shut, tramped back.

"Naa," he said. "All gone. Like that lady said that time, and you said, there never are any safety pins when you want 'em. They disap— Ferd? What're—"

Ferd jerked open the closet door, jumped back as a shoal of clothes hangers clattered out.

"And like *you* say," Ferd said with a twist of his mouth, "on the other hand, there are always plenty of clothes hangers. There weren't any here before."

Oscar shrugged. "I don't see what you're getting at. But anybody could of got in here and took the pins and left the hangers. *I* could of—but I didn't. Or *you* could of. Maybe——" He narrowed his eyes. "Maybe you walked in your sleep and done it. You better see a doctor. Jeez, you look rotten."

Ferd went back and sat down, put his head in his hands. "I *feel* rotten. I'm scared, Oscar. Scared of what?" He breathed noisily. "I'll tell you. Like I explained before, about how things that live in the wild places, they mimic other things there. Twigs, leaves . . . toads that look like rocks. Well, suppose there are . . . things . . . that live in people places. Cities. Houses. These things could imitate—well, other kinds of things you find in people places——"

"*People* places, for crise sake!"

"Maybe they're a different kind of life form. Maybe they get their nourishment out of the elements in the air. You know what safety pins *are*—these other kinds of them? Oscar, the safety pins are the pupa forms and then they, like, *hatch*. Into the larval forms. Which look just like coat hangers. They feel like them, even, but they're not. Oscar, they're not, not really, not really, not . . ."

He began to cry into his hands. Oscar looked at him. He shook his head.

After a minute Ferd controlled himself somewhat. He snuffled. "All these bicycles the cops find, and they hold them waiting for owners to show up, and then we buy them at the sale because no owners show up because there aren't any, and the same with the ones the kids are always trying to sell us, and they say they just found them, and they really did because they were never made in a factory. They grew. They grow. You smash them and throw them away, they regenerate."

Oscar turned to someone who wasn't there and waggled his head. "Hoo, boy," he said. Then, to Ferd: "You mean one day there's a safety pin and the next day instead there's a coat hanger?"

Ferd said, "One day there's a cocoon; the next day there's a moth. One day there's an egg; the next day there's a chicken. But with . . . these it doesn't happen in the open daytime where you can see it. But at night, Oscar—at night you can *hear* it happening. All the little noises in the nighttime, Oscar——"

Oscar said, "Then how come we ain't up to our belly button in bikes? If I had a bike for every coat hanger——"

But Ferd had considered that, too. If every codfish egg, he explained, or every oyster spawn grew to maturity, a man could walk across the ocean on the backs of all the codfish or oysters there'd be. So many died, so many were eaten by predatory creatures, that Nature had to produce a maximum in order to allow a minimum to arrive at maturity. And Oscar's question was: then who, uh, eats the, uh, coat hangers?

Ferd's eyes focused through wall, buildings, park, more buildings, to the horizon. "You got to get the picture. I'm not talking about real pins or hangers. I got a name for the others—'false friends,' I call them. In high-school French, we had to watch out for French words that looked like English words, but really were different. '*Faux amis*,' they call them. False friends. Pseudo pins. Pseudo hangers . . . Who eats them? I don't know for sure. Pseudo vacuum cleaners, maybe?"

His partner, with a loud groan, slapped his hands against his thighs. He said, "Ferd, Ferd, for crise sake. You know what's the trouble with you? You talk about oysters, but you forgot what they're good for. You forgot there's two kinds of people in the world. Close up them books, them bug books and French books. Get out, mingle, meet people. Soak up some brew. You know what? The next time Norma—that's this broad's name with the racing bike—the next time she comes here, *you* take the red racer and *you* go out in the woods with her. I won't mind. And I don't think she will, either. Not *too* much."

But Ferd said no. "I never want to touch the red racer again. I'm afraid of it."

At this, Oscar pulled him to his feet, dragged him protestingly out to the back and forced him to get on the French machine. "Only way to conquer your fear of it!"

Ferd started off, white-faced, wobbling. And in a moment was on the ground, rolling and thrashing, screaming.

Oscar pulled him away from the machine.

"It threw me!" Ferd yelled. "It tried to kill me! Look—blood!"

His partner said it was a bump that threw him—it was his own fear. The blood? A broken spoke. Grazed his cheek. And he insisted Ferd get on the bicycle again, to conquer his fear.

But Ferd had grown hysterical. He shouted that no man was

safe—that mankind had to be warned. It took Oscar a long time to pacify him and to get him to go home and into bed.

He didn't tell all this to Mr. Whatney, of course. He merely said that his partner had gotten fed up with the bicycle business.

"It don't pay to worry and try to change the world," he pointed out. "I always say take things the way they are. If you can't lick 'em, join 'em."

Mr. Whatney said that was his philosophy, exactly. He asked how things were, since.

"Well . . . not *too* bad. I'm engaged, you know. Name's Norma. Crazy about bicycles. Everything considered, things aren't bad at all. More work, yes, but I can do things all my own way, so . . ."

Mr. Whatney nodded. He glanced around the shop. "I see they're still making drop-frame bikes," he said, "though, with so many women wearing slacks, I wonder they bother."

Oscar said, "Well, I dunno. I kinda like it that way. Ever stop to think that bicycles are like people? I mean, of all the machines in the world, only bikes come male and female."

Mr. Whatney gave a little giggle, said that was *right,* he had never thought of it like that before. Then Oscar asked if Mr. Whatney had anything in particular in mind—not that he wasn't always welcome.

"Well, I wanted to look over what you've got. My boy's birthday is coming up——"

Oscar nodded sagely. "Now here's a job," he said, "which you can't get it in any other place but here. Specialty of the house. Combines the best features of the French racer and the American standard, but it's made right here, and it comes in three models —Junior, Intermediate and Regular. Beautiful, ain't it?"

Mr. Whatney observed that, say, that might be just the ticket. "By the way," he asked, "what's become of the French racer, the red one, used to be here?"

Oscar's face twitched. Then it grew bland and innocent and

he leaned over and nudged his customer. "Oh, *that* one. Old Frenchy? Why, I put *him* out to stud!"

And they laughed and they laughed, and after they told a few more stories they concluded the sale, and they had a few beers and they laughed some more. And then they said what a shame it was about poor Ferd, poor old Ferd, who had been found in his own closet with an unraveled coat hanger coiled tightly around his neck.

THE GUN WITHOUT A BANG
xxxxxxxxxxx by Finn O'Donnevan xxxxxxxxxxx

DID A TWIG SNAP? DIXON LOOKED BACK AND
thought he saw a dark shape melt into the underbrush. Instantly
he froze, staring back through the green-boled trees. There was
a complete and expectant silence. Far overhead, a carrion bird
balanced on an updraft, surveying the sunburned landscape, waiting, hoping.

Then Dixon heard a low, impatient cough from the underbrush.

Now he knew he was being followed. Before, it had only been
an assumption. But those vague, half-seen shapes had been real.
They had left him alone on his trek to the signal station, watching,
deciding. Now they were ready to try something.

He removed the Weapon from its holster, checked the safeties,
reholstered it and continued walking.

He heard another cough. Something was patiently trailing him,
probably waiting until he left the bush and entered the forest.
Dixon grinned to himself.

Nothing could hurt him. He had the Weapon.

Without it, he would never have ventured so far from his spaceship. One simply didn't wander around on an alien planet. But Dixon could. On his hip was the weapon to end all weapons, absolute insurance against anything that walked or crawled or flew or swam.

It was the last word in hand guns, the ultimate in personal armament.

It was the Weapon.

He looked back again. There were three beasts, less than fifty yards behind him. From that distance, they resembled dogs or hyenas. They coughed at him and moved slowly forward.

He touched the Weapon, but decided against using it immediately. There would be plenty of time when they came closer.

Alfred Dixon was a short man, very broad in the chest and shoulders. His hair was streaky blond, and he had a blond mustache which curled up at the ends. This mustache gave his tanned face a frank, ferocious appearance.

His natural habitat was Terra's bars and taverns. There, dressed in stained khakis, he could order drinks in a loud, belligerent voice, and pierce his fellow drinkers with narrow gun-metal-blue eyes. He enjoyed explaining to the drinkers, in a somewhat contemptuous tone, the difference between a Sykes needler and a Colt three-point, between the Martian horned adleper and the Venusian scom, and just what to do when a Rannarean horntank is charging you in thick brush, and how to beat off an attack of winged glitterflits.

Some men considered Dixon all bluff, but they were careful not to call it. Others thought he was a good man in spite of his inflated opinion of himself. He was just overconfident, they explained. Death or mutilation would correct this flaw.

Dixon was a great believer in personal armament. To his way of thinking, the winning of the American West was simply a contest between bow and arrow and Colt .44. Africa? The spear against the rifle. Mars? The Colt three-point against the spinknife. H-bombs smeared cities, but individual men with small arms took the territory. Why look for fuzzy economic, philosophical or political reasons when everything was so simple?

He had, of course, utter confidence in the Weapon.

Glancing back, he saw that half a dozen doglike creatures had joined the original three. They were walking in the open now, tongues lolling out, slowly closing the distance.

Dixon decided to hold fire just a little longer. The shock effect would be that much greater.

He had held many jobs in his time—explorer, hunter, prospector, asteroider. Fortune seemed to elude him. The other man always stumbled across the lost city, shot the rare beast, found the ore-bearing stream. He accepted his fate cheerfully. Damned poor luck, but what can you do? Now he was a radioman, checking the automatic signal stations on a dozen unoccupied worlds.

But more important, he was giving the ultimate hand gun its first test in the field. The gun's inventors hoped the Weapon would become standard. Dixon hoped he would become standard with it.

He had reached the edge of the rain forest. His ship lay about two miles ahead in a little clearing. As he entered the forest's gloomy shade, he heard the excited squeaking of arboreals. They were colored orange and blue, and they watched him intently from the tree tops.

It was definitely an *African* sort of place, Dixon decided. He hoped he would encounter some big game, get a decent trophy head or two. Behind him, the wild dogs had approached to twenty yards. They were gray and brown, the size of terriers, with a hyena's jaws. Some of them had moved into the underbrush, racing ahead to cut him off.

It was time to show the Weapon.

Dixon unholstered it. The Weapon was pistol-shaped and quite heavy. It also balanced poorly. The inventors had promised to reduce the weight and improve the heft in subsequent models. But Dixon liked it just the way it was. He admired it for a moment, then clicked off the safeties and adjusted for single shot.

The pack came loping toward him, coughing and snarling. Dixon took casual aim and fired.

The Weapon hummed faintly. Ahead, for a distance of a hundred yards, a section of forest simply vanished.

Dixon had fired the first disintegrator.

From a muzzle aperture of less than an inch, the beam had fanned out to a maximum diameter of twelve feet. A conic section, waist high and a hundred yards long, appeared in the forest. Within it, nothing remained. Trees, insects, plants, shrubs, wild dogs, butterflies, all were gone. Overhanging boughs caught in the blast area looked as though they had been sheared by a giant razor.

Dixon estimated he had caught at least seven of the wild dogs in the blast. Seven beasts with a half-second burst! No problems of deflection or trajectory, as with a missile gun. No need to reload, for the Weapon had a power span of eighteen duty-hours.

The perfect weapon!

He turned and walked on, reholstering the heavy gun.

There was silence. The forest creatures were considering the new experience. In a few moments, they recovered from their surprise. Blue and orange arboreals swung through the trees above him. Overhead, the carrion bird soared low, and other black-winged birds came out of the distant sky to join it. And the wild dogs coughed in the underbrush.

They hadn't given up yet. Dixon could hear them in the deep foliage on either side of him, moving rapidly, staying out of sight.

He drew the Weapon, wondering if they would dare try again. They dared.

A spotted greyhound burst from a shrub just behind him. The gun hummed. The dog vanished in mid-leap, and the trees shivered slightly as air clapped into the sudden vacuum.

Another dog charged and Dixon disintegrated it, frowning slightly. These beasts couldn't be considered stupid. Why didn't they learn the obvious lesson—that it was impossible to come against him and his Weapon? Creatures all over the Galaxy had quickly learned to be wary of an armed man. Why not these?

Without warning, three dogs leaped from different directions. Dixon clicked to automatic and mowed them down like a man swinging a scythe. Dust whirled and sparkled, filling the vacuum.

He listened intently. The forest seemed filled with low coughing sounds. Other packs were coming to join in the kill.

Why didn't they learn?

It suddenly burst upon him. *They didn't learn,* he thought, *because the lesson was too subtle!*

The Weapon—disintegrating silently, quickly, cleanly. Most of the dogs he hit simply vanished. There were no yelps of agony, no roars or howls or screams.

And above all, there was no loud boom to startle them, no smell of cordite, no click of a new shell levered in. . . .

Dixon thought, *Maybe they aren't smart enough to know this is a killing weapon. Maybe they haven't figured out what's going on. Maybe they think I'm defenseless.*

He walked more rapidly through the dim forest. He was in no danger, he reminded himself. Just because they couldn't realize it was a killing weapon didn't alter the fact that it was. Still, he would insist on a noisemaker in the new models. It shouldn't be difficult. And the sound would be reassuring.

The arboreals were gaining confidence now, swinging down almost to the level of his head, their fangs bared. Probably carnivorous, Dixon decided. With the Weapon on automatic, he slashed great cuts in the tree tops.

The arboreals fled, screaming at him. Leaves and small branches rained down. Even the dogs were momentarily cowed, edging away from the falling debris.

Dixon grinned to himself—just before he was flattened. A big bough, severed from its tree, had caught him across the left shoulder as it fell.

The Weapon was knocked from his hand. It landed ten feet away, still on automatic, disintegrating shrubs a few yards from him.

He dragged himself from under the bough and dived for the Weapon. An arboreal got to it first.

Dixon threw himself face down on the ground. The arboreal, screaming in triumph, whirled the disintegrator around its head. Giant trees, cut through, went crashing to the forest floor. The air was dark with falling twigs and leaves, and the ground was cut into trenches. A sweep of the disintegrator knifed through the tree next to Dixon, and chopped the ground a few inches from his feet. He jumped away, and the next sweep narrowly missed his head.

He had given up hope. But then the arboreal became curious. Chattering gaily, it turned the Weapon around and tried to look into the muzzle.

The animal's head vanished—silently.

Dixon saw his chance. He ran forward, leaping a trench, and recovering the disintegrator before another arboreal could play with it. He turned it off automatic.

Several dogs had returned. They were watching him closely.

Dixon didn't dare fire yet. His hands were shaking so badly, there was more risk to himself than to the dogs. He turned and stumbled in the direction of the ship.

The dogs followed.

Dixon quickly recovered his nerve. He looked at the glittering Weapon in his hand. He had considerably more respect for it now, and more than a little fear. *Much* more fear than the dogs had. Apparently they didn't associate the forest damage with the disintegrator. It must have seemed like a sudden, violent storm to them.

But the storm was over. It was hunting time again.

He was in thick brush now, firing ahead to clear a path. The dogs were on either side, keeping pace. He fired continually into the foliage, occasionally getting a dog. There were several dozen of them, pressing him closely.

Damn it, Dixon thought, *aren't they counting their losses?*

Then he realized they probably didn't know how to count.

He struggled on, not far from the spaceship. A heavy log lay in his path. He stepped over it.

The log came angrily to life and opened enormous jaws directly under his legs.

He fired blindly, holding the trigger down for three seconds and narrowly missing his own feet. The creature vanished. Dixon gulped, swayed, and slid feet-first into the pit he had just dug.

He landed heavily, wrenching his left ankle. The dogs ringed the pit, snapping and snarling at him.

Steady, Dixon told himself. He cleared the beasts from the pit's rim with two bursts, and tried to climb out.

The sides of the pit were too steep and had been fused into glass.

Frantically he tried again and again, recklessly expending his strength. Then he stopped and forced himself to think. The Weapon had got him into this hole; the Weapon could get him out.

This time he cut a shallow ramp out of the pit, and limped painfully out.

His left ankle could hardly bear weight. Even worse was the pain in his shoulder. That bough must have broken it, he decided. Using a branch as a crutch, Dixon limped on.

Several times the dogs attacked. He disintegrated them, and the gun grew increasingly heavy in his right hand. The carrion birds came down to pick at the neatly slashed carcasses. Dixon felt darkness crawl around the edges of his vision. He fought it back. He must not faint now, while the dogs were around him.

The ship was in sight. He broke into a clumsy run, and fell immediately. Some of the dogs were on him.

He fired, cutting them in two and removing half an inch from his right boot, almost down to the toe. He struggled to his feet and went on.

Quite a weapon, he thought. Dangerous to anyone, including the wielder. He wished he had the inventor in his sights.

Imagine inventing a gun without a bang!

He reached the ship. The dogs ringed him as he fumbled with the air lock. Dixon disintegrated the closest two and stumbled inside. Darkness was crawling around his vision again and he could feel nausea rising thickly in his throat.

With his last strength, he swung the air lock shut and sat down. Safe at last!

Then he heard the low cough.

He had shut one of the dogs inside with him.

His arm felt too weak to lift the heavy Weapon, but slowly he swung it up. The dog, barely visible in the dimly lighted ship, leaped at him.

For a terrifying instant, Dixon thought he couldn't squeeze the trigger. The dog was at his throat. Reflex must have clenched his hand.

The dog yelped once and was silent.

Dixon blacked out.

When he recovered consciousness, he lay for a long time, just savoring the glorious sensation of being alive. He was going to rest for a few minutes. Then he was getting out of here, away from alien planets, back to a Terran bar. He was going to get roaring drunk. Then he was going to find that inventor and ram the Weapon down the man's throat, crossways.

Only a homicidal maniac would invent a gun without a bang.

But that would come later. Right now it was a pleasure just to be alive, to lie in the sunlight, enjoying the . . .

Sunlight? Inside a spaceship?

He sat up. At his feet lay the tail and one leg of the dog. Beyond it there was an interesting zigzag slashed through the side of the spaceship. It was about three inches wide and four feet long. Sunlight filtered through it.

Outside, four dogs were sitting on their haunches, peering in. He had cut through his spaceship while killing the last dog.

Then he saw other slashes in the ship. Where had they come from?

Oh, yes, when he was fighting his way back to the ship. That last hundred yards. A few shots must have touched the spaceship.

He stood up and examined the cuts. *A neat job,* he thought, with the calm that sometimes accompanies hysteria. *Yes, sir, very neat indeed.*

Here were the severed control cables. That was where the radio had been. Over there he had managed to nick the oxygen and water tanks in a single burst, which was good shooting by anybody's standards. And here—yes, he'd done it, all right. A really clever hook shot had cut the fuel lines. And the fuel had all run out in obedience to the law of gravity and formed a pool around the ship and sunk into the ground.

Not bad for a guy who wasn't even trying, Dixon thought crazily. *Couldn't have done better with a blowtorch.*

As a matter of fact, he couldn't have done it with a blowtorch. Spaceship hulls were too tough. But not too tough for the good old little old sure-fire never-miss Weapon. . . .

A year later, when Dixon still hadn't reported, a ship was sent out. They were to give him decent burial, if any remains could be found, and bring back the prototype disintegrator, if that could be found.

The recovery ship touched down near Dixon's ship, and the crew examined the slashed and gutted hull with interest.

"Some guys," said the engineer, "don't know how to handle a gun."

"I'll say," said the chief pilot.

They heard a banging noise from the direction of the rain forest. They hurried over and found that Dixon was not dead. He was very much alive, and singing as he worked.

He had constructed a wooden shack and planted a vegetable garden around it. Surrounding the garden was a palisade. Dixon was hammering in a new sapling to replace a rotten one when the men came up.

Quite predictably, one of the men cried, "You're alive!"

"Damned right," Dixon said. "Touch and go for a while before I got the palisade built. Nasty brutes, those dogs. But I taught them a little respect."

Dixon grinned and touched a bow that leaned against the palisade within easy reach. It had been cut from a piece of seasoned, springy wood, and beside it was a quiver full of arrows.

"They learned respect," Dixon said, "after they saw a few of their pals running around with a shaft through their flanks."

"But the Weapon—" the chief pilot asked.

"Ah, the Weapon!" exclaimed Dixon, with a mad, merry light in his eyes. "Couldn't have survived without it."

He turned back to his work. He was hammering the sapling into place with the heavy, flat butt of the Weapon.

MAN IN A QUANDARY
∽∽∽∽∽∽∽ by L. J. Stecher, Jr. ∽∽∽∽∽∽∽∽

DEAR MISS DIX VI:

I have a problem. In spite of rumors to the contrary, my parents were properly married, and were perfectly normal people at the time I was born. And so was I—normal, I mean. But that all contributed to the creation of my problem.

I do not know if you can help me resolve it, but you have helped so many others that I am willing to try you. I enjoin you not to answer this letter in your column; write me privately, please.

You know all about me, of course. Who doesn't? But most of what you know about me is bound to be almost entirely wrong. So I will have to clarify my background before I present my problem.

Know, then, that I am Alfred the Magnificent. It surprises you, I imagine, that I would be writing a letter to Miss Dix VI. After all, in spite of the tax rate, I am one of the richest—I will say it! —one of the richest *men* in the world.

Every word of that last statement is true. My parents were enormously wealthy, but I have accumulated even more of the world's goods than they ever did. And if they had not been loaded with loot, I would not be here now to be writing this letter to you.

Please excuse any lack of smoothness in the style and execution of this letter. I'm doing this all myself. Usually I dictate to a secretary—a live secretary—but you understand that that would not be advisable for a letter of this kind, I'm sure.

So. My background. I was born in 2352 and, having passed my infantile I.Q. test with flying colors, was admitted to the Harvard Crèche for Superior Children at the usual age of three months.

The name of Alfred Vanderform naturally had been entered on the rolls much earlier. Ten years earlier, in point of fact. My parents had been fortunate enough to be selected to have three children and I was to be their first. They chose to begin with a son. They had known that they would be chosen, and that I would be a superior child, and had taken the wise precaution of signing me up for Harvard Crèche as soon as the planners had finished drawing up their preliminary charts.

In spite of what you may have heard, there was absolutely no chance of falsifying the initial I.Q. examination; in those days, at least. I was a physically normal, mentally superior child. My progress at the crèche was entirely satisfactory. I was an ordinarily above-average genius in every way.

At age six, I left the crèche for my sabbatical year at home with my parents, and it was there that my first disaster occurred.

My mother and father moved into the same house while I was there, which was the custom then (and may still be, for all I know) in order to provide a proper homelike atmosphere for me. Through some carelessness in original planning, this was also the year that had been selected for the birth of their second child, which was to be a girl. Both parents were to be the same for all three of their children. Under usual circumstances, they would have paid enough attention to me so that the disaster would never have been allowed to take place, but plans for their second child must have made them a trifle careless.

At any rate, in spite of my early age, an embolism somehow

developed and major damage to my heart resulted. It was here that the great wealth of my parents proved invaluable.

Prognosis was entirely unfavorable for me. The routine procedure for a three-offspring couple would have been to cancel the unsuccessful quota and reissue it for immediate production. However, it was too late to arrange for twins in their second quota and my parents decided to attempt to salvage me.

An artificial heart was prepared and substituted for the original. It had a built-in atomic battery which would require renovation no oftener than every twenty years. Voluntary control was provided through connection with certain muscles in my neck, and I soon learned to operate it at least as efficiently as a normal heart with the normal involuntary controls.

The mechanism was considerably bigger than the natural organ, but the salvage operation was a complete success. The bulge between my shoulder blades for the battery and the one in front of my chest for the pump were not excessively unsightly. I entered the Princeton Second Stage Crèche for Greatly Superior Children on time, being accepted without objection in spite of my pseudo deformity.

It cannot be proved that any special emolument was offered to or accepted by the crèche managers in order to secure my acceptance. My personal belief is that nobody had to cough up.

Three years at Princeton passed relatively uneventfully for me. In spite of the best efforts and assurances of the crèche psychologists, there was naturally a certain lack of initial acceptance of me by some of my crèche mates. However, they soon became accustomed to my fore-and-aft bulges, and since I had greater endurance than they, with voluntary control over my artificial heart, I eventually gained acceptance, and even a considerable measure of leadership—insofar as leadership by an individual is possible in a crèche.

Shortly after the beginning of my fourth year at the Princeton Crèche, the second great personal disaster struck.

Somehow or other—the cause has not been determined to this

day—my artificial heart went on the blink. I did not quite die immediately, but the prognosis was once again entirely unfavorable. Considerable damage had somehow eventuated to my lungs, my liver and my kidneys. I was a mess.

By this time, my parents had made such a huge investment in me, and my progress reports had been so uniformly excellent, that in spite of all the advice from the doctors, they determined to attempt salvage again.

A complete repackaging job was decided upon. Blood was to be received, aerated, purified and pumped back to the arterial system through a single mechanism which would weigh only about thirty-five pounds. Of course, this made portability an important factor. Remember that I was only ten years old. I could probably have carried such a weight around on my back, but I could never have engaged in the proper development of my whole body and thus could never have been accepted back again by Princeton.

It was therefore determined to put the machinery into a sort of cart, which I would tow around behind me. Wheels were quickly rejected as being entirely unsatisfactory. They would excessively inhibit jumping, climbing and many other boyish activities.

The manufacturers finally decided to provide the cart with a pair of legs. This necessitated additional machinery and added about twenty-five pounds to the weight of the finished product. They solved the problem of how I would handle the thing with great ingenuity by making the primary control involuntary. They provided a connection with my spinal cord so that the posterior pair of legs, unless I consciously ordered otherwise, always followed in the footsteps of the anterior pair. If I ran, they ran. If I jumped, they jumped.

In order to make the connection to my body, the manufacturers removed my coccyx and plugged in at and around the end of my spinal column. In other words, I had a very long and rather flexible tail, at the end of which was a smoothly streamlined flesh-colored box that followed me around on its own two legs.

A human has certain normally atrophied muscles for control of his usually nonexistent tail. Through surgery and training, those muscles became my voluntary controllers for my tail and the cart. That is, I could go around waggin' my tail while draggin' my wagon.

Pardon me, Miss Dix VI. That just slipped out.

Well, the thing actually worked. You should have seen me in a high-hurdle race—me running along and jumping over the hurdles, with that contraption galloping along right behind me, clearing every hurdle I cleared. I kept enough slack in my tail so I wouldn't get pulled up short, and then just forgot about it.

Going off a diving board was a little bit different. I learned to do things like that with my back legs under voluntary control.

Speaking of diving boards, maybe you wonder how I could swim while towing a trailer. No trouble at all. I would just put my tail between my legs and have my cart grab me around the waist with a kind of body scissors. The cart's flexible air sac was on its top when it was in normal position, so this held it away from my body, where it would not get squeezed. I would take in just enough air so that it was neutrally buoyant, and with its streamlined shape, it didn't slow me down enough to notice.

I usually "breathed"—or took in my air—through the intakes of the cart, and they stayed under water, but there was an air connection through my tail up to the lung cavity anyway, allowing me to talk. So I just breathed through my mouth in the old-fashioned way.

Backing up was rather a problem, with my posterior legs leading the way, and dancing was nearly impossible until I got the idea of having my trailer climb up out of the way onto my shoulders while I danced. That got me by Princeton's requirements, but I must confess that I was never very much in demand as a dancing partner.

At any rate, that system got me through to my sixth and last year at Princeton. I sometimes believe that I may be considered to be what is occasionally called an "accident-prone." I seem to have had more than my share of tough luck. During my last year at Princeton, I got my throat cut.

It was an accident, of course. No Princeton man would ever dream of doing away with someone he had taken a dislike to quite so crudely. Or messily.

By voluntary control of my heart, I slowed the action down to the point where I managed to keep from bleeding to death, but my larynx was destroyed beyond repair. That was when I got my Voder installation. It fitted neatly where my lungs used to be, and because it used the same resonant cavities, I soon learned to imitate my own voice well enough so that nobody could tell the difference, "before" or "after."

Actually, it was a minor accident, but I thought I'd mention it because of what the news media sometimes call my "inhuman voice." It even enables me to sing, something I never was much good at before that accident. Also, I could imitate a banjo and sing at the same time, a talent that made me popular at picnics.

That was the last real accident I had for quite a while. I got through my second (and last) home sabbatical, my Upper School, my First College and my Second College. I was chosen for, and got through, Advanced College with highest honors. Counting sabbaticals, that took a total of twenty-nine years, plus the last of my time at Princeton. And then, an eager youth of forty-two, I was on my own—ready to make my way in the world.

I was smart to avoid the government service that catches so many of us so-called super-geniuses. It's very satisfying work and all that, I suppose, but there's no money in it, and I was rich enough to want to get richer.

The cart containing my organs didn't get in my way too much. With my athletic days behind me, I taught it to come to heel instead of striding along behind me. It was less efficient, but it was a lot less conspicuous. I had a second involuntary control system built in so it would stay at heel without conscious thought on my part, once I put it there.

In my office, I would have it curl up at my feet like a sleeping dog. People told me it was hardly noticeable—even people who didn't work for me. It certainly didn't bother me or hold me back. I started to make money as though I had my own printing press and managed to hang onto most of it.

In spite of what the doom criers say, as long as there is an element of freedom in this country—and I think there always will be—there will be ways, and I mean legal ways, of coming into large hunks of cash. Within ten years, I was not only Big Rich; I was one of the most important people in the world. A Policy Maker. A Power.

It was about that time that I drank the bottle of acid.

Nobody was trying to poison me. I wasn't trying to kill myself, either. Not even subconsciously. I was just thirsty. All I can say is I did a first-rate job with what was left of my insides.

Well, they salvaged me again, and what I ended up with was a pair of carts, one trotting along beside each heel. The leash for the second one was plugged into me in front instead of in the back, naturally, but with my clothes on, nobody could tell, just by looking, that they were attached to me at all.

The doctors offered to get me by without the second trailer. They figured they could prepare predigested food and introduce it into my blood stream through the mechanism of my original wagon. I refused to let them; I had gotten too used to eating.

So whatever I ate was ground up and pumped into my new trailer—or should it be "preceder"? There it would be processed and the nutriments passed into my blood stream as required. I couldn't overeat if I tried. It was all automatic, not even hooked into my nervous system. Unusable products were compressed and neatly packaged for disposal at any convenient time. In cellophane. There was, of course, interconnection inside of me between the two carts.

I'm told I started quite a fad for walking dogs in pairs. It didn't affect me at all. I never got very good at voluntary control of my second trailer, but by that time my habit patterns were such that I hardly noticed it.

Oh, yes—about swimming. I still enjoyed swimming and I worked it out this way: Wagon number two replaced number one in straddling me, and wagon number one hung onto number two. It slowed me down, but it still let me swim. I quit diving. I couldn't spare the time to figure out how to manage it.

That took care of the next five years. I kept on getting richer. I was a happy man. Then came the crowning blow. What was left of me developed cancer.

It attacked my brain, among other things. And it was inoperable. It looked as if I had only a couple of years before deterioration of my mental powers set in, and then it would be the scrap heap for me.

But I didn't give up. By that time, I had gotten used to the parts-replacement program. And I was very rich. So I told them to get busy and build me an artificial brain as good as my own.

They didn't have time to make a neat package job this time. They took over three big buildings in the center of town and filled them with electronics. You should see the cable conduits connecting those buildings together! Then they bought the Broadway Power Plant and used most of its output. They ran in new water mains to provide the coolant.

They used most of my money, and it took all of my influence to speed things up, but they got the job done in time.

It won't do you any good to ask me how they transferred my memories and my personality to that mass of tubes and wires and tapes and transistors. I don't know. They tell me that it was the easiest part of the job, and I know that they did it perfectly. My brain power and my personality came through unchanged. I used them to get rich again in mighty short order. I had to, to pay my water and power bills.

I came out of it "Alfred the Magnificent" and still I'm just as human as you are, even if a lot of people—a few billions of them,

I guess—won't believe it. Granted, there isn't much of the Original
Me left, but there's an old saying that Glands Make the Man. Underneath it all, I'm the same Alfred Vanderform, the same old
ordinary super-genius that I have always been.

I have almost finished with the background material, Miss Dix
VI, and am nearly ready to present you my problem. I am now
approaching the age of sixty—and have therefore reached the
time of Selection for Fatherhood. I have, in fact, been fortunate
enough to be one of the few selected to father three children.

If you have chanced to hear rumors that money changed hands
in getting me selected, let me tell you that they are entirely true.
The only thing wrong about the rumors is that none of them has
named a big enough amount—not nearly big enough. It isn't that
I don't qualify by any honest evaluation. I do. But there has been
a good deal of prejudice against me as a Father, and even some
skepticism about my capability. But that doesn't matter; what
does is that I *have* been selected.

What is more, a single superior female was chosen to be mother
of all three of my children. By what is not at all a coincidence,
this woman happens to be my private secretary. She is, I may
add, very beautiful.

I am just old-fashioned enough to want my children to have
all of the advantages that I had myself, including parents who
are fully married, in the same way that my own mother and father were. Legal ceremony—religious service—everything!

So I have asked the chosen mother of my children-to-be to
marry me, and Gloria—that's her name—has been gracious enough
to accept. We are to be married week after next.

Now, Miss Dix VI, we come to my problem. How can I tell if
Gloria is in love with me, or is just marrying me for my money?

> Perplexed,
> Alfred Vanderform
> (The Magnificent)

BLANK FORM

❊❊❊❊❊❊❊ by Arthur Sellings ❊❊❊❊❊❊❊

THE CAR CAME, FINALLY, TO A SHUDDERING HALT,
slewed violently across the road.

Fletcher gave himself a moment to recover. He had never run
a man down before. But it needed no prior experience to know
that if it happened at seventy-five—and if the man stepped
straight in front of your headlights—what was left of the victim
was beyond urgency.

He backed the car to the side of the road and got out on trembling legs. He peered back along the highway. The moon was up,
but the scrawling skid marks were still as black where they
stemmed from the shadows of night a hundred yards away.

The sight snapped into focus the reality of what had just happened. Fletcher broke into a run, retracing the black lines, the
darkness stumbling back before him.

He stopped abruptly.

The lines came to an end, luridly wide and black, where he had
slammed on the brakes. And—there was nothing else. No body, no
trace of anything he had told himself to be prepared to find. No
blood or tattered flesh, no mangled shoe horribly alone.

He wondered if his car had carried the body along in front of it. He turned to go back before he realized that in that case he would surely have seen some trace on the road between.

The thought came that he hadn't actually *felt* the impact. You probably didn't at that speed, he told himself, and peered into the tree-lined darkness of the roadside. The collision must have hurled the man clear.

His eye caught a stir in the scrub then. Something moved into a patch of moonlight before it slithered behind the trunk of a big tree.

For a frantic moment, Fletcher tried to tell himself that he had been mistaken; the victim had somehow survived, dragged himself clear—and that was what he had seen. But the explanation withered. He had seen it too clearly—a snake, a big one. Python-size. Snakes that huge weren't native for several thousands of miles around.

His defensive reaction was to forget it and resume his search for the victim's body. If a python had escaped from a local zoo, it wasn't his affair—certainly not right now.

But a stronger impulse guided his feet toward the tree. He was a psychiatrist. Either he had seen a snake or he was having traumatic delusions. He had to know which. He skirted the tree warily.

"Good evening." A man stepped out from the tree's shadow.

Fletcher jumped. "Who are you?" he blurted inanely.

"My name's Lewis," the stranger said. "I live in Sanderville, three miles on."

"What are you doing here?" Fletcher's voice was shaky. He had killed a man—and hadn't found a trace of him yet. He had seen a big snake in country where there weren't such things. And now, silently and unconcernedly, as if from his own front door, stepped this stranger.

"Just an evening walk." The man half smiled. "A habit of mine." He frowned, as slightly as he had smiled. "Why?"

"Didn't you *hear* anything? I ran someone down in my car a minute ago."

The man shrugged. "The main line's just beyond the woods. A freight train just went through."

True enough, Fletcher could hear the noise of a train rumbling into the distance. "But didn't you see a——"

He stopped, suddenly alerted to the danger of appearing crazy. But this one could be nailed. He leaped behind the tree. Behind it was a clear tract of turf. No room to conceal anything, let alone a snake of the size he had seen . . . or thought he had seen. And the stranger obviously hadn't seen it, or he would surely have mentioned it. Then Fletcher *must* have imagined it.

Strangely, the certainty didn't disturb him. Nobody needed to remind him the mind could do odd things as a result of shock. And he still had to find the body of his victim. He turned back to the stranger, who was looking at him curiously.

"Help me, will you?" Fletcher asked. He went back to the highway. The stranger accompanied him willingly enough. They beat the roadside for yards around the scene of the accident, but without success.

They straightened simultaneously.

"Are you sure there *was* an accident?" the stranger said.

Fletcher looked at him coldly. "You can see the skid marks."

The man nodded. "But that doesn't prove there was a victim. You can get things wrong. An unlit road, moonlight, tree shadows."

"Maybe," Fletcher growled. But the startled image that had sprung up in the road had been no accidental pattern of moonlight and shade. That was one certainty, even if he couldn't find the body. "Anyway, I'm reporting the accident at Sanderville. I——"

He broke off as something registered. The stranger had said he lived at Sanderville, three miles on. Not *back* or *up the road*.

On. That meant the stranger knew which way Fletcher had been traveling. Or did it? Was his disturbed brain putting unnecessary stress on an innocent enough phrase? Fletcher didn't care.

He looked directly into the stranger's eyes. "I'll want you to come along as witness." The next moment, he cursed himself. He should have merely offered a lift.

The man looked indignant. "But I wasn't a witness. I told you I——"

"All the same"—Fletcher took a grip on the other's arm—"if you don't mind——"

The man squirmed in his grasp, which tightened warily. The stranger was not tall, but seemed wiry. Fletcher was bigger, though, and—he felt—stronger. But suddenly there wasn't a man in his grasp any more. The arm seemed to waver—then, for a moment so brief that Fletcher couldn't be sure that it actually happened, melt into formlessness.

Instantly there was another creature—a stag, already poised for flight.

Reason promptly abdicated. It was something much more primitive, *fear*, that hurled Fletcher onto the stag, grappling blindly with it.

The shape became man again and lashed out at Fletcher. He half turned his head. The blow hit his ear. It hurt, but didn't stun. His own right plunged into the other's solar plexus. The man's eyes popped foolishly as his breath stopped. Fletcher didn't give him a chance to change into any other shape. He slammed a cross to the jaw.

Panting, Fletcher looked down at the senseless body. Somewhere an owl hooted, and Fletcher was aware of the craziness of what he was doing—standing over an unconscious man, on guard against him changing his shape!

But he—it—didn't. Whatever strange power this man had evidently didn't work when he was unconscious.

What power was it? Hypnosis? Fletcher didn't know. He *did* know now that his own senses hadn't been playing him tricks. At least, not without outside influence. He bent down and slung the man over his shoulder.

Getting back to the car, he bundled the body into the trunk and locked it. On his way to the driving seat, he took a belated look at the front of the car. There wasn't a mark on it. He pursed his lips thoughtfully, then climbed in and drove off.

And he drove straight through Sanderville. There was no reason to believe that the police were competent to deal with creatures that seemed able to change their shape at will.

There was no reason to believe he was, either—but he intended to try.

The stranger groaned and stirred on the couch. Fletcher, seated rather more distant from him than if he had been a patient, craned forward.

Eyes blinked open, stared blankly up at the lamp angled above, then moved to Fletcher.

"You're safe here," Fletcher said quickly but softly. In a firmer tone, he added, "The door's locked and the windows are shuttered."

The alarm in the stranger's eyes died to a smoldering resignation. He sat up, rubbing his jaw. "Where is this?" he asked finally. "The police?"

"No, it's my office. I'm a psychiatrist. You gave me an almighty fright tonight, walking under my car the way you did—apart from what happened afterward. I brought you here to hear your explanation."

"You worked that one out then?"

"Does it take much working out? I run a man down, can't find the body, do see a snake, then don't see it, but find a man. When the man changes into a stag and back again, there's something going on. Something so irrational that it's not irrational to figure that the man was also the snake. That he changed shape to escape sudden death the way an ordinary man might duck. Right?"

The man nodded dumbly.

Fletcher waited for him to say something. When he didn't, he added levelly: "The question is—what kind of man *are* you?"

The man was sitting with shoulders bowed, his gaze downcast. Now he raised melancholy eyes to look straight into Fletcher's. "I don't know."

Fletcher, returning his gaze, felt a twinge of sympathy—and a conviction that the other was speaking the truth. "Do you mind if I try to help?"

The man smiled bitterly. "I don't think anyone could. But you've got me backed into a corner."

"Hell, I don't want you in a corner. It may take time and I can't keep you locked up here. You've got to be convinced of my good will, otherwise that power of yours might panic."

"It might. Especially if it got suspicious of your motives. If, for instance, you tried to publicize my case."

Fletcher laughed. "Would anyone believe it?"

The other laughed, too, briefly, as if despite himself. "I guess not." He was suddenly dead serious. "If you knew what it was like to be . . . the way I am, you——"

"We're all odd in some respect," Fletcher murmured, then, seeing the look in the other's face, "I'm sorry. Stock response. You can trust me."

"All right. I haven't been able to find the answer myself. But it's your risk."

"I'll take that chance." Fletcher poised his pen. "Full name?"

"John Lewis." The man smiled wryly. "Or Bill Smith or Fred Jones. I chose John Lewis."

"I see. Will all the rest be made up, too?"

Lewis shrugged. "There isn't much to make up. They don't ask many questions, the circles I've been moving in. On forms I say I'm twenty-eight, born in Alaska—that's far enough away to put people off checking."

"Amnesia, then. But for the rest of this, let me have it straight.

Just when and where did you find yourself without a name and a past?"

"Up in Oregon. There was a big project going on up there, a new town being built. One of the men found me in the woods."

"What kind of shape were you in? Damn, I mean——"

Lewis gave a flicker of a smile. "That's all right. To answer the question I don't believe you meant, I was this shape. And I was in fair condition. But I was pretty helpless. I couldn't even speak English."

Fletcher's eyebrows rose. "When did that come back?"

"It—didn't come back."

"You mean you learned it all over again?"

"That's right. Only I don't think it was again."

"How long ago was this?"

"Not quite three years ago."

"Hm-mm." Fletcher made a note, a single word, *Intelligent*. For the other had perfect command of the language now. "What happened then? How did you get by?"

"It wasn't hard. All they wanted up there was a strong arm and a broad back. And there was an acute labor shortage. After a couple of years, I'd stacked up a good roll, so I came down here to find out about myself if I could."

"You think you came from these parts, then?"

"Nothing so easy. It was just that there weren't so many books up there. I had to read to find out the answer, if there was one. I read books on psychiatry, medicine, folklore, myth, the occult, heaven knows what else." He looked up at Fletcher, as the latter made two lines under the word *Intelligent*. "But I drew a blank."

"Then your other—ah—talent had already shown itself by then." The other looked at him warily, so he added, "If yours had been an ordinary amnesia case, you would already have gone to see somebody like me, wouldn't you?"

Lewis relaxed, suspicion yielding to a respect for Fletcher's understanding. "Yes, this talent, as you call it—it first happened when

I'd been on the job about six months. The iron fighters botched setting a girder. They'd got one end bolted, and the other end came free. It's quite a sight to see a solid-steel flange bend like cardboard. The girder came swinging down, crashed through a platform and headed for me.

"The next thing I clearly remember was finding myself in the woods nearby, trembling. I seemed to have fallen down, my head was so near the ground. But I was still standing on my feet—*all four of them*. They were yellow, and I had a tail. I felt it thrashing as I looked out from cover at the confusion of the accident. I had changed into a mountain lion. Just like that. I realized I was safe —and I suddenly changed back. I returned to the job.

"Nobody had noticed. There had been too much going on. Three men had been injured. Someone did start to say that it was funny but he could have sworn he'd seen—then he stopped and shook his head.

"There was only one other time. I was swimming in a lake up there. I went out further than I should have and got into difficulties. I changed into a fish."

Fletcher finished his notation. "These changes have happened in an emergency, just like this evening. But have you ever *tried* to change?"

"It doesn't work," Lewis said. "It seems to work only like a reflex."

"As I thought." Fletcher pondered. "You said you've read folklore, myth, the occult. There *are* accounts there, of course, of men changing into other creatures."

"I know. But not the way I change. Anyway, I don't feel bewitched, if that doesn't sound like a stupid thing to say."

"No. Besides, if it were witchcraft, I wouldn't be qualified to help at all. So let's examine other possibilities. You've lived with this for three years. Do you have any theory at all?"

Lewis framed his lips to speak, stopped, framed his lips again. Fletcher waited.

Lewis seemed finally to make up his mind. "I think I came from another world."

He looked at Fletcher almost defiantly, but Fletcher said only, "Yes?"

"Yes. I believe that I crashed, that I lost not only my memory but my shape. Heaven knows what I was originally, but I must have been of some species that could change its shape at need, which would be an asset on the different worlds it visited. Does that make sense?"

"More sense than anything I can think up on the spur of the moment. Whatever the truth, the only way to discover it is to get beyond the traumatic block that is sealing off your previous existence." He looked deliberately at Lewis. "That might be dangerous."

"How?"

"Because a traumatic block is set up in the mind in self-defense. Penetrate it—there's no knowing how the mind may react. And, in your case, another danger occurs to me. If your make-up is nonhuman, the treatment itself might have a totally unexpected effect on you."

Lewis considered that. "I'm game, if you are. But I think you face two dangers, too. First, my peculiar talent might not take kindly to my being treated and might run amok. It hasn't been entirely fear for my own safety that's stopped me visiting a psychiatrist before. What treatment do you have in mind?"

"Narco-analysis. I put you under narcosis and, by asking you questions, try to dig your past out of your subconscious. I'll just have to keep my fingers crossed that your talent will keep quiet. But what's the other danger?"

"Well, if I did come from another world, I must have been on some kind of mission. What if the mission . . . was a hostile one?"

Glancing up suddenly at him, Fletcher smiled. "There you sit, decent enough to be concerned about my welfare, and you're trying to convince me that you might be a monster!"

"I'm serious," Lewis insisted.

"Then I'm ready to take both chances. You may have suffered a loss of memory, and a loss of shape, but I think that if you had had a hostile intent, at least a trace of that attitude would have remained." He looked at his wrist. "It's midnight. My apartment's in this building. Unless you've got other commitments, how about staying with me while you're under treatment? It would make it easier to fit you in with my other patients."

"All right." Lewis looked at Fletcher quizzically. "You're going to a lot of trouble for me. I don't quite get it."

Fletcher laughed. "Scratch a psychiatrist and you'll find a repressed Sherlock Holmes. You chose the wrong man to get run down by."

Lewis smiled. "You know, I'm beginning to hope I chose the right one."

By noon the next day, Fletcher knew narco-analysis wasn't going to be the answer. To all questions relating to Lewis's existence before his discovery in the Oregon woods, his mind, freed from conscious control, made no answer at all. Even to suggestions of a crash, response was negative.

Fletcher was beginning to weigh the possibilities of more drastic methods, like shock treatment, when a fresh idea hit him.

"Change into a Saint Bernard dog," he said, feeling for a wild moment the ludicrousness of the command.

Lewis promptly changed into a Saint Bernard.

"Now back again." Lewis's subconscious dutifully re-formed its owner.

"Mm-mm," Fletcher said to himself. A glimmer of light was dawning.

When Lewis came to, he told him what had happened.

"Your talent is a true reflex. It's automatic. It responds to suggestion when your conscious control is relaxed. If we could get your memory back, you'd naturally remember what your original shape was. But your memory is obviously not going to yield easily. So, say we reverse the process. Say we experiment on finding your shape. It might take a hell of a while, but if we hit on it, it should trigger the rest of your memory."

For the first time, something like elation came into Lewis's eyes. "*Yes*. I thought of that myself—that if I could only get back my original shape—but I gave up the thought as hopeless when I found I couldn't will it. But if you can do it——"

Fletcher cut across his excitement. "Don't be too optimistic. There's no guarantee we'll hit on it, for one thing. Another is that amnesia may be proof against that, too. But if I do hit it, if I do give your subconscious the right command, it should create quite a stir in your psyche."

His smile was rather grim.

During the next two weeks Fletcher did a drastic streamlining of his appointment book, putting off all but the most urgent and persistent cases.

It was the most fantastic fortnight he had ever spent. He kept his consulting room locked and shuttered whenever Lewis was in there. And he was there most of the time. He was tough, physically and mentally, and kept coming back for more, in between demanding to be told all the shapes that Fletcher successively dictated to his subconscious.

Fletcher set up every possible permutation and combination imaginable—but without a single response, except that Lewis's subconscious went through the motions as docilely as a trained seal. He did become a seal once—and every other creature in the world's catalogue, except for an occasional gap. The first time that happened, Fletcher thought he had hit on the right shape. Then he found, to his disgust, that it was due to the simple fact that Lewis just didn't have that particular creature in his stock of acquired knowledge.

So when that happened, Fletcher described the creature, and Lewis took it from there. The same routine was followed with all the fantastic imaginary shapes that Fletcher thought up. For, in the second week, the Earth was left behind. Local magazine stores did an unusual trade in science fiction magazines, and hundreds of illustrations took fleeting shape on Fletcher's couch.

Once, on Fletcher's instruction to assume some particularly fantastic shape, the willing subject gave a groan, and Fletcher tensed. That was the kind of reaction he'd been praying for. But his hopes immediately evaporated, for, with a contented sigh, Lewis made it. It had been only a temporary constructional difficulty.

At the end of the fortnight, Fletcher was ready to give in. He told Lewis so.

Lewis looked dismayed.

"Well, can you think of anything else?" Fletcher challenged him, for Lewis had taken over the task of indexing.

"No. Perhaps you can only get a response by an exact prompt —every detail, color and all."

"I know. That would put it on a par with the monkeys on the typewriters—a job for eternity. Before I tackle that, I think I'll take a look up in Oregon. I might get a clue there."

"*I* didn't."

"Maybe you were too close to it."

"But—you won't rouse any suspicion about me? I mean——"

"Yes?"

Lewis bit his lip. "I'm sorry."

"That's all right. I'll just say I'm a doctor handling your case. Strictly amnesia. I won't mention the rest."

Lewis beamed. "Right. And while you're away, I'll really analyze those shapes, just in case we overlooked or forgot one."

Fletcher went by plane. A bus from the airport took him to the construction job. The township was nearly finished now, and most of the workers had been paid off. But he was lucky enough to contact the man who had found Lewis—a towering Irish foreman called Brannigan.

"He was stark naked and lost," Brannigan told him over a beer. "But he wasn't any trouble. Doc checked him and passed him as okay. Apart from his loss of memory or whatever it was. But he was a good worker, one of the best I ever had. Some of these good-for-nothing loafers, they——"

Fletcher waited patiently through a long complaint about the present-day worker—it was obvious that Brannigan had been reared in tougher days—then said: "Did you ever find anything round about?"

"Like what?"

"Well, did your workmen ever turn up anything like—well, documents, scraps of metal, anything? I'm trying to get a lead on Lewis's real identity."

Brannigan scratched his head. "I didn't hear of anything. We found a lot of Indian remains—pots, weapons, but nothing else. If anybody had, I'd have heard about it. And we cleared several miles around this project."

Fletcher sighed. "Okay, thanks."

On the plane back, he tried to add it up. But nothing plus nothing wasn't a very profitable sum. He might be a moderately successful psychiatrist—on ordinary cases, anyway—but as a Sherlock Holmes he was definitely deficient, he thought with disgust.

Then something clicked. Sherlock Holmes . . . the dog in the night . . . the dog that didn't bark. The spaceship that wasn't there. That didn't have to mean a thing, of course. If you could accept the fact of a man who could change shape and the conjecture of a spaceship, then you could accept a matter transmitter, or whatever else writers employed to move their heroes between worlds.

But if there *had* been a spaceship, and there were no remains, that meant there hadn't been a crash. That, in turn, meant that——

By the time the plane touched down, Fletcher had explored a long avenue of conjecture. It had kept branching off into realms of possibility that it would have been hopeless to follow. But, keeping to a path he *could* follow, he had tracked it out to the end, and at the end was one last possibility.

Lewis was waiting for him glumly in his office. "I've analyzed all the shapes."

"Well?"

Lewis shook his head sadly. "You covered the ground one hundred per cent."

"Only ninety-nine point nine nine nine," Fletcher told him. "Ready for one more try?"

Lewis nodded, a light of hope reawakening in his eyes.

"Mind you, it's only a try," Fletcher warned. "*One* try—after the thousands we've made already. So don't expect too much."

Fletcher gave him a minimum dose, waited, then said the word.

It worked.

A cry broke from the lips of the figure on the couch, accompanied by a great writhing of features and of form. Nothing like this had ever happened before. Then the figure sighed and changed. Eyes looked sightlessly up at Fletcher; strange words broke from a newly shaped mouth.

Fletcher waited tensely.

The drug was thrown off. The body straightened up. The eyes gained focus. They also changed color—to violet—and the rest of the shape altered slightly as if changing from the general outline that had just been triggered to the particular, the original.

"How do you feel?" Fletcher asked.

"All right. It's all so confusing, having it come back to me. But how did you guess?" The voice had changed, which wasn't surprising, but still spoke English perfectly.

"I'll tell you. You just correct me if I'm wrong. All right? Oh . . . what do I call you now?"

"Ruvil."

"Is that first name or last?"

"Both."

"Right. Now—no trace of any spaceship was found near where you thought you had crashed. So I started figuring on what that meant. It could only mean that you were landed here by a ship that took off again. That, in turn, meant that you were already amnesiac. That could have meant that you were just dumped here because you were no longer any use as a member of the crew or whatever.

"But somehow I couldn't conceive of a race with a culture that could build spaceships abandoning one of its members as callously as that. But a race that could build spaceships *could* conceivably introduce an artificial amnesia into a subject. Artificial and permanent. Endangered by only one thing—the talent that your species has for changing shape.

"Now I tried to place myself in the skin of a creature of another world that I didn't know a thing about. And I reasoned like this:

"First, for some reason, powers on your world wanted you out of the way. But they were too humane to kill you. Why didn't they just dump you on another world? Because you had some knowledge that they feared you could use. So—without at this stage going into what that knowledge might be—they gave you this artificial memory block before they dumped you.

"But there was always the danger that you might get into a spot that would cause you to change to your original shape—and trigger your memory. Now the really tough part came. Why did they choose this planet? Because they had never visited it before? But perhaps they had—incognito. Perhaps they're incognito on every world they visit, having the power they have. Obviously I couldn't get far on that tack.

"So then I pondered on just *where* on Earth they had dumped you. And then it clicked. They had left you with this artificial memory block—and probably in some neutral state, physically. You were just a blank, in mind and shape, when you saw a man approach, as they figured was bound to happen before long.

"Your reflex acted. You became a man—the one shape you would never have reason to change from into your original. At least, not foreseeably. I wondered whether the difference was such as to matter. It obviously was."

Ruvil laughed now. "Believe me, it is. Didn't you know that?"

"On Earth, yes. Some men have said that your species is the most widely divergent from Man imaginable. But one or two things still have me puzzled. Just what did you know that was so dangerous to your own kind?"

Ruvil laughed again. "You know, that's one thing that hasn't come back yet. Anyway, I'm not worried. Oh, the intrigues back on Varn—that's the name of my world. They're extremely intelligent—*and* humane, as you correctly diagnosed—but also slightly cockeyed. It seems that the more developed a culture you get, the bigger the neuroses."

"But why have they never visited Earth? Openly, I mean."

"Because they never contact a world that's already well on the way to space travel itself. When a race is at that point, it's likely to go off the handle, before it gets its sights adjusted. There have been one or two unhappy incidents in the past. *Yes*, of course—that's the knowledge they were frightened I'd use or pass on. Not the reason they banished me. That was some dreadful palace conspiracy. I am—*was*—a member of one of the dynastic families back on Varn."

"But why didn't they dump you on a more primitive world where your knowledge would be of no use to you?" asked Fletcher.

"Because—well, because Varn ships are in regular contact with them, I suppose. They had to choose a world like Earth—and any other developed culture is always humanoid. Yes, it was really clever of them to banish me here and to dump me in a practically all-man area. And"—Ruvil's violet eyes shone admiringly—"it was very clever of you to work it all out."

Fletcher coughed nervously and leaned back. "Yes, well . . . what are your plans now? To show us how to build spaceships and lead a fleet back to Varn?"

Ruvil laughed tinklingly. "Of course not. They overestimated the attention I paid to my lessons at school. I wouldn't know how to start. Besides, what would *I* want with spaceships?"

Ruvil stretched luxuriously, and Fletcher had to admit that, in with such other obvious endowments, a knowledge of spaceship construction *would* have been rather redundant.

"No." Ruvil smoothed her long golden hair with delicate fingers. "There's lots of other Varnian lore that's much more worth knowing."

She got up from the couch in one lithe movement, far too quickly for Fletcher to have moved, even if he had wanted to. "For instance . . ."

THE MINIMUM MAN

∞∞∞∞∞∞ by Robert Sheckley ∞∞∞∞∞∞

EVERYBODY HAS HIS SONG, THOUGHT ANTON PER-
ceveral. A pretty girl is like a melody, and a brave spaceman like
a flurry of trumpets. Wise old men on the Interplanetary Council
make one think of richly blended woodwinds. There are geniuses
whose lives are an intricate counterpoint endlessly embellished,
and scum of the planets whose existence seems nothing more than
the wail of an oboe against the inexorable pounding of a bass
drum.

Perceveral thought about this, loosely gripping a razor blade
and contemplating the faint blue veins in his wrist.

For if everybody has his song, his could be likened to a poorly
conceived and miserably executed symphony of errors.

There had been muted horns of gladness at his birth. Bravely,
to the sound of muffled drums, young Perceveral had ventured
into school. He had excelled and been promoted to a small work-
shop class of five hundred pupils, where he could receive a measure of individual attention. The future had looked promising.

But he was congenitally unlucky. There was a constant series of small accidents with overturned inkwells, lost books and misplaced papers. Things had a damnable propensity for breaking under his fingers; or sometimes his fingers broke under things. To make matters worse, he caught every possible childhood disease, including proto-Measles, Algerian Mumps, Impetigo, Foxpox, Green Fever and Orange Fever.

These things in no way reflected upon Perceveral's native ability; but one needs more than ability in a crowded and competitive world. One needs considerable luck, and Perceveral had none. He was transferred to an ordinary class of ten thousand students, where his problems were intensified and his opportunities for catching disease expanded.

He was a tall, thin, bespectacled, goodhearted, hard-working young man whom the doctors early diagnosed as accident-prone, for reasons which defied their analysis. But whatever the reasons, the facts remained. Perceveral was one of those unhappy people for whom life is difficult to the point of impossibility.

Most people slip through the jungle of human existence with the facility of prowling panthers. But, for the Perceverals, the jungle is continually beset with traps, snares and devices, sudden precipices and unfordable streams, deadly fungus and deadlier beasts. No way is safe. All roads lead to disaster.

Young Perceveral won his way through college in spite of his remarkable talent for breaking his leg on winding staircases, twisting his ankle on curbstones, fracturing his elbow in revolving doors, smashing his glasses against plate-glass windows, and all the rest of the sad, ludicrous, painful events which beset the accident-prone. Manfully he resisted the solace of hypochondria and kept trying.

Upon graduation from college, Perceveral took himself firmly in hand and tried to reassert the early clear theme of hope set by his stalwart father and gentle mother. With a ruffle of drums and a trilling of chords, Perceveral entered the island of Manhattan, to forge his destiny. He worked hard to conquer his unhappy predisposition, and to stay cheerful and optimistic in spite of everything.

But his predisposition caught up with him. The noble chords dissolved into vague mutterings, and the symphony of his life degenerated to the level of *opéra bouffe*. Perceveral lost job after job in a snarl of broken voxwriters and smeared contracts, forgotten file cards and misplaced data sheets; in a mounting crescendo of ribs wrenched in the subway rush, ankles sprained on gratings, glasses smashed against unseen projections, and in a bout of illnesses which included Hepatitis Type J, Martian Flu, Venusian Flu, Waking Sickness and Giggling Fever.

Perceveral still resisted the lure of hypochondria. He dreamed of space, of the iron-jawed adventurers advancing Man's frontier, of the new settlements on distant planets, of vast expanses of open land where, far from the hectic plastic jungles of Earth, a man could really find himself. He applied to the Planetary Exploration & Settlement Board, and was turned down. Reluctantly he pushed the dream aside and tried a variety of jobs. He underwent Analysis, Hypnotic Suggestion, Hypnotic Hypersuggestion and Countersuggestion Removal—all to no avail.

Every man has his limits and every symphony has its end. Perceveral gave up hope at the age of thirty-four when he was fired, after three days, from a job he had sought for two months. That, as far as he was concerned, provided the final humorous off-key cymbal clash to something which probably shouldn't have been started in the first place.

Grimly he took his meager paycheck, accepted a last wary handshake from his former employer, and rode the elevator to the lobby. Already vague thoughts of suicide were crossing his mind in the form of truck wheels, gas pipes, tall buildings and swift rivers.

The elevator reached the great marble lobby with its uniformed riot policemen and its crowds waiting admittance to the mid-town streets. Perceveral waited in line, idly watching the Population

Density Meter fluctuate below the panic line, until his turn came. Outside, he joined a compact body of people moving westward in the direction of his housing project.

Suicidal thoughts continued to flow through his mind, more slowly now, taking more definite forms. He considered methods and means until he reached home. There he disengaged himself from the crowd and slipped in through an entry port.

He struggled against a flood of children pouring through corridors, and reached his city-provided cubicle. He entered, closed and locked the door, and took a razor blade from his shaving kit. He lay down on the bed, propping his feet against the opposite wall, and contemplated the faint blue veins of his wrist.

Could he do it? Could he do it cleanly and quickly, without error and without regret? Or would he bungle this job, too, and be dragged screaming to a hospital, a ludicrous sight for the interns to snicker about?

As he was thinking, a yellow envelope was slipped under his door. It was a telegram, arriving pat on the hour of decision, with a melodramatic suddenness which Perceveral considered quite suspect. Still, he put down the razor blade and picked up the envelope.

It was from the Planetary Exploration & Settlement Board, the great organization that controlled every Earthman's movements in space. With trembling fingers, Perceveral opened the envelope and read:

> Mr. Anton Perceveral
> Temporary Housing Project 1993
> District 43825, Manhattan 212, N.Y.
> Dear Mr. Perceveral:
> Three years ago you applied to us for a position in any off-Earth capacity. Regretfully we had to turn you down at that time. Your records have been kept on file, however, and have re-

*cently been brought up to date. I am happy to
inform you that a position is immediately available for you, one which I consider well suited
to your particular talents and qualifications. I
believe this job will meet with your approval,
carrying, as it does, a salary of $20,000 a year,
all government fringe benefits, and an unex-
celled opportunity for advancement.*

Could you come in and discuss it with me?

> *Sincerely,*
> *William Haskell*
> *Asst. Placement Director*

WH/ibm3dc

Perceveral folded the telegram carefully and put it back in its
envelope. His first feeling of intense joy vanished, to be replaced
by a sense of apprehension.

What talents and qualifications did he have for a job command-
ing twenty thousand a year and benefits? Could they be confusing
him with a different Anton Perceveral?

It seemed unlikely. The Board just didn't do that sort of thing.
And presuming that they knew him and his ill-starred past—what
could they possibly want from him? What could *he* do that practically any man, woman or child couldn't do better?

Perceveral put the telegram in his pocket and replaced the razor
blade in his shaving kit. Suicide seemed a little premature now.
First he would find out what Haskell wanted.

At the headquarters of the Planetary Exploration & Settlement
Board, Perceveral was admitted at once to William Haskell's
private office. The Assistant Placement Director was a large, blunt-
featured, white-haired man who radiated a geniality which Perceveral found suspicious.

"Sit down, sit down, Mr. Perceveral," Haskell said. "Cigarette?
Care for a drink? Awfully glad you could make it."

"Are you sure you have the right man?" Perceveral asked.

Haskell glanced through a dossier on his desk. "Let's see. Anton Perceveral; age thirty-four; parents, Gregory James Perceveral and Anita Swaans Perceveral, Laketown, New Jersey. Is that right?"

"Yes," Perceveral said. "And you have a job for me?"

"We have indeed."

"Paying twenty thousand a year and benefits?"

"Perfectly correct."

"Could you tell me what the job is?"

"That's what we're here for," Haskell said cheerfully. "The job I have in mind for you, Mr. Perceveral, is listed in our catalogue as Extraterrestrial Explorer."

"I beg your pardon?"

"Extraterrestrial or alien-planet explorer," Haskell said. "The explorers, you know, are the men who make the first contacts on alien planets, the primary settlers who gather our essential data. I think of them as the Drakes and Magellans of this century. It is, I think you'll agree, an excellent opportunity."

Perceveral stood up, his face a dull red. "If you're finished with the joke, I'll leave."

"Eh?"

"Me an extraterrestrial explorer?" Perceveral said with a bitter laugh. "Don't try to kid me. I read the papers. I know what the explorers are like."

"What are they like?"

"They're Earth's finest," Perceveral said. "The very best brains in the very best bodies. Men with trigger-quick reactions, able to tackle any problem, cope with any situation, adjust to any environment. Isn't that true?"

"Well," Haskell said, "it *was* true back in the early days of planetary exploration. And we have allowed that stereotype to remain in the public eye, to instill confidence. But that type of explorer is now obsolete. There are plenty of other jobs for men such as you describe. But not planetary exploration."

"Couldn't your supermen make the grade?" Perceveral asked with a faint sneer.

"Of course they could," Haskell said. "No paradox is involved here. The record of our early explorers is unsurpassed. Those men managed to survive on every planet where human survival was even remotely possible, against overwhelming odds, by sheer grit and tenacity. The planets called for their every resource and they rose to meet the challenge. They stand as an eternal monument to the toughness and adaptability of Homo sapiens."

"Then why did you stop using them?"

"Because our problems on Earth changed," Haskell told him. "In the early days, the exploration of space was an adventure, a scientific achievement, a defense measure, a symbol. But that passed. Earth's overpopulation trend continued—explosively. Millions spilled into relatively empty lands like Brazil, New Guinea and Australia. But the population explosion quickly filled them. In major cities, the population panic point was reached and produced the Weekend Riots. And the population, bolstered by geriatrics and a further sharp decrease in infant mortality, continued to grow."

Haskell rubbed his forehead. "It was a mess. But the ethics of population increase aren't my business. All we at the Board knew was, we had to have new land fast. We needed planets which—unlike Mars and Venus—would be rapidly self-supporting. Places to which we could siphon millions, while the scientists and politicians on Earth tried to straighten things out. We had to open these planets to colonization as rapidly as possible. And that meant speeding up the initial exploratory process."

"I know all that," Perceveral said. "But I still don't see why you stopped using the optimum explorer type."

"Isn't it obvious? We were looking for places where *ordinary* people could settle and survive. Our optimum explorer type was not ordinary. Quite the contrary, he almost approximated a new species. And he was no judge of *ordinary* survival conditions. For example, there are bleak, dreary, rain-swept little planets that the average colonist finds depressing to the point of insanity; but our optimum explorer is too sound to be disturbed by climatic monotony. Germs which devastate thousands give him, at most, a bad time for a while. Dangers which can push a colony to the brink of disaster, our optimum explorer simply evades. He can't assess these things in everyday terms. They simply don't touch him."

"I'm beginning to see," Perceveral said.

"Now the best way," Haskell said, "would have been to attack these planets in stages. First an explorer, then a basic research team, then a trial colony composed largely of psychologists and sociologists, then a research group to interpret the findings of the other groups, and so forth. But there's never enough time or money for all that. We need those colonies right now, not in fifty years."

Mr. Haskell paused and looked hard at Perceveral. "So, you see, we must have *immediate knowledge* as to whether a group of ordinary people could live and thrive on any new planet. That's why we changed our qualifications for explorers."

Perceveral nodded. "Ordinary explorers for ordinary people. There's just one thing, however."

"Yes?"

"I don't know how well you know my background . . ."

"Quite well," Haskell assured him.

"Then you might have noticed that I have certain tendencies toward—well, a certain accident-proneness. To tell you the honest truth, I have a hard time surviving right here on Earth."

"I know," Mr. Haskell said pleasantly.

"Then how would I make out on an alien planet? And why would you want me?"

Mr. Haskell looked slightly ill at ease. "Well, you stated our position wrongly when you said 'ordinary explorers for ordinary people.' It isn't that simple. A colony is composed of thousands, often millions of people, who vary considerably in their survival potentialities. Humanity and the law state that all of them must have a fighting chance. The people themselves must be reassured before they'll leave Earth. We must convince them—and the law—and ourselves—that even the weakest will have a chance for survival."

"Go on," Perceveral said.

"Therefore," Haskell said quickly, "some years ago we stopped using the optimum-survival explorer, and began using the minimum-survival explorer."

Perceveral sat for a while digesting this information. "So you want me because any place *I* can live in, *anyone* can live in."

"That more or less sums up our thinking on the problem," Haskell said, smiling genially.

"But what would *my* chances be?"

"Some of our minimum-survival explorers have done very well."

"And others?"

"There are hazards, of course," Haskell admitted. "And aside from the potential dangers of the planet itself, there are other risks involved in the very nature of the experiment. I can't even tell you what they are, since that would destroy our only control element on the minimum-survival test. I simply tell you that they are present."

"Not a very good outlook," Perceveral said.

"Perhaps not. But think of the rewards if you won through! You would, in effect, be the founding father of a colony! Your value as an expert would be immeasurable. You would have a permanent place in the life of the community. And equally important, you might be able to dispel certain insidious self-doubts concerning your place in the scheme of things."

Perceveral nodded reluctantly. "Tell me one thing. Your telegram arrived today at a particularly crucial moment. It seemed almost——"

"Yes, it was planned," Haskell said. "We've found that the people we want are most receptive when they've reached a certain psychological state. We keep close watch over the few who fit our requirements, waiting for the right moment to make our presentation."

"It might have been embarrassing if you'd been an hour later," Perceveral said.

"Or unfruitful if we'd been a day earlier." Haskell arose from behind his desk. "Would you join me for lunch, Mr. Perceveral? We can discuss final details over a bottle of wine."

"All right," Perceveral said. "But I'm not making any promises yet."

"Of course not," Haskell said, opening the door for him.

After lunch Perceveral did some hard thinking. The explorer's job appealed to him strongly in spite of the risks. It was, after all, no more dangerous than suicide, and much better paying. The rewards were great if he won; the penalty for failure was no more than the price he had been about to pay for failure on Earth.

He hadn't done well in thirty-four years on Earth. The best he had shown were flashes of ability marred by a strong affinity for illness, accident and blunder. But Earth was crowded, cluttered and confused. Perhaps his accident-proneness had been not some structural flaw in him but the product of intolerable conditions.

Exploration would give him a new environment. He would be alone, dependent only on himself, answerable only to himself. It would be tremendously dangerous—but what could be more dangerous than a glittering razor blade held in his own hand?

This would be the supreme effort of his life, the ultimate test. He would fight as he had never fought before to conquer his fatal tendencies. And this time he would throw every ounce of strength and determination into the struggle.

He accepted the job. In the next weeks of preparation he ate and drank and slept determination, hammered it into his brain and wove it between his nerves, mumbled it to himself like a Buddhist prayer, dreamed about it, brushed his teeth and washed his hands with it, meditated upon it until the monotonous refrain buzzed in his head waking and sleeping, and began slowly to act as a check and restraint upon action.

The day arrived when he was assigned a year's tour of duty upon a promising planet in the East Star Ridge. Haskell wished him luck and promised to stay in touch by L-phase radio. Perceveral and his equipment were put aboard the picket ship *Queen of Glasgow,* and the adventure was begun.

During the months in space, Perceveral continued to think obsessively of his resolve. He handled himself carefully in no-weight, watched his every movement and cross-checked his every motive. This continuous inspection slowed him down considerably; but gradually it became habitual. A set of new reflexes began to form, struggling to conquer the old reflex system.

But progress was spasmodic. In spite of his efforts, Perceveral caught a minor skin irritation from the ship's purification system, broke one of his ten pairs of glasses against a bulkhead, and suffered numerous headaches, backaches, skinned knuckles and stubbed toes.

Still, he felt he had made progress, and his resolution hardened accordingly. And at last his planet came into view.

The planet was named Theta. Perceveral and his equipment were set down on a grassy, forested upland near a mountain range. The area had been preselected by air survey for its promising qualities. Water, wood, local fruits and mineral-bearing ores were all nearby. The area could make an excellent colony site.

The ship's officers wished him luck, and departed. Perceveral watched until the ship vanished into a bank of clouds. Then he went to work.

First he activated his robot. It was a tall, gleaming, black multipurpose machine, standard equipment for explorers and settlers.

It couldn't talk, sing, recite or play cards like the more expensive models. Its only response was a headshake or a nod; dull companionship for the year ahead. But it was programed to handle verbal work commands of a considerable degree of complexity, to perform the heaviest labor, and to show a degree of foresight in problem situations.

With the robot's help, Perceveral set up his camp on the plain, keeping a careful check on the horizon for signs of trouble. The air survey had detected no signs of an alien culture, but you could never tell. And the nature of Theta's animal life was still uninvestigated.

He worked slowly and carefully, and the silent robot worked beside him. By evening, he had set up a temporary camp. He activated the radar alarm and went to bed.

He awoke just after dawn to the shrilling of the radar alarm bell. He dressed and hurried outside. There was an angry humming in the air, like the sound of a locust horde.

"Get two beamers," he told the robot, "and hurry back. Bring the binoculars, too."

The robot nodded and lurched off. Perceveral turned slowly, shivering in the gray dawn, trying to locate the direction of the sound. He scanned the damp plain, the green edge of forest, the cliffs beyond. Nothing moved. Then he saw, outlined against the sunrise, something that looked like a low dark cloud. The cloud was flying toward his camp, moving very quickly against the wind.

The robot returned with the beamers. Perceveral took one and directed the robot to hold the other, awaiting orders to fire. The robot nodded, his eye cells gleaming dully as he turned toward the sunrise.

When the cloud swept nearer, it resolved into a gigantic flock of birds. Perceveral studied them through his binoculars. They were about the size of Terran hawks, but their darting, erratic flight resembled the flight of bats. They were heavily taloned and their long beaks were edged with sharp teeth. With all that lethal armament, they had to be carnivorous.

The flock circled them, humming loudly. Then, from all directions, with wings swept back and talons spread, they began to dive. Perceveral directed the robot to begin firing.

He and the robot stood back to back, blasting into the onslaught of birds. There was a whirling confusion of blood and feathers as battalions of birds were scythed out of the sky. Perceveral and the robot were holding their own, keeping the aerial wolf pack at a distance, even beating it back. Then Perceveral's beamer failed.

The beamers were supposed to be fully charged and guaranteed for seventy-five hours at full automatic. A beamer couldn't fail! He stood for a moment, stupidly clicking the trigger. Then he flung down the weapon and hurried to the supplies tent, leaving the robot to continue the fight alone.

He located his two spares and came out. When he rejoined the battle, he saw that the robot's beamer had stopped functioning. The robot stood erect, beating off the swarm of birds with his arms. Drops of oil sprayed from his joints as he flailed at the dense flock. He swayed, dangerously close to losing his balance, and Perceveral saw that some birds had evaded his swinging arms and were perched on his shoulders, pecking at his eye cells and kinesthetic antenna.

Perceveral swung up both beamers and began to cut into the swarm. One weapon failed almost immediately. He continued chopping with the last, praying it would retain its charge.

The flock, finally alarmed by its losses, rose and wheeled away, screaming and hooting. Miraculously unhurt, Perceveral and the robot stood knee-deep in scattered feathers and charred bodies.

Perceveral looked at the four beamers, three of which had failed him entirely. Then he marched angrily to the communications tent.

He contacted Haskell and told him about the attack of the birds and the failure of three beamers out of four. Red-faced with outrage, he denounced the men who were supposed to check an explorer's equipment. Then, out of breath, he waited for Haskell's apology and explanation.

"That," Haskell said, "was one of the control elements."

"Huh?"

"I explained it to you months ago," Haskell said. "We are testing for minimum-survival conditions. *Minimum,* remember? We have to know what will happen to a colony composed of people of varying degrees of proficiency. Therefore, we look for the lowest denominator."

"I know all that. But the beamers——"

"Mr. Perceveral, setting up a colony, even on an absolute minimum basis, is a fantastically expensive operation. We supply our colonists with the newest and best in guns and equipment, but we can't replace things that stop functioning or are used up. The colonists have to use irreplaceable ammunition, equipment that breaks and wears out, food stores that become exhausted or spoiled——"

"And that's what you've given me?" Perceveral asked.

"Of course. As a control, we have equipped you with the minimum of survival equipment. That's the only way we'll be able to predict how the colonists will make out on Theta."

"But it isn't fair! Explorers always get the best equipment!"

"No," Haskell said. "The old-style optimum-survival explorers did, of course. But we're testing for least potential, which must extend to equipment as well as to personality. I told you there would be risks."

"Yes, you did," Perceveral said. "But . . . All right. Do you have any other little secrets in store for me?"

"Not really," Haskell said, after a momentary pause. "Both you and your equipment are of minimum-survival quality. That about sums it up."

Perceveral detected something evasive in this answer, but

Haskell refused to be more specific. They signed off and Perceveral returned to the chaos of his camp.

Perceveral and the robot moved their camp to the shelter of the forest for protection against further assaults by the birds. In setting up again, Perceveral noted that fully half of his ropes were badly worn, his electrical fixtures were beginning to burn out, and the canvas of his tents showed mildew. Laboriously he repaired everything, bruising his knuckles and skinning his palms. Then his generator broke down.

He sweated over it for three days, trying to figure out the trouble from the badly printed instruction book, written in German, that had been sent with the machine. Nothing seemed to be set up right in the generator and nothing worked. At last he discovered, by pure accident, that the book was meant for an entirely different model. He lost his temper at this and kicked the generator, almost breaking the little toe of his right foot.

Then he took himself firmly in hand and worked for another four days, figuring out the differences between his model and the model described, until he had the generator working again.

The birds found that they could plummet through the trees into Perceveral's camp, snatch food and be gone before the beamer could be leveled at them. Their attacks cost Perceveral a pair of glasses and a nasty wound on the neck. Laboriously he wove nets, and, with the robot's help, strung them in the branches above his camp.

The birds were baffled. Perceveral finally had time to check his food stores, and to discover that many of his dehydrated staples had been poorly processed, and others had become a host to an ugly air-borne fungus. Either way, it added up to spoilage. Unless he took measures now, he would be short of food during the Thetan winter.

He ran a series of tests on local fruits, grains, berries and vegetables. They showed several varieties to be safe and nourishing. He ate these, and broke into a spectacular allergy rash. Painstaking work with his medical kit gave him a cure for the allergy, and he set up a test to discover the guilty plant. But just as he was checking final results, the robot stamped in, upsetting test tubes and spilling irreplaceable chemicals.

Perceveral had to continue the allergy tests on himself, and to exclude one berry and two vegetables as unfit for his consumption.

But the fruits were excellent and the local grains made a fine bread. Perceveral collected seed, and, late in the Thetan spring, directed the robot to the tasks of plowing and planting.

The robot worked tirelessly in the new fields, while Perceveral did some exploring. He found pieces of smooth rock upon which characters had been scratched, and what looked like numbers, and even little stick-pictures of trees and clouds and mountains. Intelligent beings must have lived on Theta, he decided. Quite probably they still inhabited some parts of the planet. But he had no time to search for them.

When Perceveral checked his fields, he found that the robot had planted the seed inches too deep, in spite of his programed instructions. That crop was lost, and Perceveral planted the next by himself.

He built a wooden shack and replaced the rotting tents with storage sheds. Slowly he made his preparations for survival through the winter. And slowly he began to suspect that his robot was wearing out.

The great black all-purpose machine performed its tasks as before. But the robot's movements were growing increasingly jerky and his use of strength was indiscriminate. Heavy jars splintered in his grip and farming implements broke when he used them. Perceveral programed him for weeding the fields, but the robot's broad splay feet trampled the grain sprouts as his fingers plucked the weeds. When the robot went out to chop firewood, he usually succeeded in breaking the ax handle. The cabin shook when the robot entered, and the door sometimes left its hinges.

Perceveral wondered and worried about the robot's deterioration. There was no way he could repair it, for the robot was a factory-sealed unit, meant to be repaired only by factory technicians with special tools, parts and knowledge. All Perceveral could do was retire the robot from service. But that would leave him completely alone.

He programed increasingly simple tasks into the robot and took more work upon himself. Still the robot continued to deteriorate. Then one evening, when Perceveral was eating his dinner, the robot lurched against the stove and sent a pot of boiling rice flying.

With his new-found survival talents, Perceveral flung himself out of the way and the boiling mess landed on his left shoulder instead of his face.

That was too much. The robot was dangerous to have around. After dressing his burn, Perceveral decided to turn the robot off and continue the work of survival alone. In a firm voice, he gave the Dormancy Command.

The robot simply glared at him and moved restlessly around the cabin, not responding to a robot's most basic command.

Perceveral gave the order again. The robot shook his head and began to stack firewood.

Something had gone wrong. He would have to turn the robot off manually. But there was no sign of the usual cut-out switch anywhere on the machine's gleaming black surface. Nevertheless, Perceveral took out his tool kit and approached the robot.

Amazingly, the robot backed away from him, arms raised defensively.

"Stand still!" Perceveral shouted.

The robot moved away until his back was against the wall.

Perceveral hesitated, wondering what was going wrong. Machines weren't permitted to disobey orders. And the willingness to give up life had been carefully structured into all robotic devices.

He advanced on the robot, determined to turn him off somehow. The robot waited until he was close, then swung an armored

fist at him. Perceveral dodged out of the way and flung a wrench
at the robot's kinesthetic antenna. The robot quickly retracted it
and swung again. This time his armored fist caught Perceveral in
the ribs.

Perceveral fell to the floor and the robot stood over him, his
eye cells flaring red and his iron fingers opening and closing. Perceveral shut his eyes and waited for the *coup de grâce*. But the
machine turned and left the shack, smashing the lock as he went.

In a few minutes Perceveral heard the sound of firewood being
cut and stacked—as usual.

With the aid of his medical kit, Perceveral taped up his side.
The robot finished work and came back for further instructions.
Shakily, Perceveral ordered him to a distant spring for water.
The robot left, showing no further signs of aggression. Perceveral
dragged himself to the radio shack.

"You shouldn't have tried to turn him off," Haskell said, when
he heard what had happened. "He isn't designed to be turned off.
Wasn't that apparent? For your own safety, don't try it again."

"But what's the reason?"

"Because—as you've probably guessed by now—the robot acts
as our quality-control over you."

"I don't understand," Perceveral said. "Why do you need a
quality-control?"

"Must I go through it all again?" Haskell asked wearily. "You
were hired as a minimum-survival explorer. Not average. Not superior. *Minimum*."

"Yes, but——"

"Let me continue. Do you recall how you were during your
thirty-four years on Earth? You were continually beset by accident, disease and general misfortune. That is what we wanted on
Theta. But you've changed, Mr. Perceveral."

"I've certainly *tried* to change."

"Of course," Haskell said. "We expected it. Most of our minimum-survival explorers change. Faced with a new environment

and a fresh start, they get a grip on themselves such as they've never had before. But it's not what we're testing for, so we have to compensate for the change. Colonists, you see, don't always come to a planet in a spirit of self-improvement. And any colony has its careless ones, to say nothing of the aged, the infirm, the feeble-minded, the foolhardy, the inexperienced children, and so forth. Our minimum-survival standards are a guarantee that all of them will have a chance. Now are you beginning to understand?"

"I think so," Perceval said.

"That's why we need a quality-control over you—to keep you from acquiring the average or superior survival qualities which we are *not* testing for."

"Therefore the robot," Perceval said bleakly.

"Correct. The robot has been programed to act as a check, a final control over your survival tendencies. He reacts to you, Perceval. As long as you stay within a preselected range of general incompetence, the robot operates at par. But when you improve, become more skillful at survival, less accident-prone, the robot's behavior deteriorates. He begins to break the things that you should be breaking, to form the wrong decisions you should be forming——"

"That isn't fair!"

"Perceval, you seem to feel that we're running some kind of sanitorium or self-aid program for your benefit. Well, we're not. We're interested only in getting the job that we bought and paid for. The job, let me add, which you chose as an alternative to suicide."

"All right!" Perceval shouted. "I'm doing the job. But is there any rule that says I can't dismantle that damned robot?"

"No rule at all," Haskell said in a quieter voice, "if you can do it. But I earnestly advise you not to try. It's too dangerous. The robot will not allow himself to be deactivated."

"That's for me to decide, not him," Perceveral said, and signed off.

Spring passed on Theta, and Perceveral learned how to live with his robot. He ordered him to scout a distant mountain range, but the robot refused to leave him. He tried giving him no orders, but the black monster wouldn't stay idle. If no work was assigned, the robot assigned work to himself, suddenly bursting into action and creating havoc in Perceveral's field and sheds.

In self-defense, Perceveral gave him the most harmless task he could think of. He ordered the robot to dig a well, hoping he would bury himself in it. But, grimy and triumphant, the robot emerged every evening and entered the cabin, showering dirt into Perceveral's food, transmitting allergies, and breaking dishes and windows.

Grimly, Perceveral accepted the status quo. The robot now seemed the embodiment of that other, darker side of himself, the inept and accident-prone Perceveral. Watching the robot on his destructive rounds, he felt as though he were watching a misshapen portion of himself, a sickness cast into solid, living form.

He tried to shake free of this fantasy. But more and more the robot came to represent his own destructive urges cut loose from the life impulse and allowed to run rampant.

Perceveral worked, and his neurosis stalked behind him, eternally destructive, yet—in the manner of neuroses—protective of itself. His self-perpetuating malady lived with him, watched him while he ate and stayed close while he slept.

Perceveral did his work and became increasingly competent at it. He took what enjoyment he could from the days, regretted the setting of the sun, and lived through the horror of the nights when the robot stood beside his bed and seemed to wonder if now were the time for a summing-up. And in the morning, still alive, Perceveral tried to think of ways of disposing of his staggering, lurching, destructive neurosis.

But the deadlock remained until a new factor appeared to complicate matters.

It had rained heavily for several days. When the weather cleared, Perceval walked out to his fields. The robot lumbered behind him, carrying the farming tools.

Suddenly a crack appeared in the moist ground under his feet. It widened, and the whole section he was standing on collapsed. Perceval leaped for firm ground. He made it to the slope, and the robot pulled him up the rest of the way, almost yanking his arm from his socket.

When he examined the collapsed section of field, he saw that a tunnel had run under it. Digging marks were still visible. One side was blocked by the fall. On the other side the tunnel continued deep into the ground.

Perceval went back for his beamer and his flashlight. He climbed down one side of the hole and flashed his light into the tunnel. He saw a great furry shape retreat hastily around a bend. It looked like a giant mole.

At last he had met another species of life on Theta.

For the next few days he cautiously probed the tunnels. Several times he glimpsed gray molelike shapes, but they fled from him into a labyrinth of passageways.

He changed his tactics. He went only a few hundred feet into the main tunnel and left a gift of fruit. When he returned the next day, the fruit was gone. In its place were two lumps of lead.

The exchange of gifts continued for a week. Then, one day when Perceval was bringing more fruit and berries, a giant mole appeared, approaching slowly and with evident nervousness. He motioned at Perceval's flashlight, and Perceval covered the lens so that it wouldn't hurt the mole's eyes.

He waited. The mole advanced slowly on two legs, his nose wrinkling, his small wrinkled hands clasped to his chest. He stopped and looked at Perceval with bulging eyes. Then he bent down and scratched a symbol in the dirt of the passageway.

Perceveral had no idea what the symbol meant. But the act itself implied language, intelligence and a grasp of abstractions. He scratched a symbol beside the mole's, to imply the same things.

An act of communication between alien races had begun. The robot stood behind Perceveral, his eye cells glowing, watching while the man and the mole searched for something in common.

Contact meant more labor for Perceveral. The fields and gardens still had to be tended, the repairs on equipment made and the robot watched; in his spare time, Perceveral worked hard to learn the moles' language. And the moles worked equally hard to teach him.

Perceveral and the moles slowly grew to understand each other, to enjoy each other's company, to become friends. Perceveral learned about their daily lives, their abhorrence of the light, their journeys through the underground caverns, their quest for knowledge and enlightenment. And he taught them what he could about Man.

"But what is the metal thing?" the moles wanted to know.

"A servant of Man," Perceveral told them.

"But it stands behind you and glares. It hates you, the metal thing. Do all metal things hate men?"

"Certainly not," Perceveral said. "This is a special case."

"It frightens us. Do all metal things frighten?"

"Some do. Not all."

"And it is hard to think when the metal thing stares at us, hard to understand you. Is it always like that with metal things?"

"Sometimes they do interfere," Perceveral admitted. "But don't worry, the robot won't hurt you."

The mole people weren't so sure. Perceveral made what excuses he could for the heavy, lurching, boorish machine, spoke of machinery's service to Man and the graciousness of life that it made possible. But the mole people weren't convinced and shrank from the robot's dismaying presence.

Nevertheless, after lengthy negotiations, Perceveral made a

treaty with the mole people. In return for supplies of fresh fruits and berries, which the moles coveted but could rarely obtain, they agreed to locate metals for future colonists and find sources of water and oil. Furthermore, the colonists were granted possession of all the surface land of Theta and the moles were confirmed in their lordship of the underground.

This seemed an equitable distribution to both parties, and Perceval and the mole chief signed the stone document with as much of a flourish as an incising tool would allow.

To seal the treaty, Perceval gave a feast. He and the robot brought a great gift of assorted fruits and berries to the mole people. The gray-furred, soft-eyed moles clustered around, squeaking eagerly to each other.

The robot set down his baskets of fruit and stepped back. He slipped on a patch of smooth rock, flailed for balance, and came crashing down across one of the moles. Immediately he regained his balance and tried, with his clumsy iron hands, to help the mole up. But he had broken the creature's back.

The rest of the moles fled, carrying their dead companion with them. And Perceval and the robot were left alone in the tunnel, surrounded by great piles of fruit.

That night, Perceval thought long and hard. He was able to see the damnable logic of the event. Minimum-survival contacts with aliens should have an element of uncertainty, distrust, misunderstanding, and even a few deaths. His dealings with the mole people had gone altogether too smoothly for minimum requirements.

The robot had simply corrected the situation and had performed the errors which Perceval should have made on his own.

But although he understood the logic of the event, he couldn't accept it. The mole people were his friends and he had betrayed them. There could be no more trust between them, no hope of co-operation for future colonists. Not while the robot clumped and stumbled down the tunnels.

Perceveral decided that the robot must be destroyed. Once and for all, he determined to test his painfully acquired skill against the destructive neurosis that walked continually beside him. And if it cost his life—well, Perceveral reminded himself, he had been willing to lose it less than a year ago, for much poorer reasons.

He re-established contact with the moles and discussed the problem with them. They agreed to help him, for even these gentle people had the concept of vengeance. They supplied some ideas which were surprisingly human, since the moles also possessed a form of warfare. They explained it to Perceveral and he agreed to try their way.

In a week, the moles were ready. Perceveral loaded the robot with baskets of fruit and led him into the tunnels, as though he were attempting another treaty.

The mole people weren't to be found. Perceveral and the robot journeyed deeper into the passageways, their flashlights probing ahead into the darkness. The robot's eye cells glowed red and he towered close behind Perceveral, almost at his back.

They came to an underground cavern. There was a faint whistle and Perceveral sprinted out of the way.

The robot sensed danger and tried to follow. But he stumbled, thwarted by his own programed ineptness, and fruit scattered across the cavern floor. Then ropes dropped from the blackness of the cavern's roof and settled around the robot's head and shoulders.

He ripped at the tough fiber. More ropes settled around him, hissing in swift flight down from the roof. The robot's eye cells flared as he ripped the cords from his arms.

Mole people emerged from the passageways by the dozens. More lines snaked around the robot, whose joints spurted oil as he strained to break the strands. For minutes, the only sounds in the cavern were the hiss of flying ropes, the creak of the robot's joints, and the dry crack of breaking line.

Perceveral ran back to join the fight. They bound the robot

closer and closer until his limbs had no room to gain a purchase. And still the ropes hissed through the air until the robot toppled over, bound in a great cocoon of rope with only his head and feet showing.

Then the mole people squeaked in triumph and tried to gouge out the robot's eyes with their blunt digging claws. But steel shutters slid over the robot's eyes. So they poured sand into his joints until Perceveral pushed them aside and attempted to melt the robot with his last beamer.

The beamer failed before the metal even grew hot. They fastened ropes to the robot's feet and dragged him down a passageway that ended in a deep chasm. They levered him over the side and listened while he bounced off the granite sides of the precipice, and cheered when he struck bottom.

The mole people held a celebration. But Perceveral felt sick. He returned to his shack and lay in bed for two days, telling himself over and over that he had not killed a man, or even a thinking being. He had simply destroyed a dangerous machine.

But he couldn't help remembering the silent companion who had stood with him against the birds, and had weeded his fields and gathered wood for him. Even though the robot had been clumsy and destructive, he had been clumsy and destructive in Perceveral's own personal way—a way that he, above all people, could understand and sympathize with.

For a while, he felt as though a part of himself had died. But the mole people came to him in the evenings and consoled him, and there was work to be done in the fields and sheds.

It was autumn, time for harvesting and storing his crops. Perceveral went to work. With the robot's removal, his own chronic propensity for accident returned briefly. He fought it back with fresh confidence. By the first snows, his work of storage and food preservation was done. And his year on Theta was coming to an end.

He radioed a full report to Haskell on the planet's risks, promises and potentialities, reported his treaty with the mole people, and recommended the planet for colonization. In two weeks, Haskell radioed back.

"Good work," he told Perceveral. "The Board decided that Theta definitely fits our minimum-survival requirements. We're sending out a colony ship at once."

"Then the test is over?" Perceveral asked.

"Right. The ship should be there in about three months. I'll probably take this batch out. My congratulations, Mr. Perceveral. You're going to be the founding father of a brand-new colony!"

Perceveral said, "Mr. Haskell, I don't know how to thank you——"

"Nothing to thank me for," Haskell said. "Quite the contrary. By the way, how did you make out with the robot?"

"I destroyed him," Perceveral said. He described the killing of the mole and the subsequent events.

"Hmm," Haskell said.

"You told me there was no rule against it."

"There isn't. The robot was part of your equipment, just like the beamers and tents and food supplies. Like them, he was also part of your survival problems. You had a right to do anything you could about him."

"Then what's wrong?"

"Well, I just hope you really destroyed him. Those quality-control models are built to last, you know. They've got self-repair units and a strong sense of self-preservation. It's damned hard to really knock one out."

"I think I succeeded," Perceveral said.

"I hope so. It would be embarrassing if the robot survived."

"Why? Would it come back for revenge?"

"Certainly not. A robot has no emotions."

"Well?"

"The trouble is this. The robot's purpose was to cancel out any gains you made in survival-quality. It did, in various destructive ways."

"Sure. So, if it comes back, I'll have to go through the whole business again."

"More. You've been separated from the robot for a few months now. If it's still functioning, it's been accumulating a backlog of accidents for you. All the destructive duties that it should have performed during those months—they'll all have to be discharged before the robot can return to normal duties. See what I mean?"

Perceveral cleared his throat nervously. "And of course he would discharge them as quickly as possible in order to get back to regular operation."

"Of course. Now look, the ship will be there in about three months. That's the quickest we can make it. I suggest you make sure that robot is immobilized. We wouldn't want to lose you now."

"No, we wouldn't," Perceveral said. "I'll take care of it at once."

He equipped himself and hurried to the tunnels. The mole people guided him to the chasm after he explained the problem. Armed with blowtorch, hacksaw, sledge hammer and cold chisel, Perceveral began a slow descent down the side of the precipice.

At the bottom, he quickly located the spot where the robot had landed. There, wedged between two boulders, was a complete robotic arm, wrenched loose from the shoulder. Further on, he found fragments of a shattered eye cell. And he came across an empty cocoon of ripped and shredded rope.

But the robot wasn't there.

Perceveral climbed back up the precipice, warned the moles and began to make what preparations he could.

Nothing happened for twelve days. Then news was brought to him in the evening by a frightened mole. The robot had appeared again in the tunnels, stalking the dark passageways with a single eye cell glowing, expertly threading the maze into the main branch.

The moles had prepared for his coming with ropes. But the robot had learned. He had avoided the silent dropping nooses and charged into the mole forces. He had killed six moles and sent the rest into flight.

Perceveral nodded briefly at the news, dismissed the mole and continued working. He had set up his defenses in the tunnels. Now he had his four dead beamers disassembled on the table in front of him. Working without a manual, he was trying to interchange parts to produce one usable weapon.

He worked late into the night, testing each component carefully before fitting it back into the casing. The tiny parts seemed to float before his eyes and his fingers felt like sausages. Very carefully, working with tweezers and a magnifying glass, he began reassembling the weapon.

The radio suddenly blared into life.

"Anton?" Haskell asked. "What about the robot?"

"He's coming," said Perceveral.

"I was afraid so. Now listen, I rushed through a priority call to the robot's manufacturers. I had a hell of a fight with them, but I got their permission for you to deactivate the robot, and full instructions on how to do it."

"Thanks," Perceveral said. "Hurry up, how's it done?"

"You'll need the following equipment. A power source of two hundred volts delivered at twenty-five amps. Can your generator handle that?"

"Yes. Go on."

"You'll need a bar of copper, some silver wire and a probe made of some non-conductor such as wood. You set the stuff up in the following——"

"I'll never have time," Perceveral said, "but tell me quickly."

His radio hummed loudly.

"Haskell!" Perceveral cried.

His radio went dead. Perceveral heard the sounds of breakage coming from the radio shack. Then the robot appeared in the doorway.

The robot's left arm and right eye cell were missing, but his self-repair units had sealed the damaged spots. He was colored a dull black now, with rust-streaks down his chest and flanks.

Perceveral glanced down at the almost-completed beamer. He began fitting the final pieces into place.

The robot walked toward him.

"Go cut firewood," Perceveral said, in as normal a tone as he could manage.

The robot stopped, turned, picked up the ax, hesitated, and started out the door.

Perceveral fitted in the final component, slid the cover into place and began screwing it down.

The robot dropped the ax and turned again, struggling with contradictory commands. Perceveral hoped he might fuse some circuits in the conflict. But the robot made his decision and launched himself at Perceveral.

Perceveral raised the beamer and pressed the trigger. The blast stopped the robot in mid-stride. His metallic skin began to glow a faint red.

Then the beamer failed again.

Perceveral cursed, hefted the heavy weapon and threw it at the robot's remaining eye cell. It just missed, bouncing off his forehead.

Dazed, the robot groped for him. Perceveral dodged his arm and fled from the cabin, toward the black mouth of the tunnel. As he entered, he looked back and saw the robot following.

He walked several hundred yards down the tunnel. Then he turned on a flashlight and waited for the robot.

He had thought the problem out carefully when he'd discovered that the robot had not been destroyed.

His first idea naturally was flight. But the robot, traveling night and day, would easily overtake him. Nor could he dodge aimlessly in and out of the maze of tunnels. He would have to stop and eat, drink and sleep. The robot wouldn't have to stop for anything.

Therefore he had arranged a series of traps in the tunnels and had staked everything on them. One of them was bound to work. He was sure of it.

But even as he told himself this, Perceveral shivered, thinking of the accumulation of accidents that the robot had for him—the months of broken arms and fractured ribs, wrenched ankles, slashes, cuts, bites, infections and diseases. All of which the robot would hound him into as rapidly as possible, in order to get back to normal routine.

He would never survive the robot's backlog. His traps *had* to work!

Soon he heard the robot's thundering footsteps. Then the robot appeared, saw him, and lumbered forward.

Perceveral sprinted down a tunnel, then turned into a smaller tunnel. The robot followed, gaining slightly.

When Perceveral reached a distinctive outcropping of rock, he looked back to gauge the robot's position. Then he tugged a cord he had concealed behind the rock.

The roof of the tunnel collapsed, releasing tons of dirt and rock over the robot.

If the robot had continued for another step, he would have been buried. But appraising the situation instantly, he whirled and leaped back. Dirt showered him, and small rocks bounced off his head and shoulders. But the main fall missed him.

When the last pebble had fallen, the robot climbed over the mound of debris and continued the pursuit.

Perceveral was growing short of wind. He was disappointed at the failure of the trap. But, he reminded himself, he had a better one ahead. The next would surely finish off the implacable machine.

They ran down a winding tunnel lit only by occasional flashes from Perceveral's flashlight. The robot began gaining again. Perceveral reached a straight stretch and put on a burst of speed.

He crossed a patch of ground that looked exactly like any other patch. But as the robot thundered over it, the ground gave way. Perceveral had calculated it carefully. The trap, which held under his weight, yielded at once under the robot's bulk.

The robot thrashed for a handhold. Dirt trickled through his fingers and he slid into the trap that Perceveral had dug—a pit with sloping sides that came together like a great funnel, designed to keep the robot immovably wedged at the bottom.

The robot, however, flung both his legs wide, almost at right angles to his body. His joints creaked as his heels bit into the sloping sides; they sagged under his weight, but held. He was able to stop himself before reaching the bottom, with both legs stiffly outspread and pressed into the soft dirt.

The robot's hand gouged deep handholds in the dirt. One leg retracted and found a foothold; then the other. Slowly the robot extricated himself, and Perceveral started running again.

His breath came short and hard now and he was getting a stitch in his side. The robot gained more easily, and Perceveral had to strain to stay ahead.

He had counted on those two traps. Now there was just one more left. A very good one, but risky to use.

Perceveral forced himself to concentrate in spite of a growing dizziness. The last trap had to be calculated carefully. He passed a stone marked in white and switched off his flashlight. He began counting strides, slowing until the robot was directly behind him, his fingers inches from his neck.

Eighteen—nineteen—twenty!

On the twentieth step, Perceveral flung himself headfirst into the darkness. For seconds, he seemed to be floating in the air. Then he struck water in a flat, shallow dive, surfaced and waited.

The robot had been too close behind to stop. There was a tremendous splash as he hit the surface of the underground lake; a sound of furious splashing; and, finally, the sound of bubbles as the heavy robot sank beneath the surface.

When he heard that, Perceveral struck out for the opposite

shore. He made it and pulled himself out of the icy water. For
minutes, he lay shuddering on the slimy rocks. Then he forced
himself to climb further ashore on hands and knees, to a cache
where he had stored firewood, matches, whisky, blankets and
clothes.

During the next hours Perceveral dried himself, changed clothes
and built a small fire. He ate and drank and watched the still
surface of the underground lake. Days ago, he had tested with a
hundred-foot line and had found no bottom. Perhaps the lake was
bottomless. More likely it fed into a swift-flowing underwater
river that would pull the robot along for weeks and months.
Perhaps . . .

He heard a faint sound in the water and trained his flashlight
in its direction. The robot's head appeared, and then his shoulders
and torso emerged.

The lake was very evidently not bottomless. The robot must
have walked across the bottom and climbed the steep slope on
the opposite side.

The robot began to climb the slimy rocks near shore. Perceveral
wearily pulled himself to his feet and broke into a run.

His last trap had failed him and his neurosis was closing in for
the kill. Perceveral headed toward a tunnel exit. He wanted the
end to come in sunlight.

At a jolting dogtrot, Perceveral led the robot out of the tunnels
toward a steep mountain slope. His breath felt like fire in his
throat and his stomach muscles were knotted painfully. He ran
with his eyes half closed, dizzy from fatigue.

His traps had failed. Why hadn't he realized the certainty of
their failure earlier? The robot was part of himself, his own
neurosis moving to destroy him. And how can a man trick the
trickiest part of himself? The right hand always finds out what
the left hand is doing, and the cleverest of devices never fools
the supreme fooler for long.

He had gone about the thing in the wrong way, Perceveral

thought, as he began to climb the mountain slope. The way to freedom is not through deception. It is . . .

The robot clutched at his heel, reminding Perceveral of the difference between theoretical and practical knowledge. He pulled himself out of the way and bombarded the robot with stones. The robot brushed them aside and continued climbing.

Perceveral cut diagonally across the steep rock face. The way to freedom, he told himself, is not through deception. That was bound to fail. The way out is through *change!* The way out is through conquest, not of the robot, but of what the robot represented.

Himself!

He was feeling lightheaded and his thoughts poured on unchecked. If, he insisted to himself, he could conquer his sense of kinship with the robot—then obviously the robot would no longer be *his* neurosis! It would simply be a neurosis, with no power over him.

All he had to do was lose his neurosis—even for ten minutes— and the robot couldn't harm him!

All sense of fatigue left him and he was flooded with a supreme and intoxicating confidence. Boldly, he ran across a mass of jumbled rocks, a perfect place for a twisted ankle or a broken leg. A year ago, even a month ago, he would infallibly have had an accident. But the changed Perceveral, striding like a demigod, traversed the rocks without error.

The robot, one-armed and one-eyed, doggedly took the accident upon himself. He tripped and sprawled at full length across the sharp rocks. When he picked himself up and resumed the chase, he was limping.

Completely intoxicated but minutely watchful, Perceveral came to a granite wall, and leaped for a fingerhold that was no more than a gray shadow above him. For a heart-stopping second, he dangled in the air. Then, as his fingers began to slip, his foot found a hold. Without hesitation, he pulled himself up.

The robot followed, his dry joints creaking loudly. He bent a finger out of commission making the climb that Perceveral should have failed.

Perceveral leaped from boulder to boulder. The robot came after him, slipping and straining, drawing near. Perceveral didn't care. The thought struck him that all his years of accident-proneness had gone into the making of this moment. The tide had turned now. He was at last what nature had intended him to be all along—an accident-*proof* man!

The robot crawled after him up a dazzling surface of white rock. Perceveral, drunk with supreme confidence, pushed boulders into motion and shouted to create an avalanche.

The rocks began to slide, and above him he heard a deep rumble. He dodged around a boulder, evaded the robot's outflung arm and came to a dead end.

He was in a small, shallow cave. The robot loomed in front of him, blocking the entrance, his iron fist pulled back.

Perceveral burst into laughter at the sight of the poor, clumsy, accident-prone robot. Then the robot's fist, driven by the full force of his body, shot out.

Perceveral ducked, but it wasn't necessary. The clumsy robot missed him anyhow, by at least half an inch. It was just the sort of mistake Perceveral had expected of the ridiculous accident-prone creature.

The force of the swing carried the robot outward. He fought hard to regain his balance, poised on the lip of the cliff. Any normal man or robot would have regained it. But not the accident-prone robot. He fell on his face, smashing his last eye cell, and began to roll.

Perceveral leaned out to accelerate the roll, then quickly crouched back inside the shallow cave. The avalanche completed the job for him, rolling a diminishing black dot down the dusty white mountainside and burying it under tons of stone.

Perceveral watched it all, chuckling to himself. Then he began to ask himself what, exactly, he had been doing.

And that was when he started to shake.

Months later, Perceveral stood by the gangplank of the colony ship *Cuchulain*, watching the colonists step down into Theta's midwinter sunshine. There were all types and kinds.

They had all come to Theta for a chance at a new life. Each of them was vitally important at least to himself, and each deserved a fighting chance at survival, no matter what his potentialities.

And he, Anton Perceveral, had scouted the minimum-survival requirements on Theta for these people; and had, in some measure, given hope and promise to the least capable among them— the incompetents who also wanted to live.

He turned away from the stream of pioneers and entered the ship by a rear ladder. He walked down a corridor and entered Haskell's cabin.

"Well, Anton," Haskell said, "how do they look to you?"

"They seem like a nice group," Perceveral said.

"They are. Those people consider you their founding father, Anton. They want you here. Will you stay?"

Perceveral said, "I consider Theta my home."

"Then it's settled. I'll just——"

"Wait," Perceveral said. "I'm not finished. I consider Theta my home. I want to settle here, marry, raise kids. But not yet."

"Eh?"

"I've grown pretty fond of exploring," Perceveral said. "I'd like to do some more of it. Maybe one or two more planets. Then I'll settle down on Theta."

"I was afraid you might want that," Haskell said unhappily.

"What's wrong with it?"

"Nothing. But I'm afraid we can't use you again as an explorer, Anton."

"Why not?"

"You know what we need. Minimum-survival personalities for staking out future colonies. You cannot by any stretch of the imagination be considered a minimum-survival personality any longer."

"But I'm the same man I always was!" Perceveral said. "Oh, sure, I improved on the planet. But you expected that and had the robot to compensate for it. And at the end——"

"Yes, what about that?"

"Well, at the end I just got carried away. I think I was drunk or something. I can't imagine how I acted that way."

"Still, that's how you did act."

"Yes. But look! Even with that, I barely survived the experience —the total experience on Theta! *Barely!* Doesn't that prove I'm still a minimum-survival personality?"

Haskell pursed his lips and looked thoughtful. "Anton, you almost convince me. But I'm afraid you're indulging in a bit of word juggling. In all honesty, I can't view you as minimum any longer. I'm afraid you'll just have to put up with your lot on Theta."

Perceveral's shoulders slumped. He nodded wearily, shook hands with Haskell and turned to go.

As he turned, the edge of his sleeve caught Haskell's inkstand, brushing it off the table. Perceveral lunged to catch it and banged his hand against the desk. Ink splattered over him. He fumbled again, tripped over a chair, fell.

"Anton," Haskell asked, "was that an act?"

"No," Perceveral said. "It wasn't, damn it."

"Hmm. Interesting. Now, Anton, don't raise your hopes too high, but maybe—I say just *maybe*——"

Haskell stared hard at Perceveral's flushed face, then burst into laughter.

"What a devil you are, Anton! You almost had me fooled. Now will you kindly get the hell out of here and join the colonists? They're dedicating a statue to you and I think they'd like to have you present."

Shamefaced, but grinning in spite of it, Anton Perceveral walked out to meet his new destiny.